J. M. BARRIE'S

ADAPTED AND DRAWN BY
STREF

COLOURED BY
FIN CRAMB

EDINBURGH

For my daughter, Amy, and my mothers (!)
with love

STREF

For my family and friends – for all your support,
thank you

FIN

Extra special thanks to Christine De Poortere, Peter Pan Director at Great Ormond Street Hospital Children's Charity. Without you, there would be no book: 'One girl is more use than twenty boys!'

Special thanks to Morris Heggie, Eli Winter, Simon Jones, Cathy Agnew and the Peter Pan Moat Brae Trust, John McKenna and the National Trust for Scotland, Louise Innes and the National Museum of Scotland, Alan Grant, Sean Watson, Lynsey May, James Cramb, Graham Clark, Jim Dallas

For their support, help and advice we would also like to thank John McShane, Patrick Evans, Alison Macintyre Collingham, Erin H. Reah, the Cramb family, Jim Alexander, Out of the Blue Drill Hall

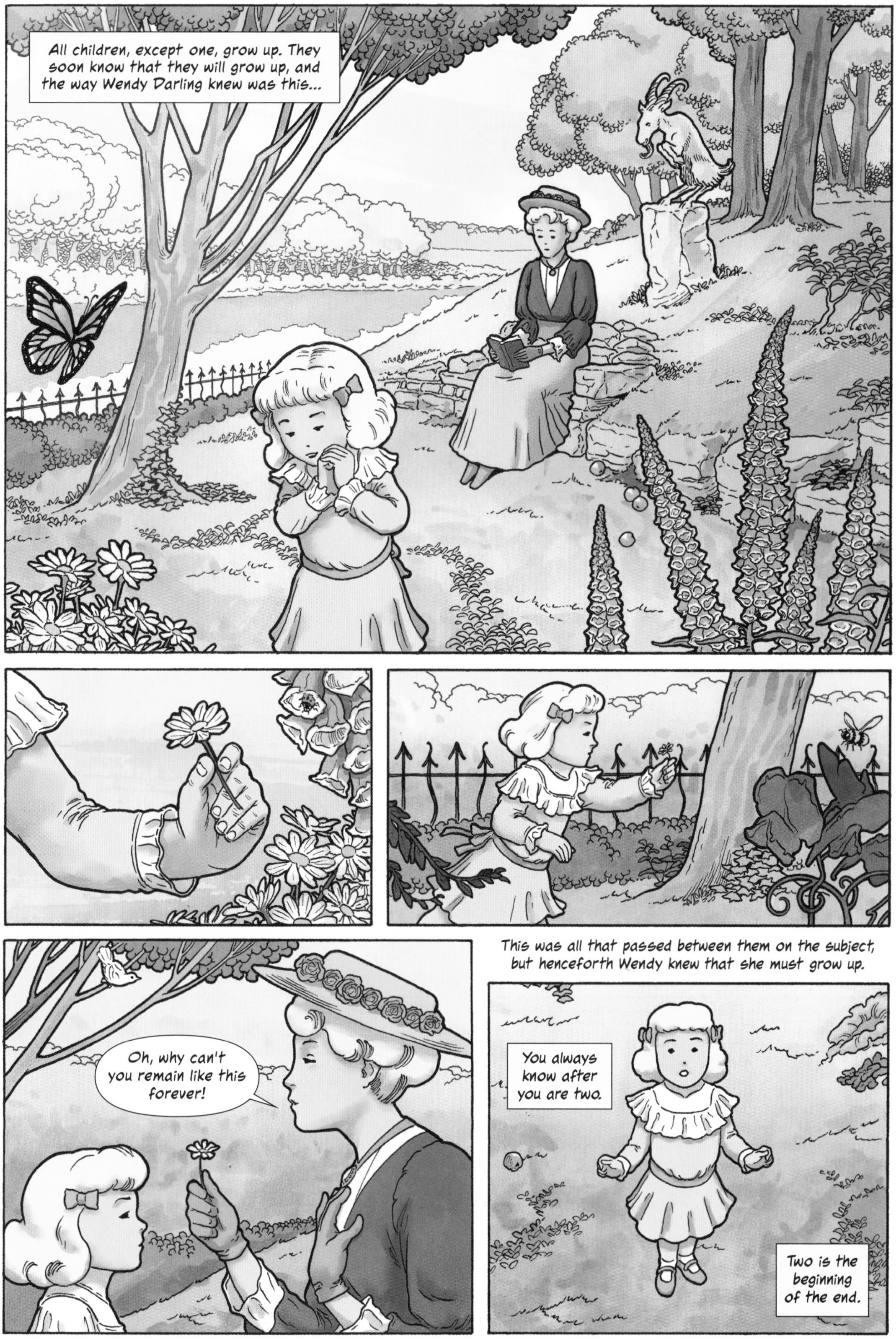
All children, except one, grow up. They soon know that they will grow up, and the way Wendy Darling knew was this...
Oh, why can't you remain like this forever!
This was all that passed between them on the subject, but henceforth Wendy knew that she must grow up.
You always know after you are two.
Two is the beginning of the end.

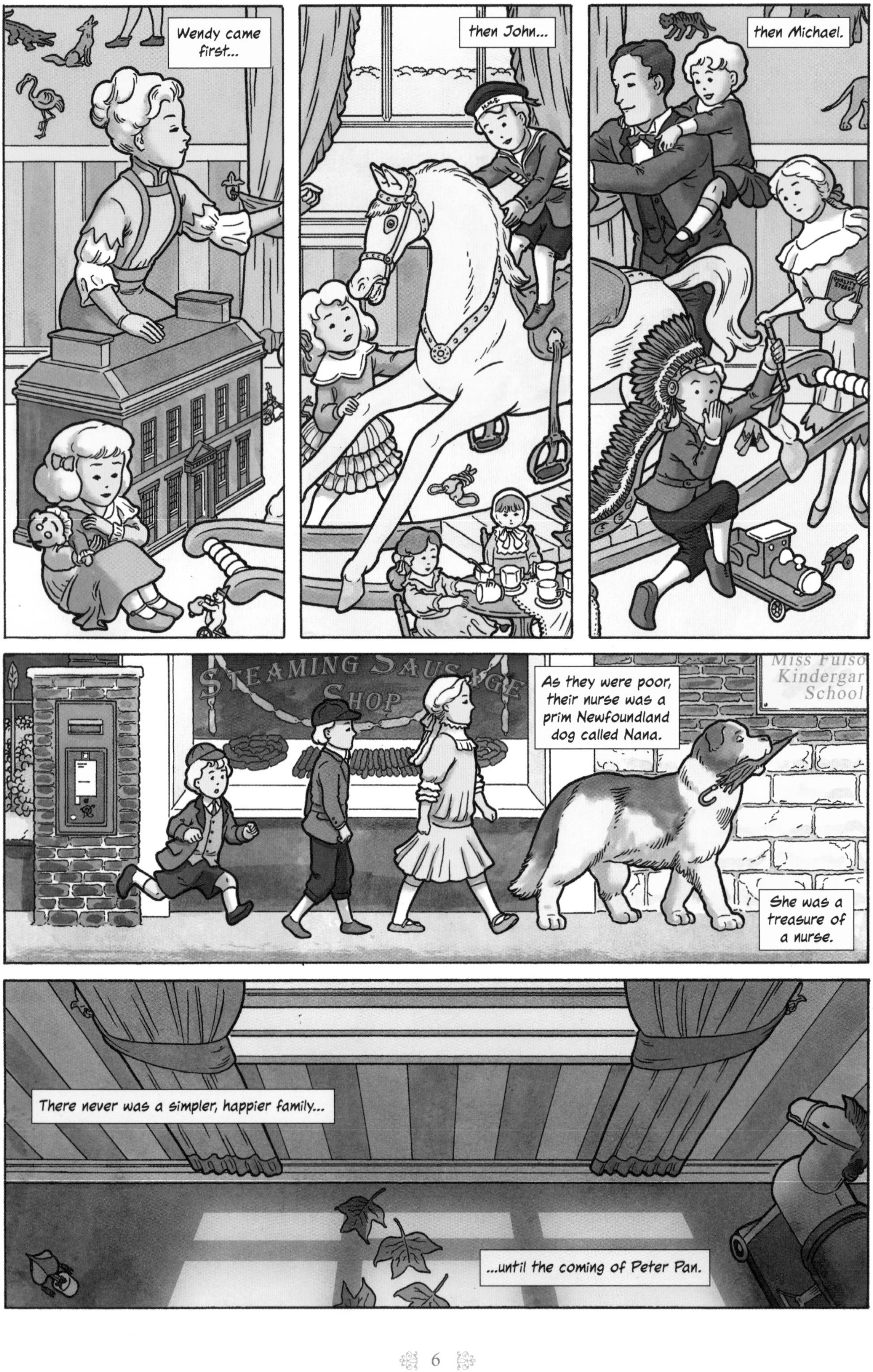
Wendy came first...
then John...
then Michael.
STEAMING SAUSAGE SHOP
As they were poor, their nurse was a prim Newfoundland dog called Nana.
She was a treasure of a nurse.
There never was a simpler, happier family...
...until the coming of Peter Pan.

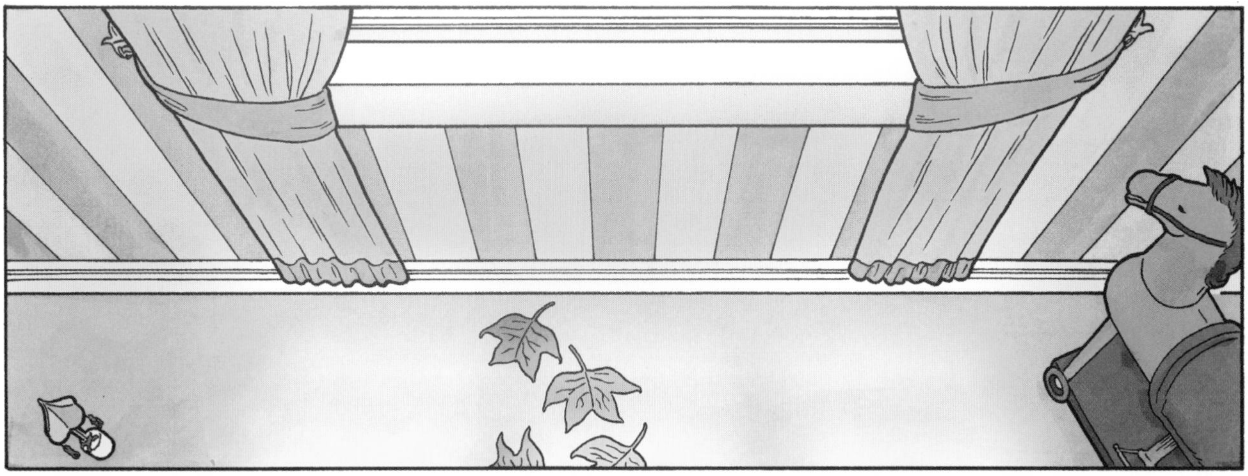

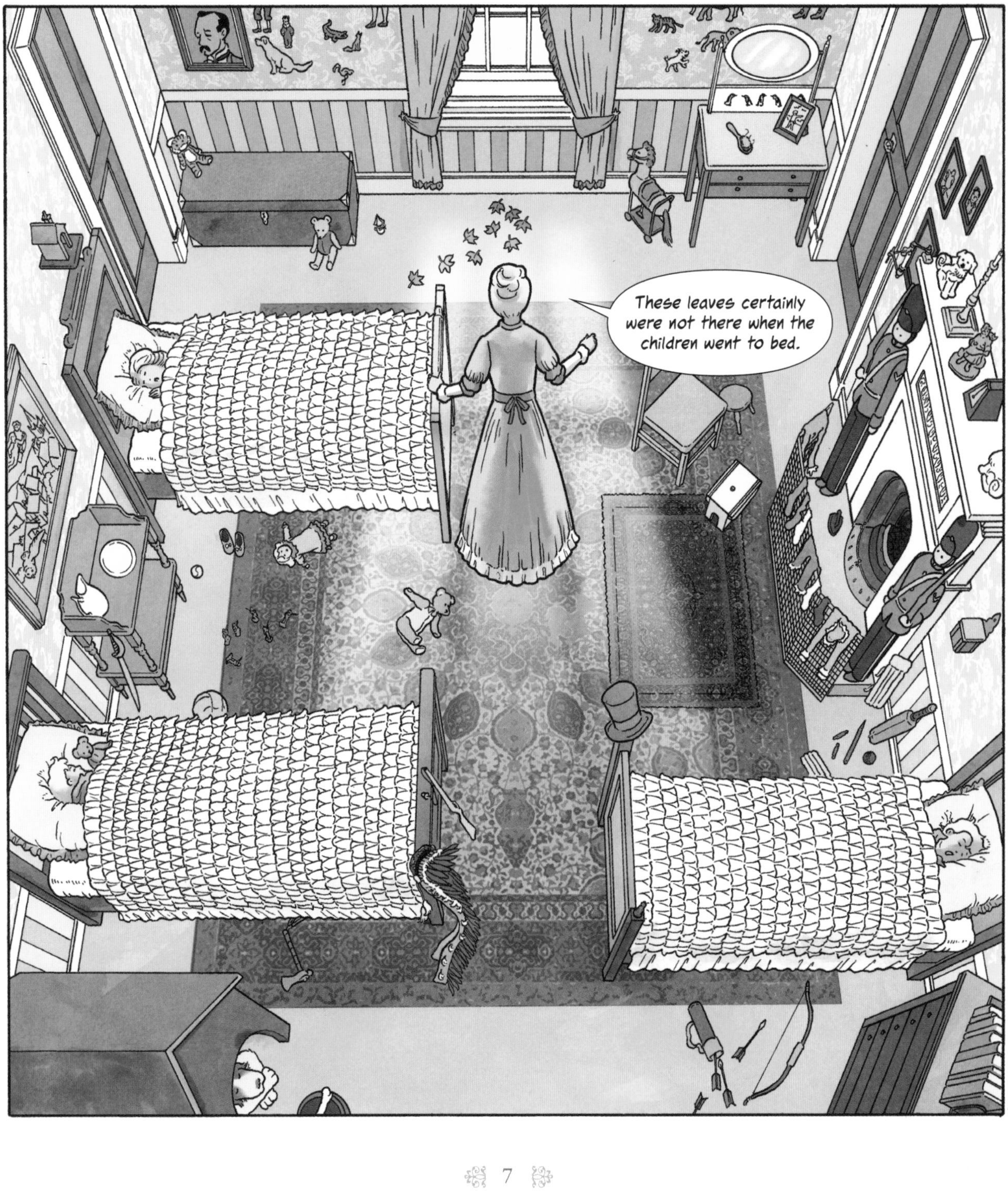
These leaves certainly were not there when the children went to bed.

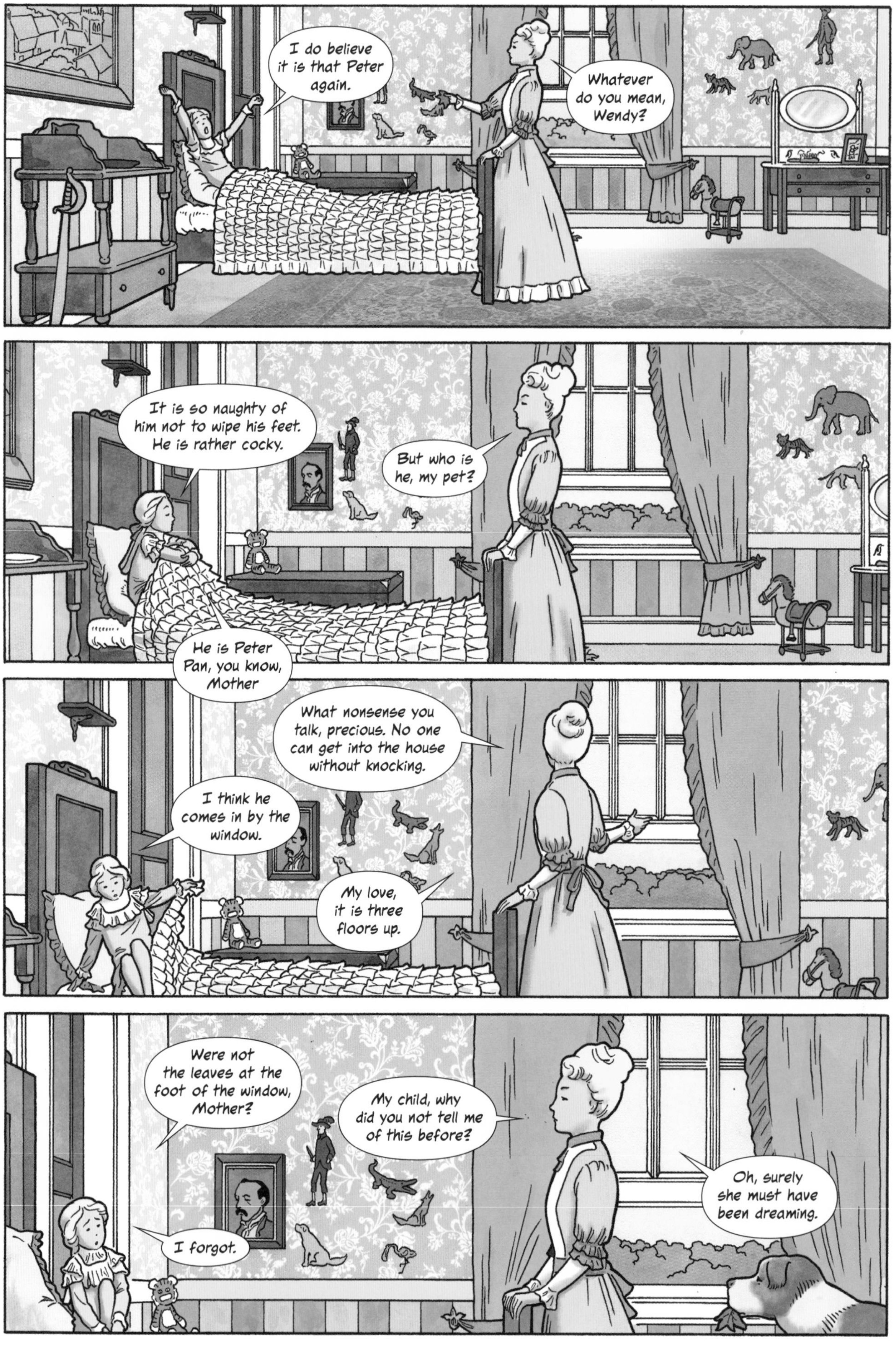
I do believe it is that Peter again.
Whatever do you mean, Wendy?
It is so naughty of him not to wipe his feet. He is rather cocky.
But who is he, my pet?
He is Peter Pan, you know, Mother
What nonsense you talk, precious. No one can get into the house without knocking.
I think he comes in by the window.
My love, it is three floors up.
Were not the leaves at the foot of the window, Mother?
My child, why did you not tell me of this before?
I forgot.
Oh, surely she must have been dreaming.

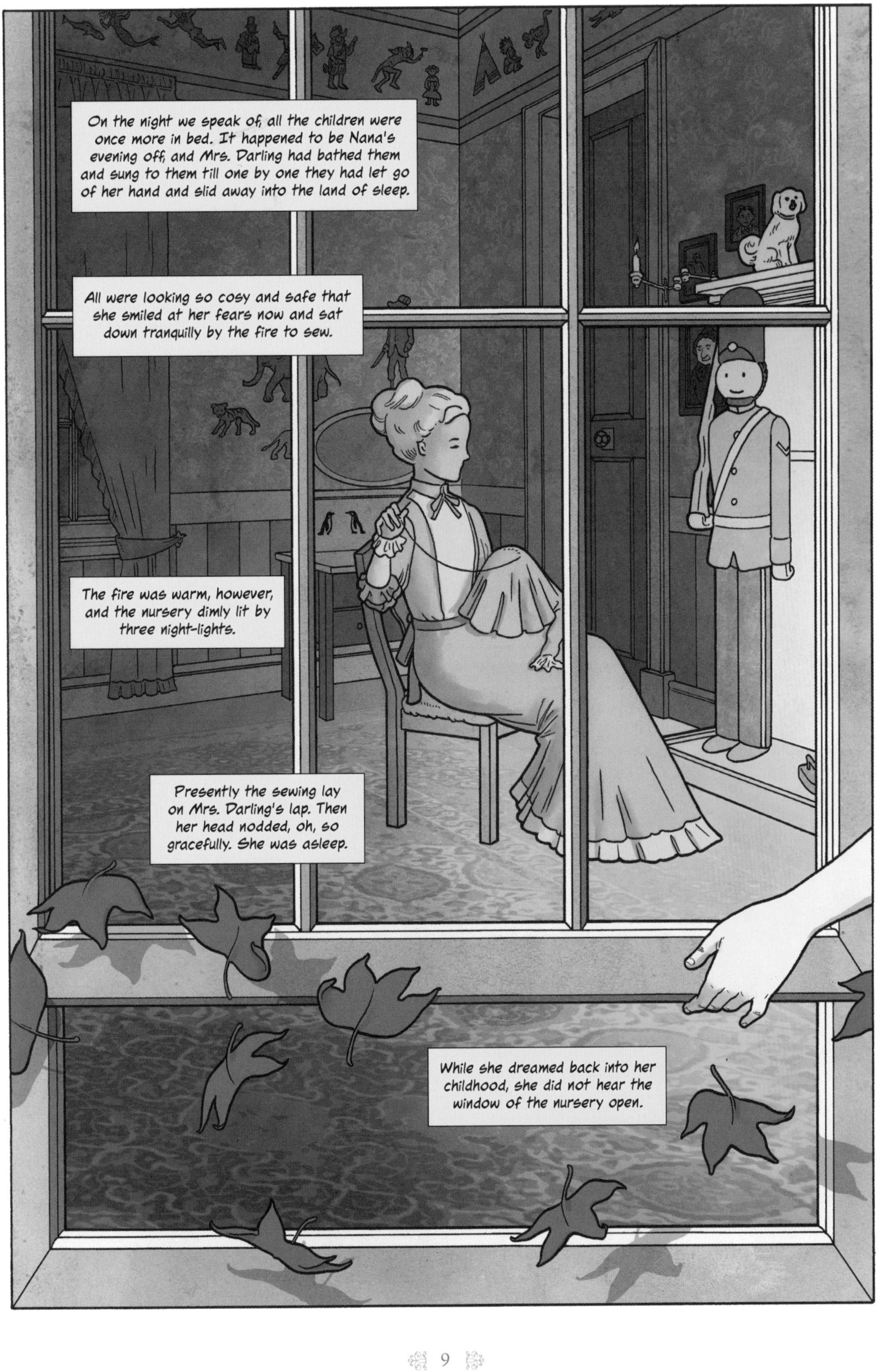
On the night we speak of, all the children were once more in bed. It happened to be Nana's evening off, and Mrs. Darling had bathed them and sung to them till one by one they had let go of her hand and slid away into the land of sleep.
All were looking so cosy and safe that she smiled at her fears now and sat down tranquilly by the fire to sew.
The fire was warm, however, and the nursery dimly lit by three night-lights.
Presently the sewing lay on Mrs. Darling's lap. Then her head nodded, oh, so gracefully. She was asleep.
While she dreamed back into her childhood, she did not hear the window of the nursery open.

She remembered a Peter Pan, who was said to live with the fairies.

There were odd stories about him...

...as when children died he went part of the way with them, so that they should not be frightened.

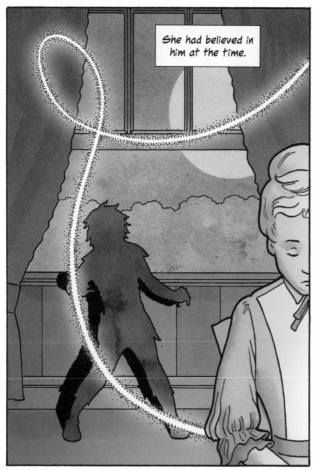

She had believed in him at the time.

But now that she was married and full of sense she quite doubted whether there was any such person.

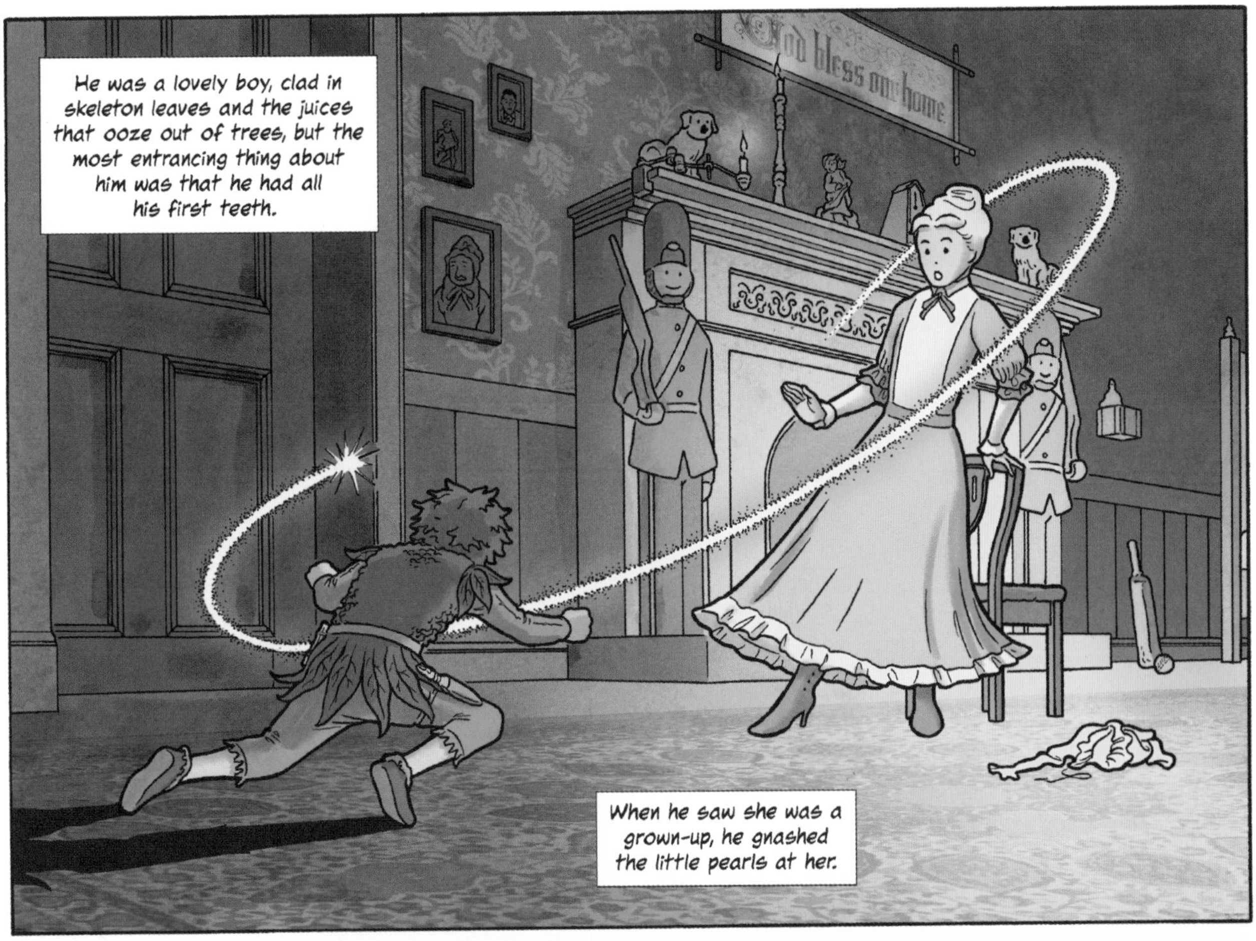
He was a lovely boy, clad in skeleton leaves and the juices that ooze out of trees, but the most entrancing thing about him was that he had all his first teeth.
God bless our home
When he saw she was a grown-up, he gnashed the little pearls at her.

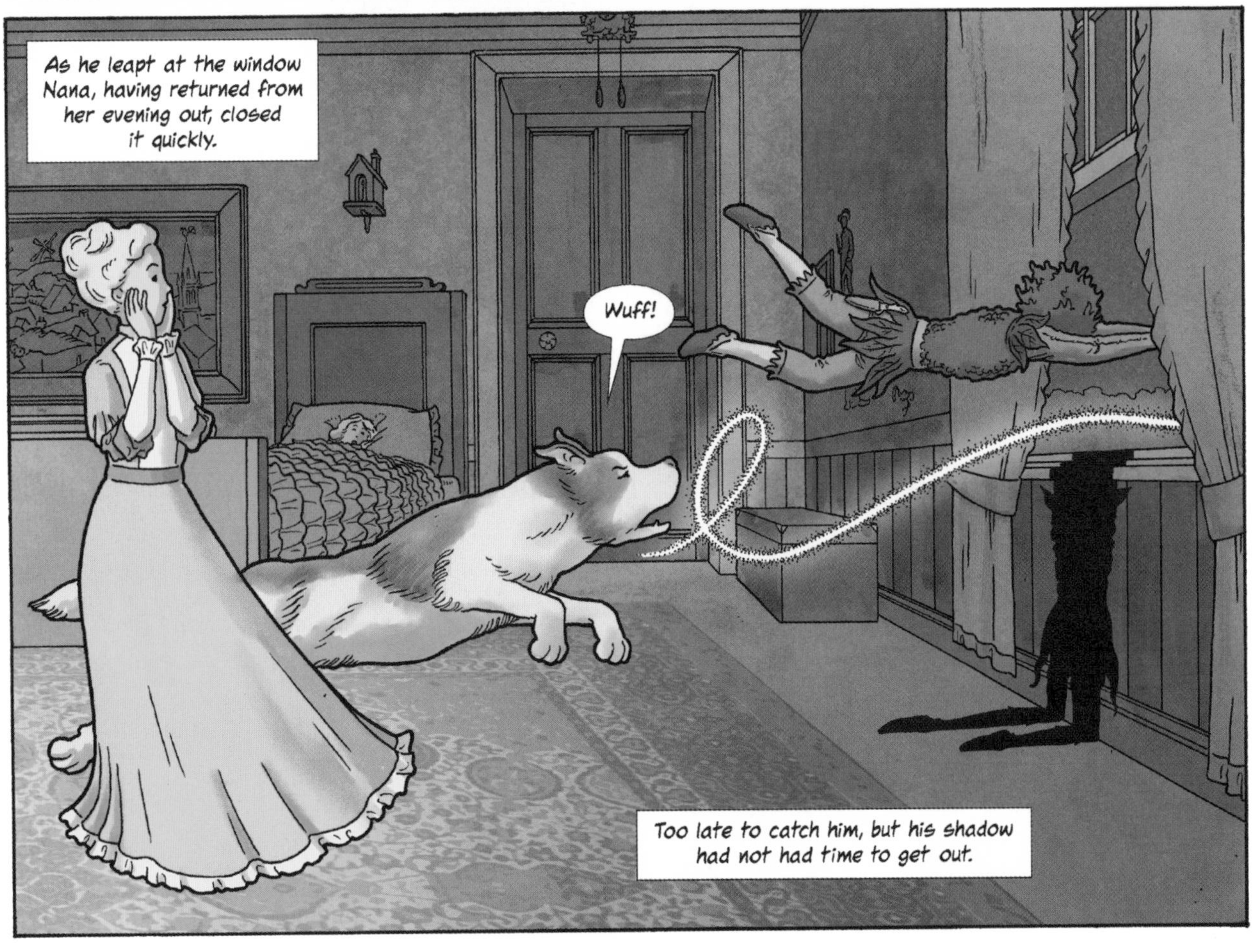
As he leapt at the window Nana, having returned from her evening out, closed it quickly.
Wuff!
Too late to catch him, but his shadow had not had time to get out.

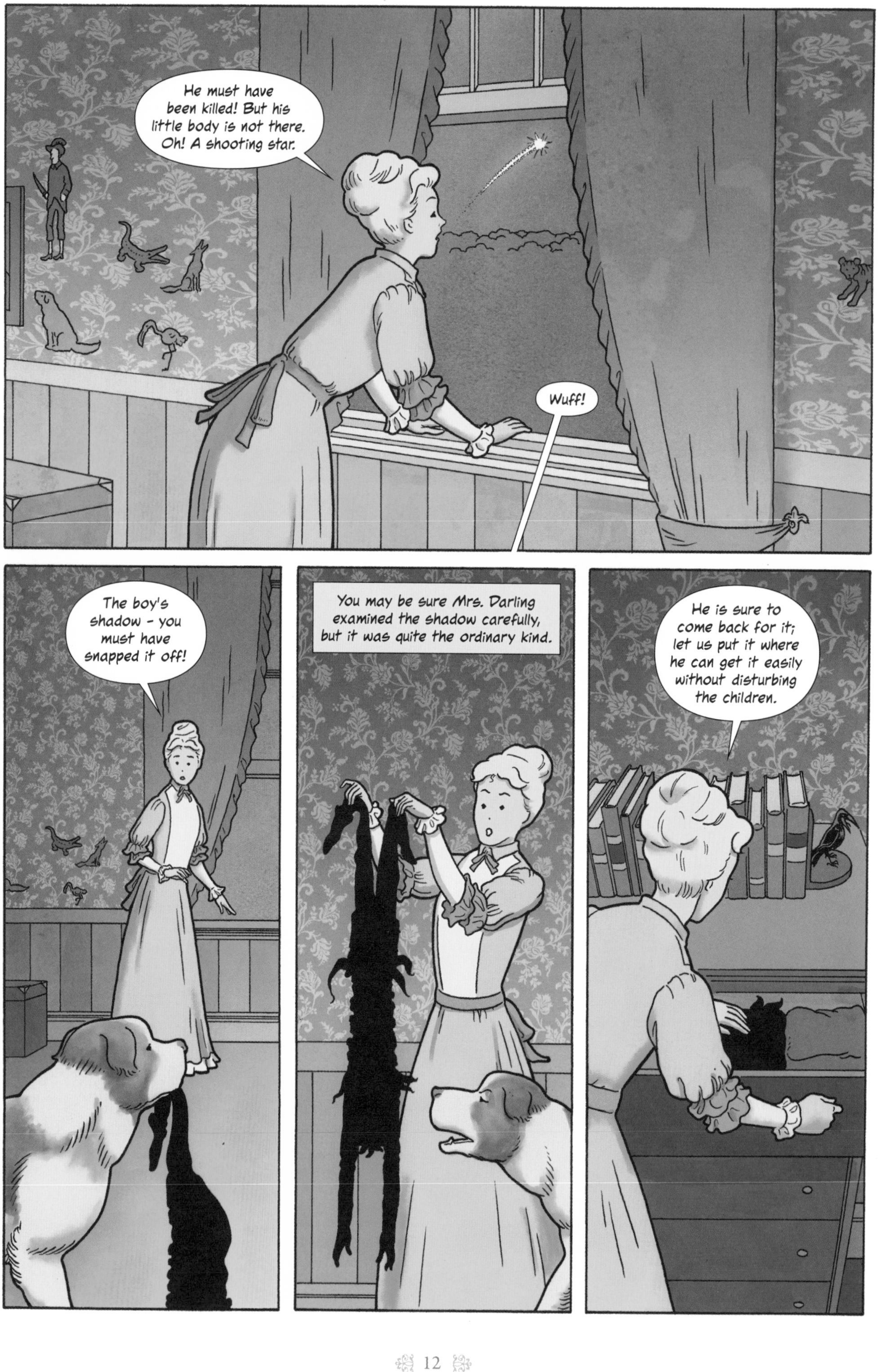
He must have been killed! But his little body is not there. Oh! A shooting star.
Wuff!
The boy's shadow - you must have snapped it off!
You may be sure Mrs. Darling examined the shadow carefully, but it was quite the ordinary kind.
He is sure to come back for it; let us put it where he can get it easily without disturbing the children.

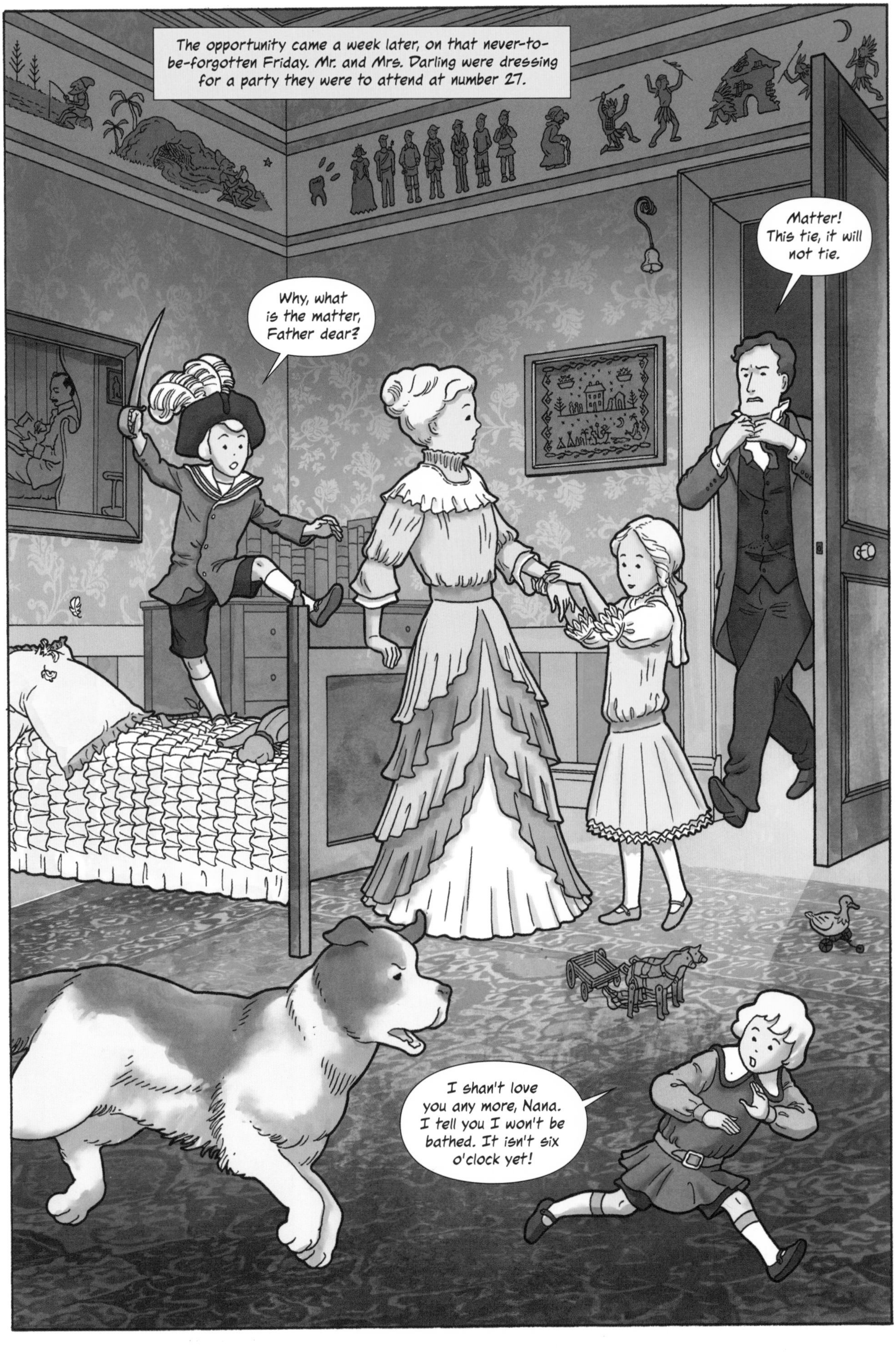
The opportunity came a week later, on that never-to-be-forgotten Friday. Mr. and Mrs. Darling were dressing for a party they were to attend at number 27.
Why, what is the matter, Father dear?
Matter! This tie, it will not tie.
I shan't love you any more, Nana. I tell you I won't be bathed. It isn't six o'clock yet!

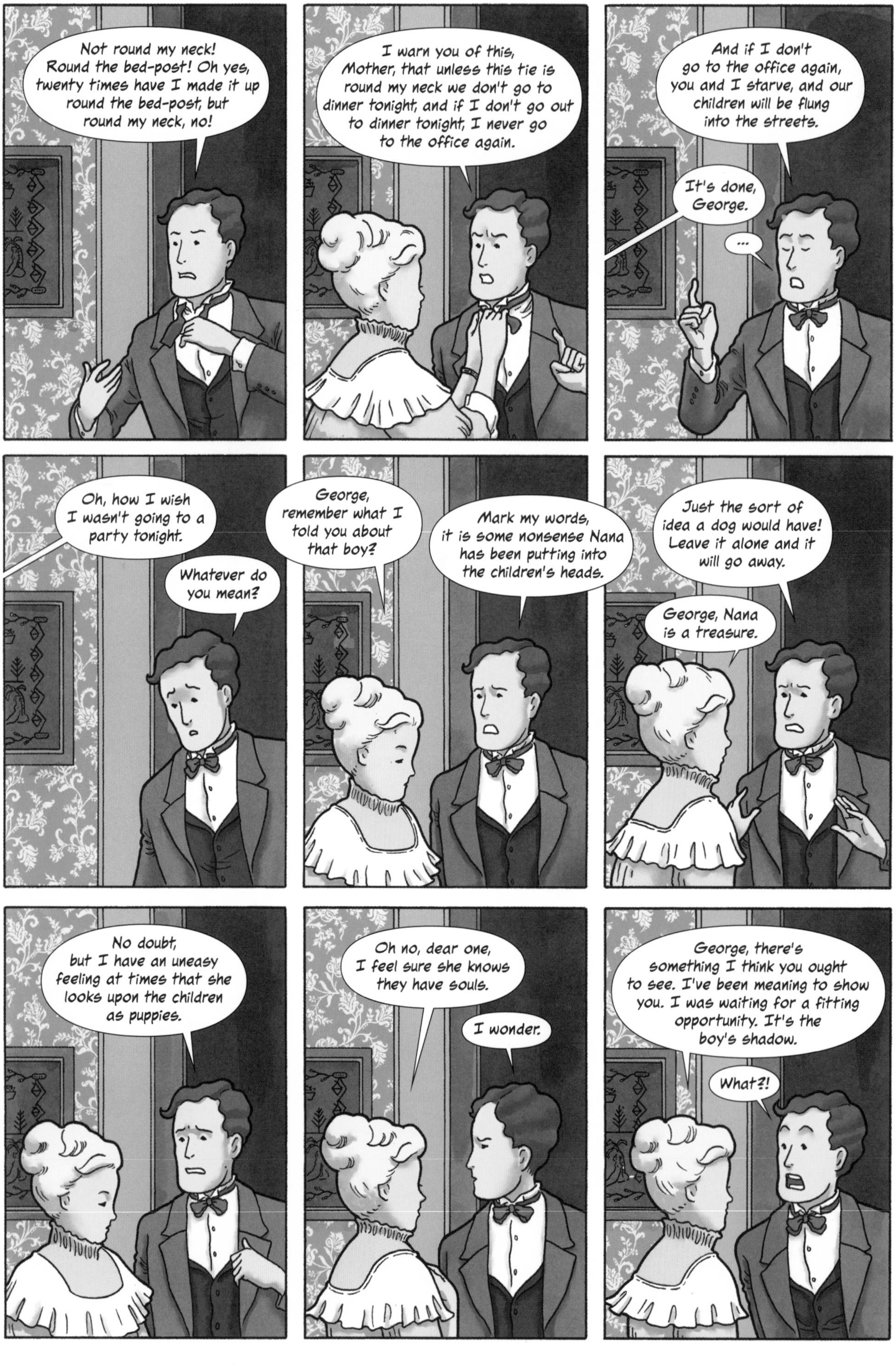
Not round my neck! Round the bed-post! Oh yes, twenty times have I made it up round the bed-post, but round my neck, no!
I warn you of this, Mother, that unless this tie is round my neck we don't go to dinner tonight, and if I don't go out to dinner tonight, I never go to the office again.
And if I don't go to the office again, you and I starve, and our children will be flung into the streets.
It's done, George.
...
Oh, how I wish I wasn't going to a party tonight.
Whatever do you mean?
George, remember what I told you about that boy?
Mark my words, it is some nonsense Nana has been putting into the children's heads.
Just the sort of idea a dog would have! Leave it alone and it will go away.
George, Nana is a treasure.
No doubt, but I have an uneasy feeling at times that she looks upon the children as puppies.
Oh no, dear one, I feel sure she knows they have souls.
I wonder.
George, there's something I think you ought to see. I've been meaning to show you. I was waiting for a fitting opportunity. It's the boy's shadow.
What?!

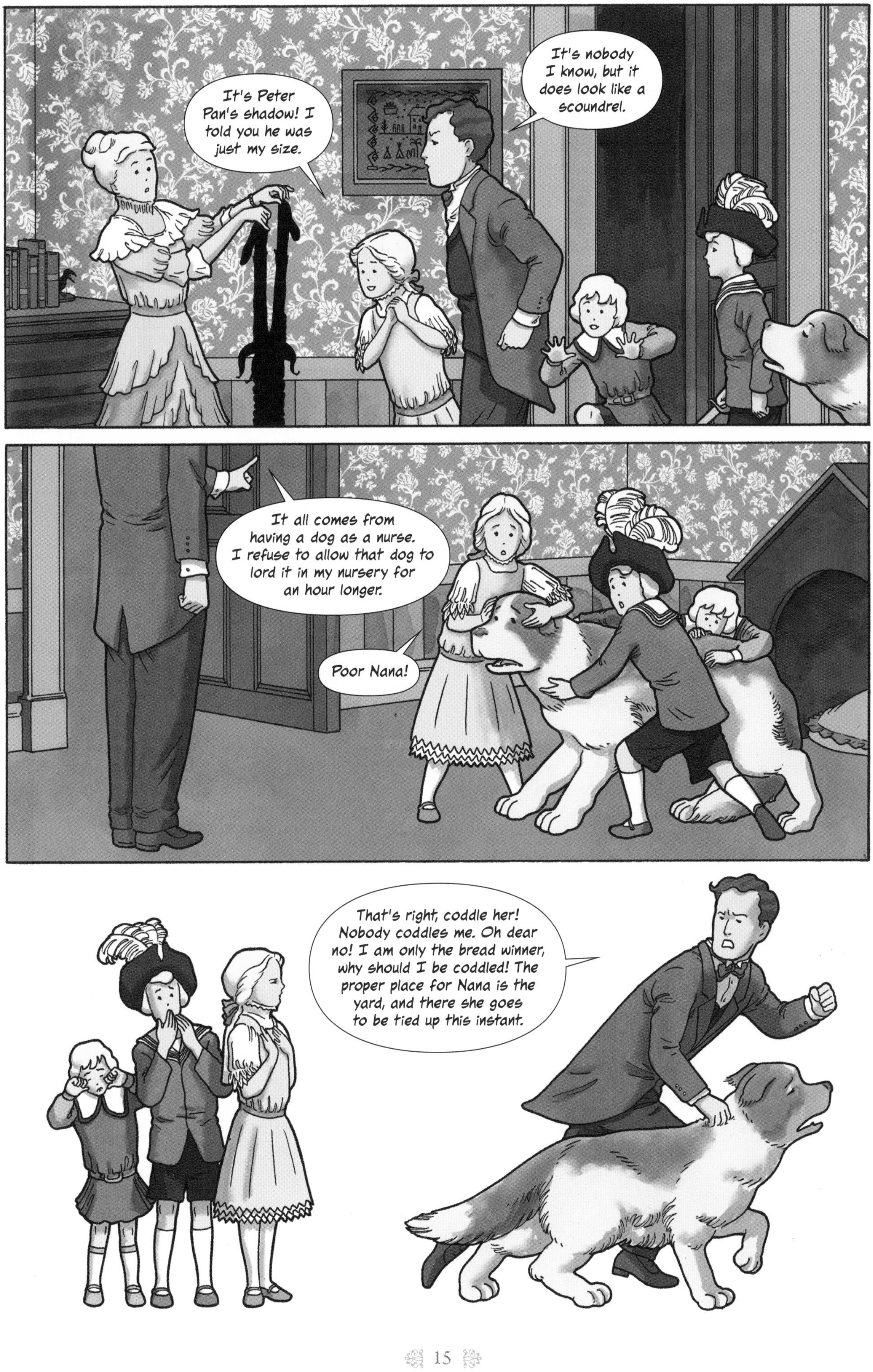
It's Peter Pan's shadow! I told you he was just my size.
It's nobody I know, but it does look like a scoundrel.
It all comes from having a dog as a nurse. I refuse to allow that dog to lord it in my nursery for an hour longer.
Poor Nana!
That's right, coddle her! Nobody coddles me. Oh dear no! I am only the bread winner, why should I be coddled! The proper place for Nana is the yard, and there she goes to be tied up this instant.

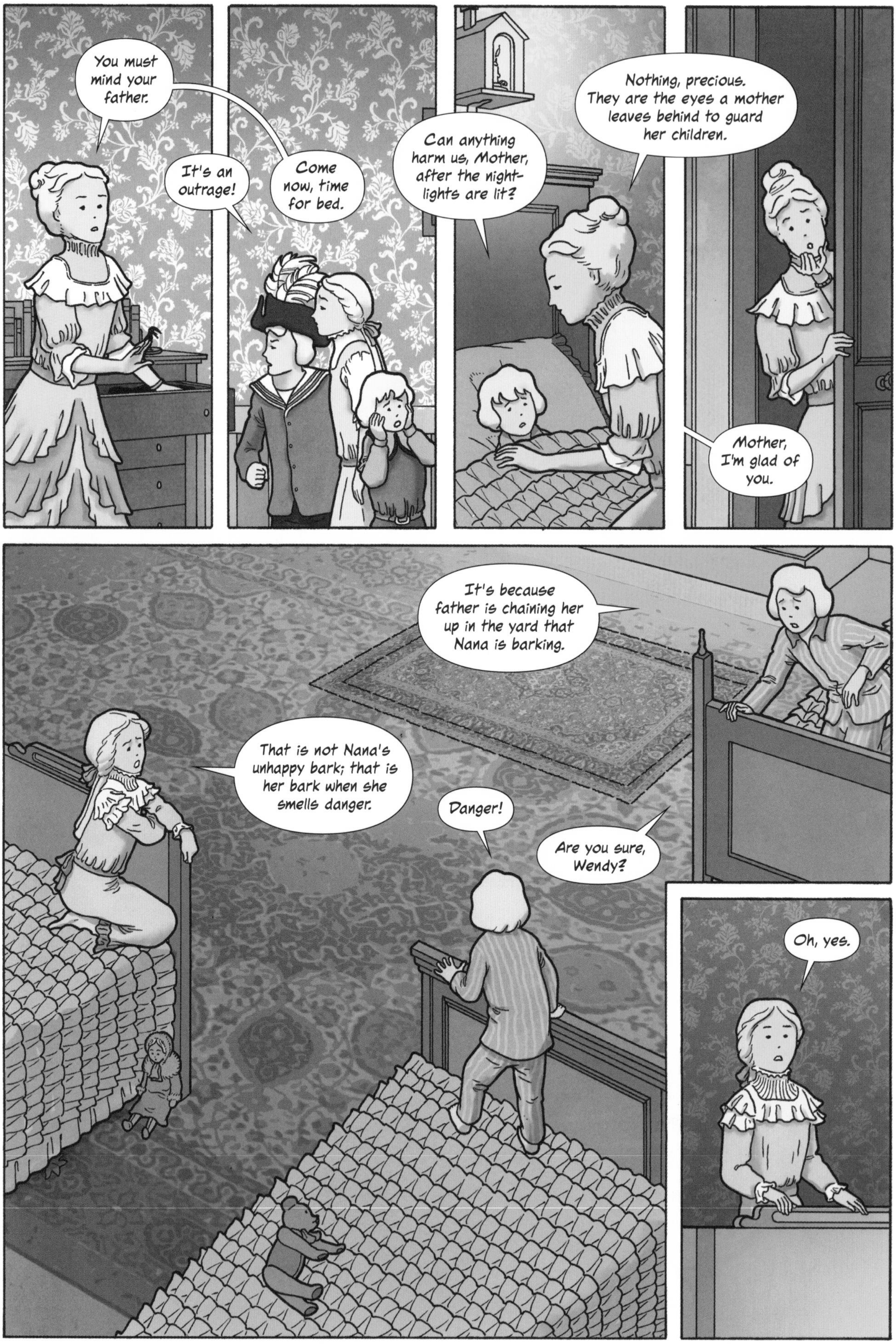
You must mind your father.
It's an outrage!
Come now, time for bed.
Can anything harm us, Mother, after the night-lights are lit?
Nothing, precious. They are the eyes a mother leaves behind to guard her children.
Mother, I'm glad of you.
It's because father is chaining her up in the yard that Nana is barking.
That is not Nana's unhappy bark; that is her bark when she smells danger.
Danger!
Are you sure, Wendy?
Oh, yes.

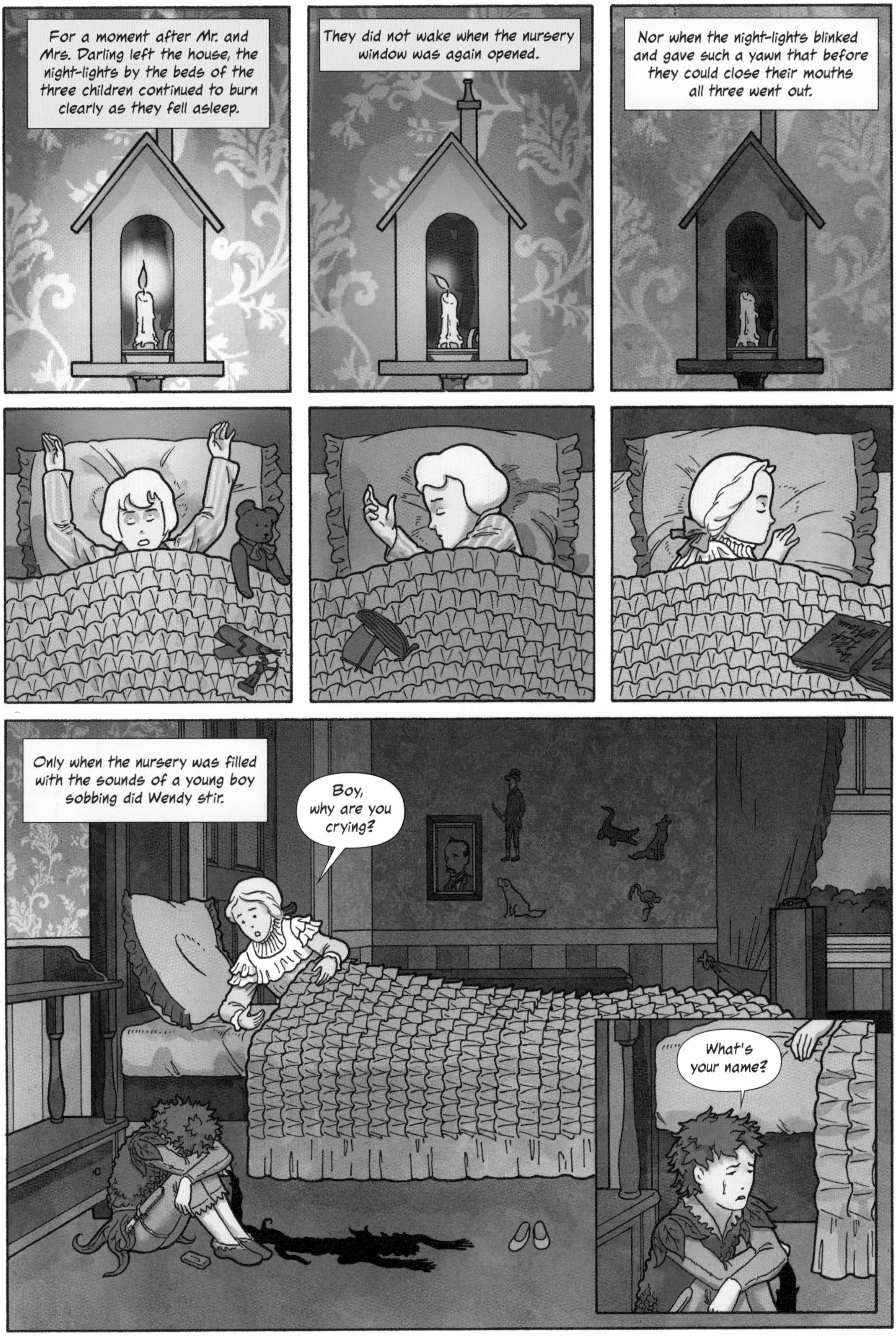
For a moment after Mr. and Mrs. Darling left the house, the night-lights by the beds of the three children continued to burn clearly as they fell asleep.
They did not wake when the nursery window was again opened.
Nor when the night-lights blinked and gave such a yawn that before they could close their mouths all three went out.
Only when the nursery was filled with the sounds of a young boy sobbing did Wendy stir.
Boy, why are you crying?
What's your name?

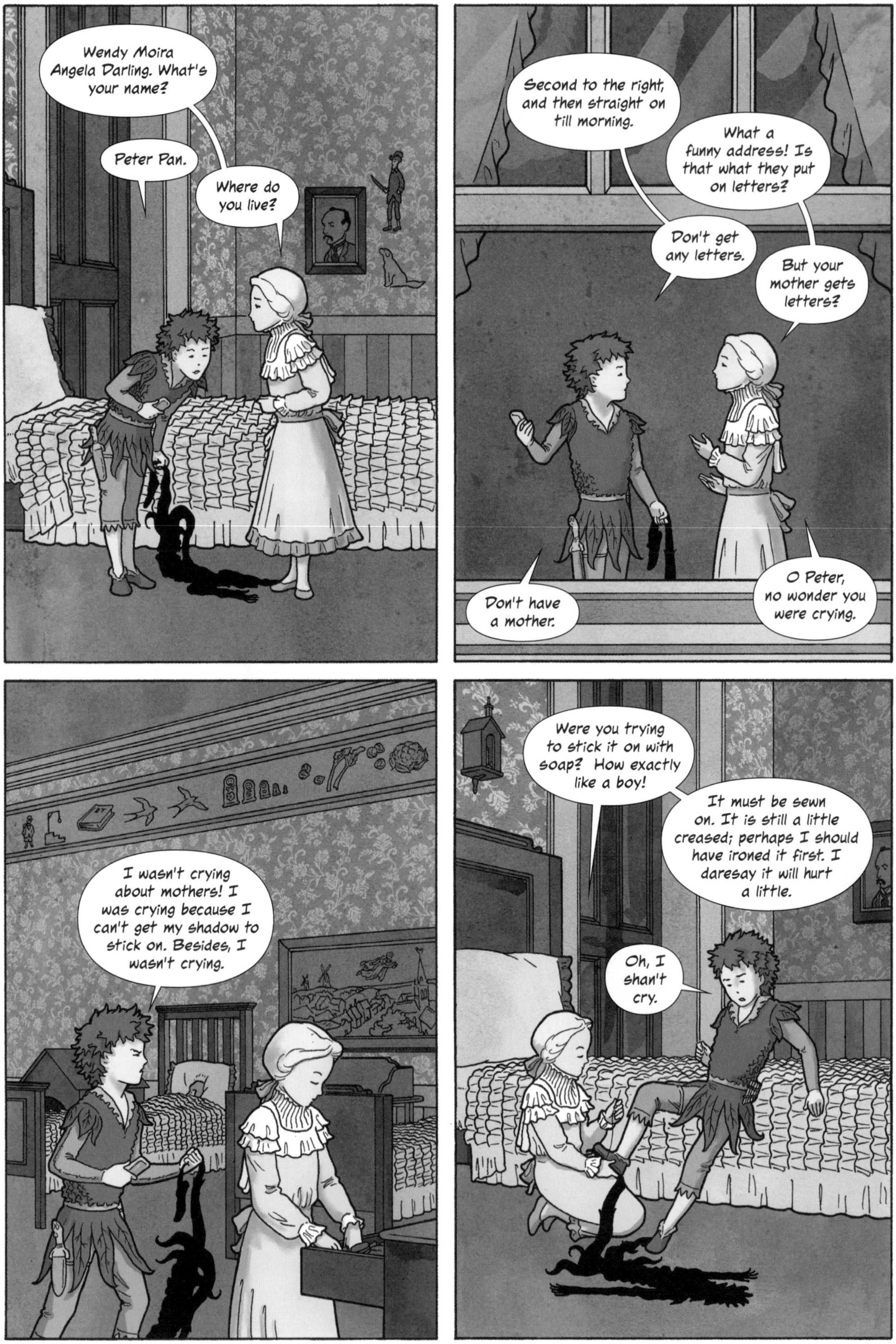
Wendy Moira Angela Darling. What's your name?
Peter Pan.
Where do you live?
Second to the right, and then straight on till morning.
What a funny address! Is that what they put on letters?
Don't get any letters.
But your mother gets letters?
Don't have a mother.
O Peter, no wonder you were crying.
I wasn't crying about mothers! I was crying because I can't get my shadow to stick on. Besides, I wasn't crying.
Were you trying to stick it on with soap? How exactly like a boy!
It must be sewn on. It is still a little creased; perhaps I should have ironed it first. I daresay it will hurt a little.
Oh, I shan't cry.

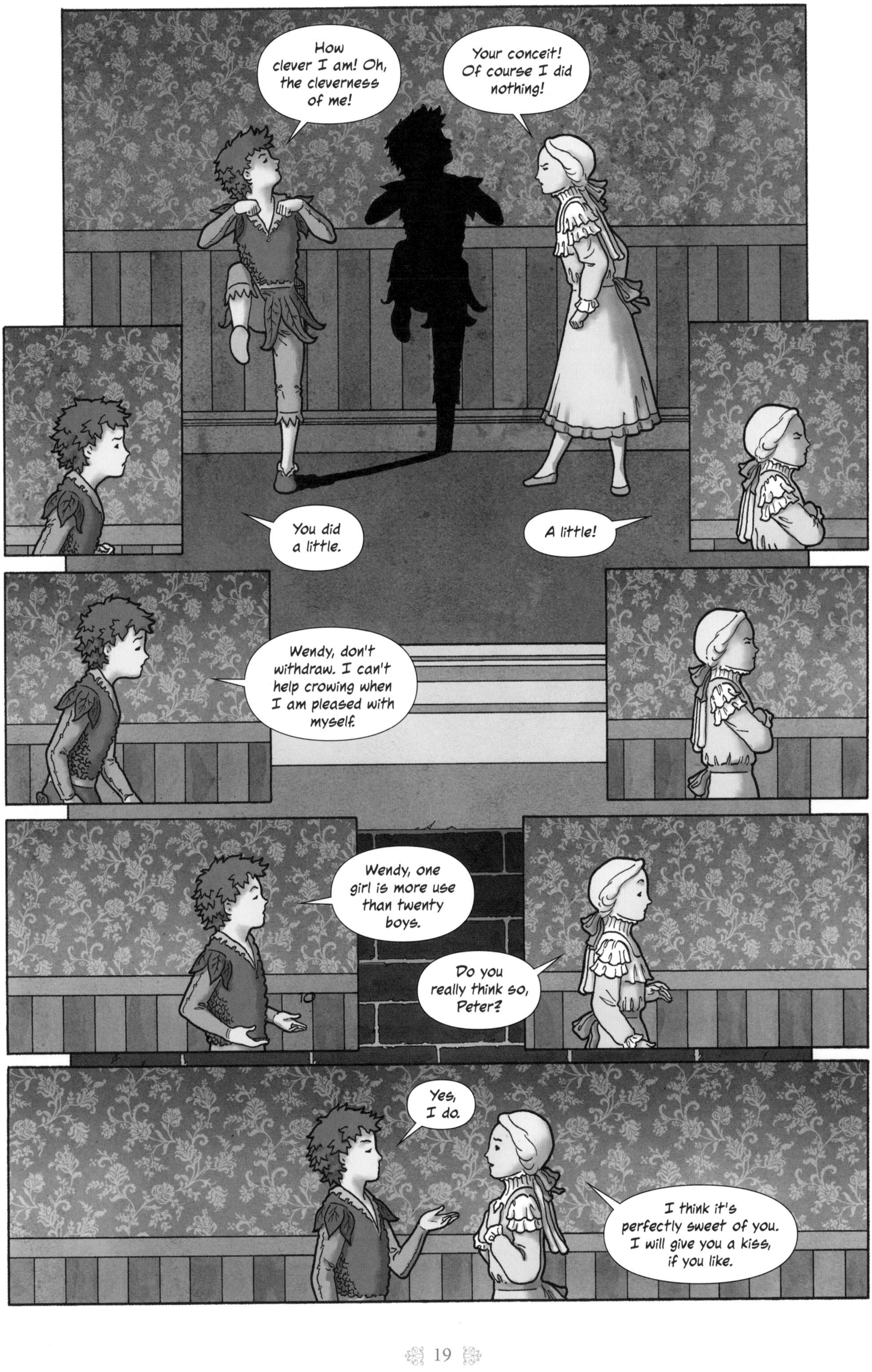
How clever I am! Oh, the cleverness of me!
Your conceit! Of course I did nothing!
You did a little.
A little!
Wendy, don't withdraw. I can't help crowing when I am pleased with myself.
Wendy, one girl is more use than twenty boys.
Do you really think so, Peter?
Yes, I do.
I think it's perfectly sweet of you. I will give you a kiss, if you like.

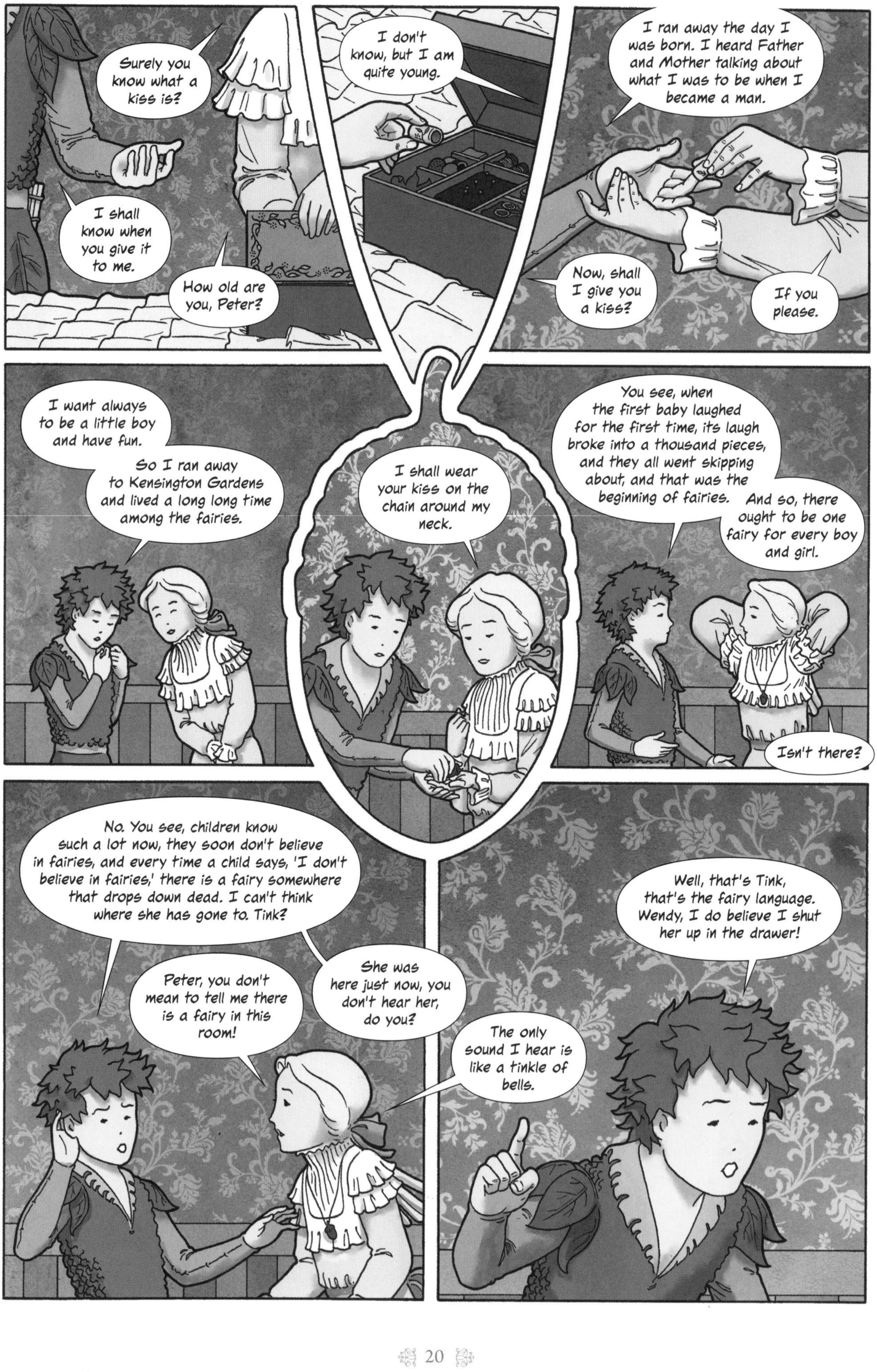
Surely you know what a kiss is?
I shall know when you give it to me.
How old are you, Peter?
I don't know, but I am quite young.
I ran away the day I was born. I heard Father and Mother talking about what I was to be when I became a man.
Now, shall I give you a kiss?
If you please.
I want always to be a little boy and have fun.
So I ran away to Kensington Gardens and lived a long long time among the fairies.
I shall wear your kiss on the chain around my neck.
You see, when the first baby laughed for the first time, its laugh broke into a thousand pieces, and they all went skipping about, and that was the beginning of fairies.
And so, there ought to be one fairy for every boy and girl.
Isn't there?
No. You see, children know such a lot now, they soon don't believe in fairies, and every time a child says, 'I don't believe in fairies,' there is a fairy somewhere that drops down dead. I can't think where she has gone to. Tink?
Peter, you don't mean to tell me there is a fairy in this room!
She was here just now, you don't hear her, do you?
The only sound I hear is like a tinkle of bells.
Well, that's Tink, that's the fairy language. Wendy, I do believe I shut her up in the drawer!

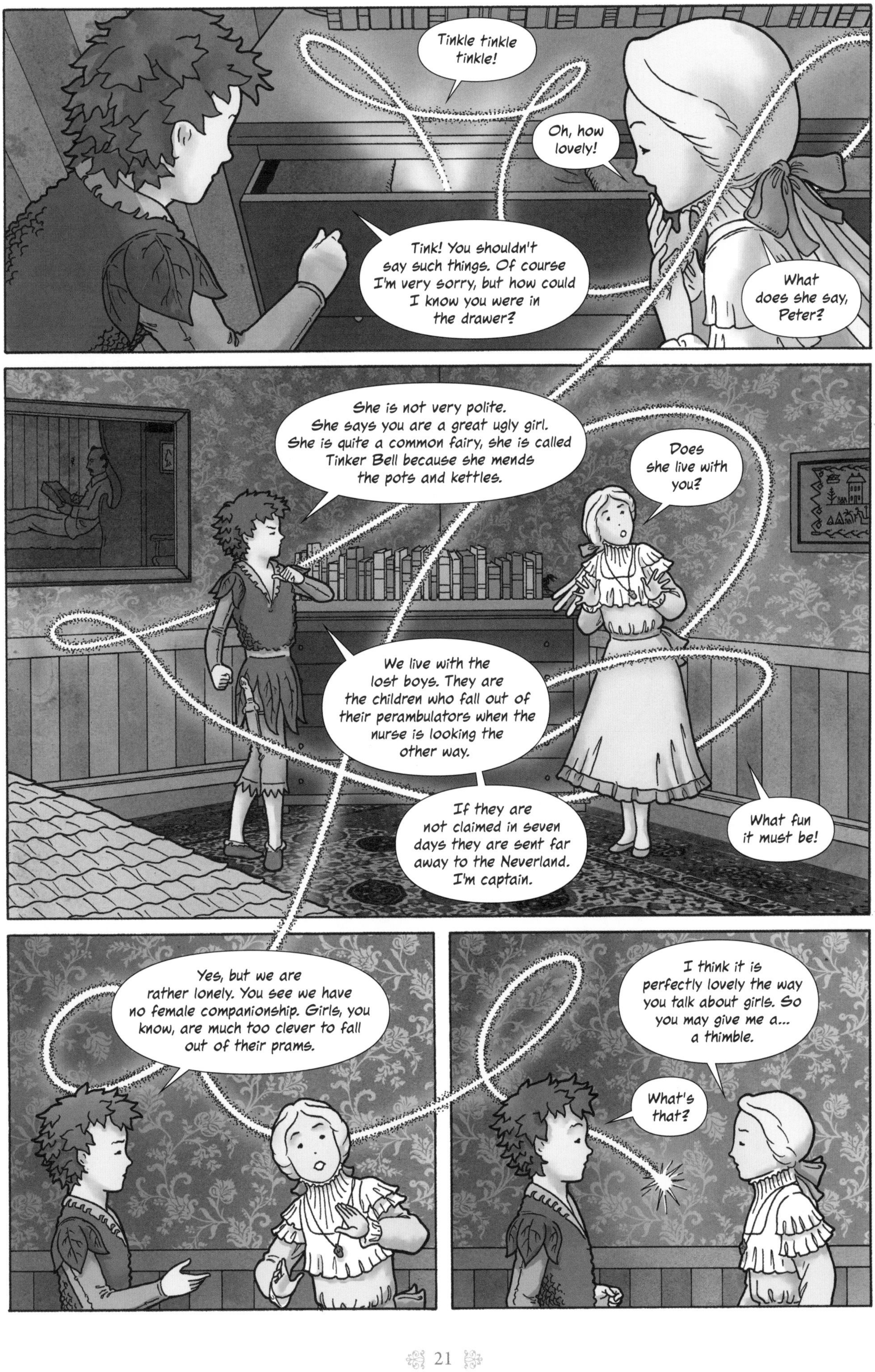
Tinkle tinkle tinkle!
Oh, how lovely!
Tink! You shouldn't say such things. Of course I'm very sorry, but how could I know you were in the drawer?
What does she say, Peter?
She is not very polite. She says you are a great ugly girl. She is quite a common fairy, she is called Tinker Bell because she mends the pots and kettles.
Does she live with you?
We live with the lost boys. They are the children who fall out of their perambulators when the nurse is looking the other way.
If they are not claimed in seven days they are sent far away to the Neverland. I'm captain.
What fun it must be!
Yes, but we are rather lonely. You see we have no female companionship. Girls, you know, are much too clever to fall out of their prams.
I think it is perfectly lovely the way you talk about girls. So you may give me a... a thimble.
What's that?

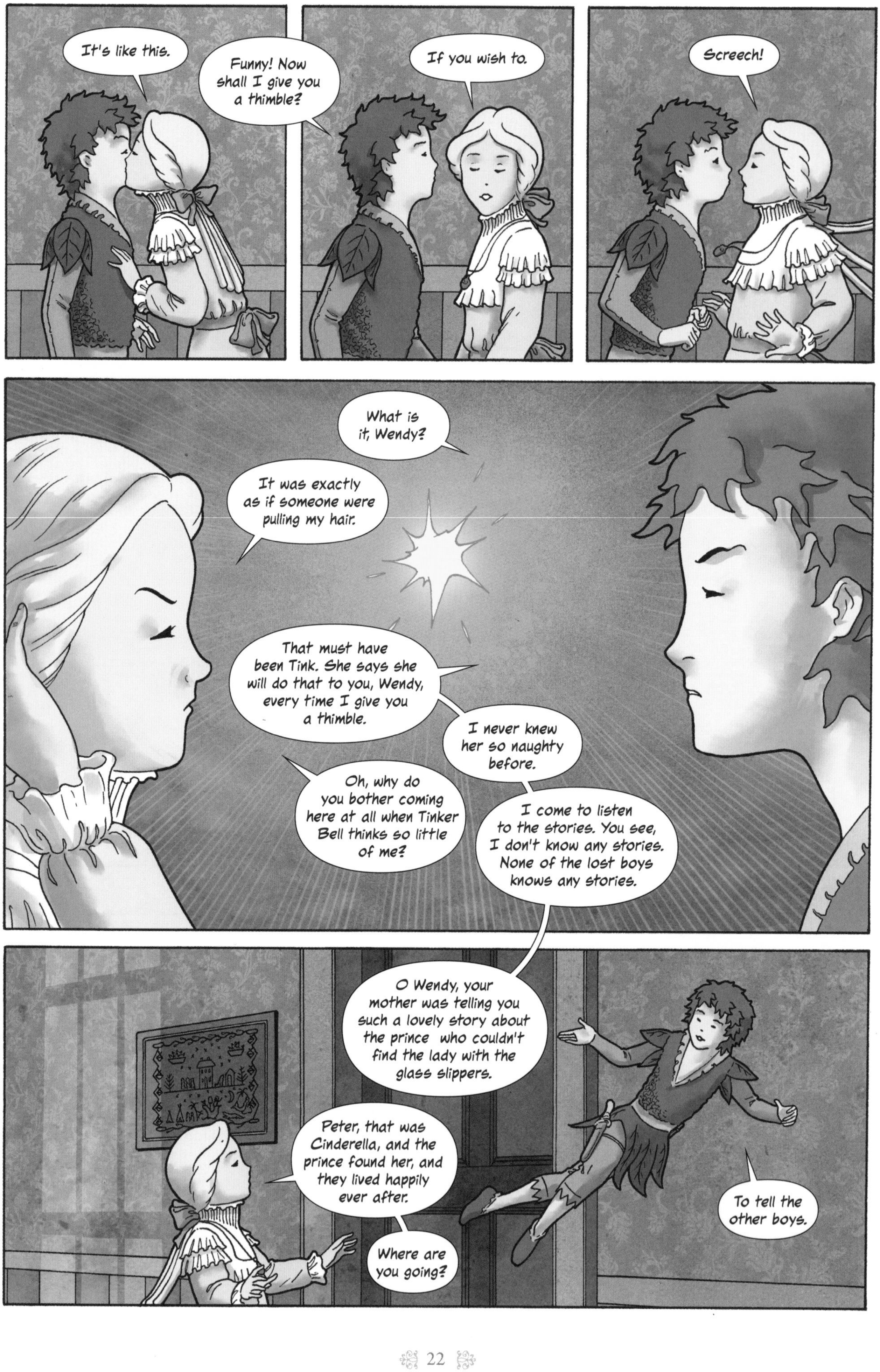
It's like this.
Funny! Now shall I give you a thimble?
If you wish to.
Screech!
What is it, Wendy?
It was exactly as if someone were pulling my hair.
That must have been Tink. She says she will do that to you, Wendy, every time I give you a thimble.
I never knew her so naughty before.
Oh, why do you bother coming here at all when Tinker Bell thinks so little of me?
I come to listen to the stories. You see, I don't know any stories. None of the lost boys knows any stories.
O Wendy, your mother was telling you such a lovely story about the prince who couldn't find the lady with the glass slippers.
Peter, that was Cinderella, and the prince found her, and they lived happily ever after.
Where are you going?
To tell the other boys.

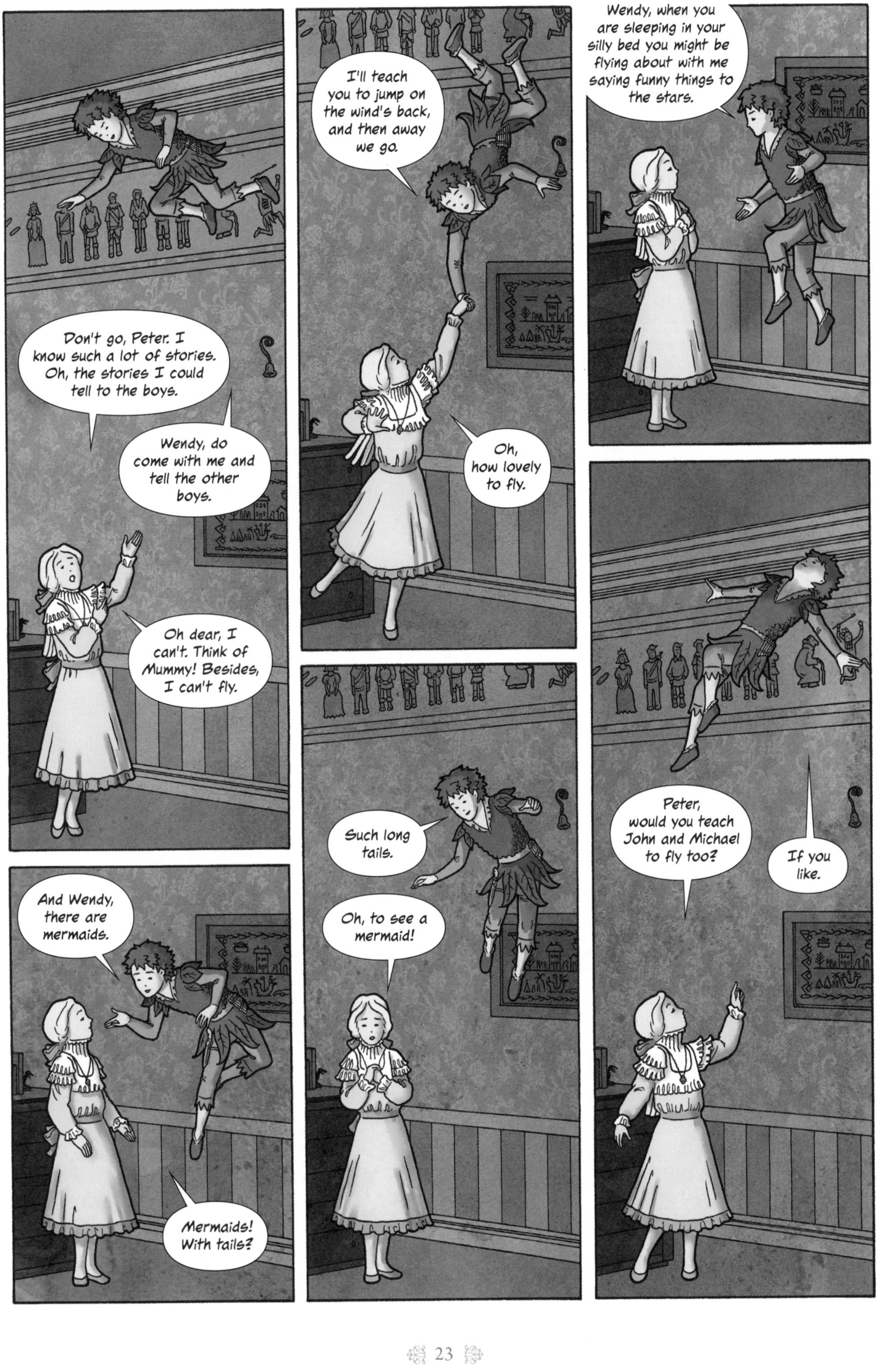
Don't go, Peter. I know such a lot of stories. Oh, the stories I could tell to the boys.
Wendy, do come with me and tell the other boys.
Oh dear, I can't. Think of Mummy! Besides, I can't fly.
I'll teach you to jump on the wind's back, and then away we go.
Oh, how lovely to fly.
Wendy, when you are sleeping in your silly bed you might be flying about with me saying funny things to the stars.
And Wendy, there are mermaids.
Mermaids! With tails?
Such long tails.
Oh, to see a mermaid!
Peter, would you teach John and Michael to fly too?
If you like.

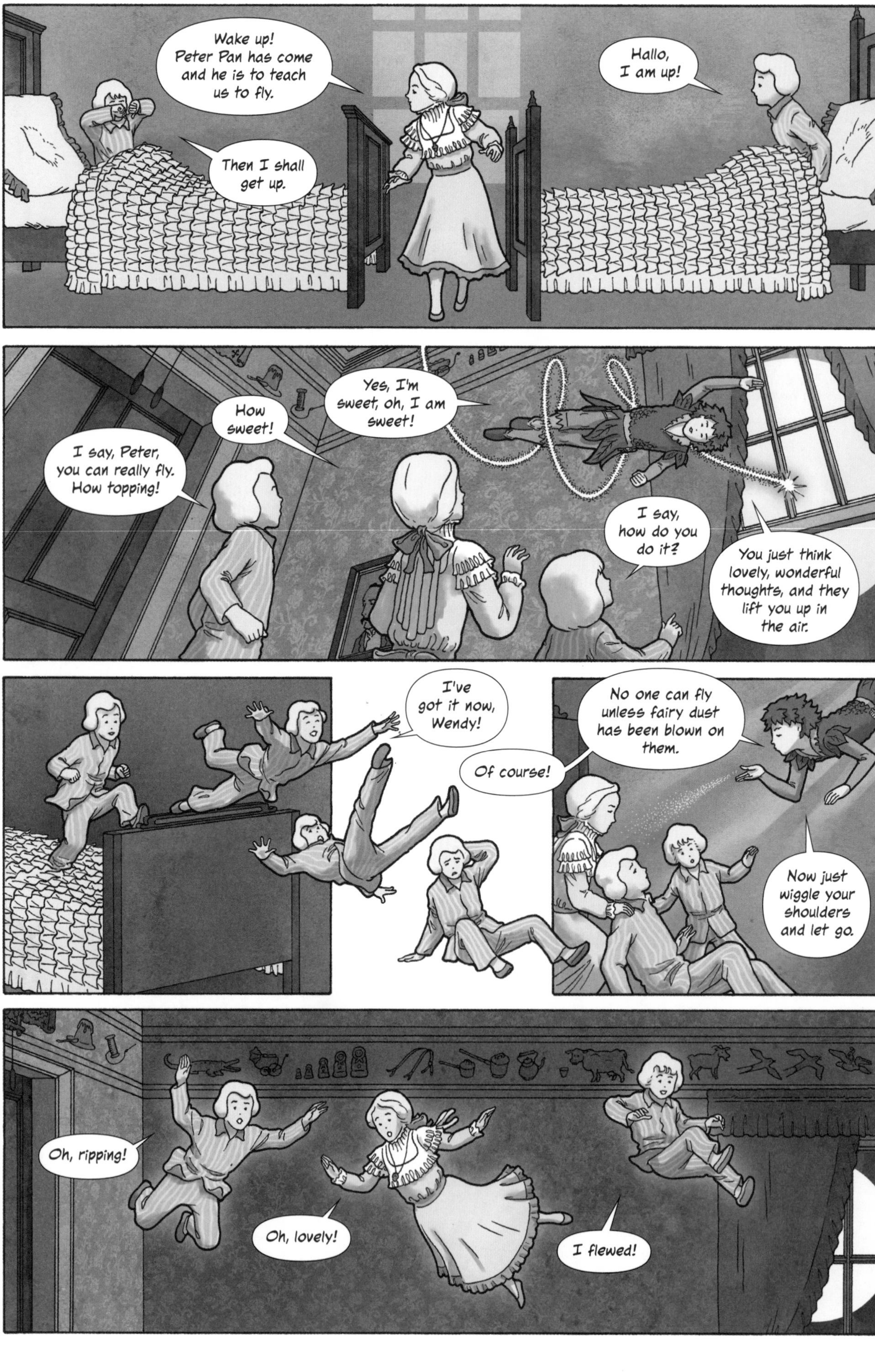
Wake up! Peter Pan has come and he is to teach us to fly.
Hallo, I am up!
Then I shall get up.
I say, Peter, you can really fly. How topping!
How sweet!
Yes, I'm sweet, oh, I am sweet!
I say, how do you do it?
You just think lovely, wonderful thoughts, and they lift you up in the air.
I've got it now, Wendy!
No one can fly unless fairy dust has been blown on them.
Of course!
Now just wiggle your shoulders and let go.
Oh, ripping!
Oh, lovely!
I flewed!

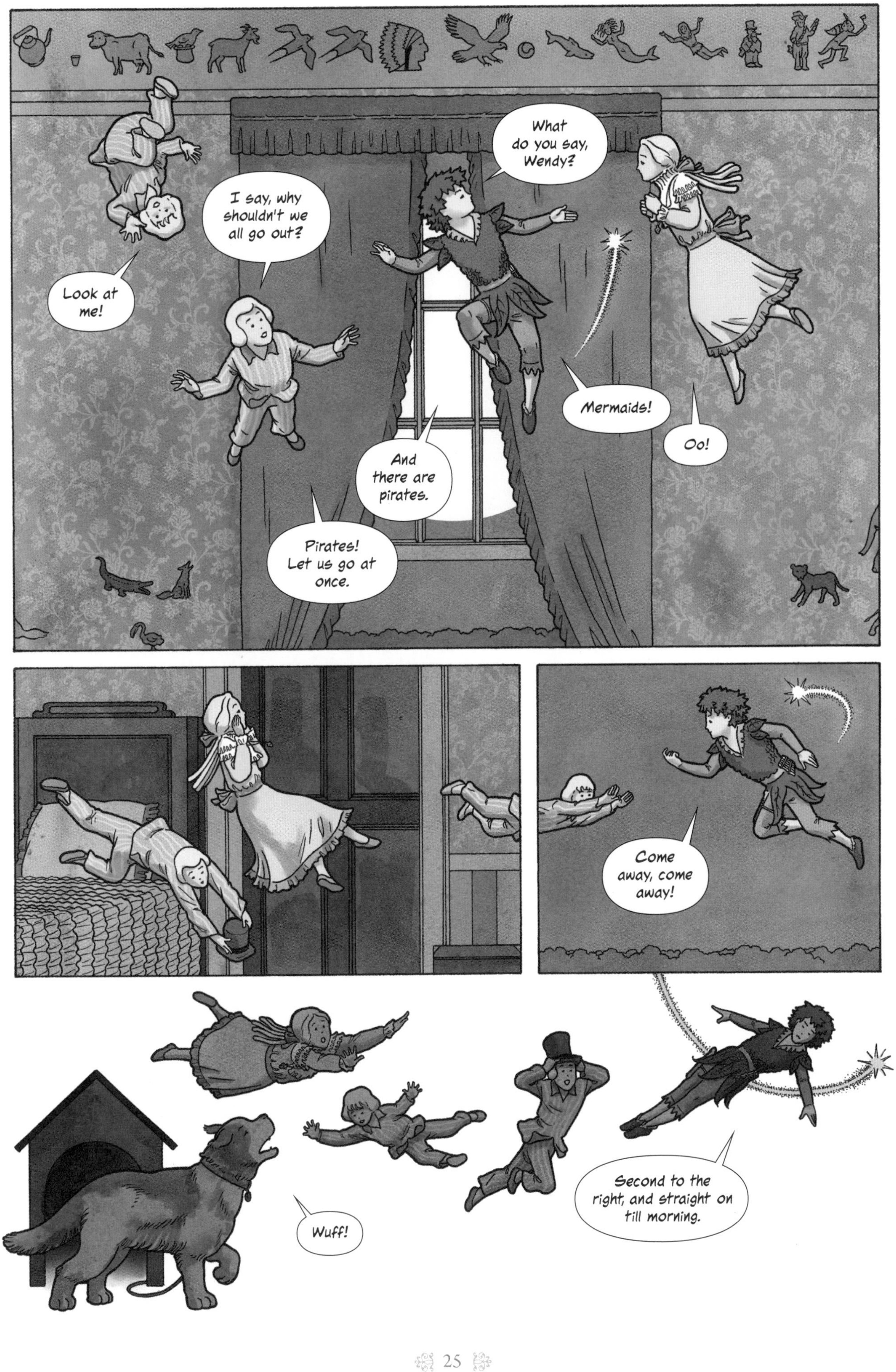
Look at me!
I say, why shouldn't we all go out?
What do you say, Wendy?
Mermaids!
Oo!
And there are pirates.
Pirates! Let us go at once.
Come away, come away!
Wuff!
Second to the right, and straight on till morning.

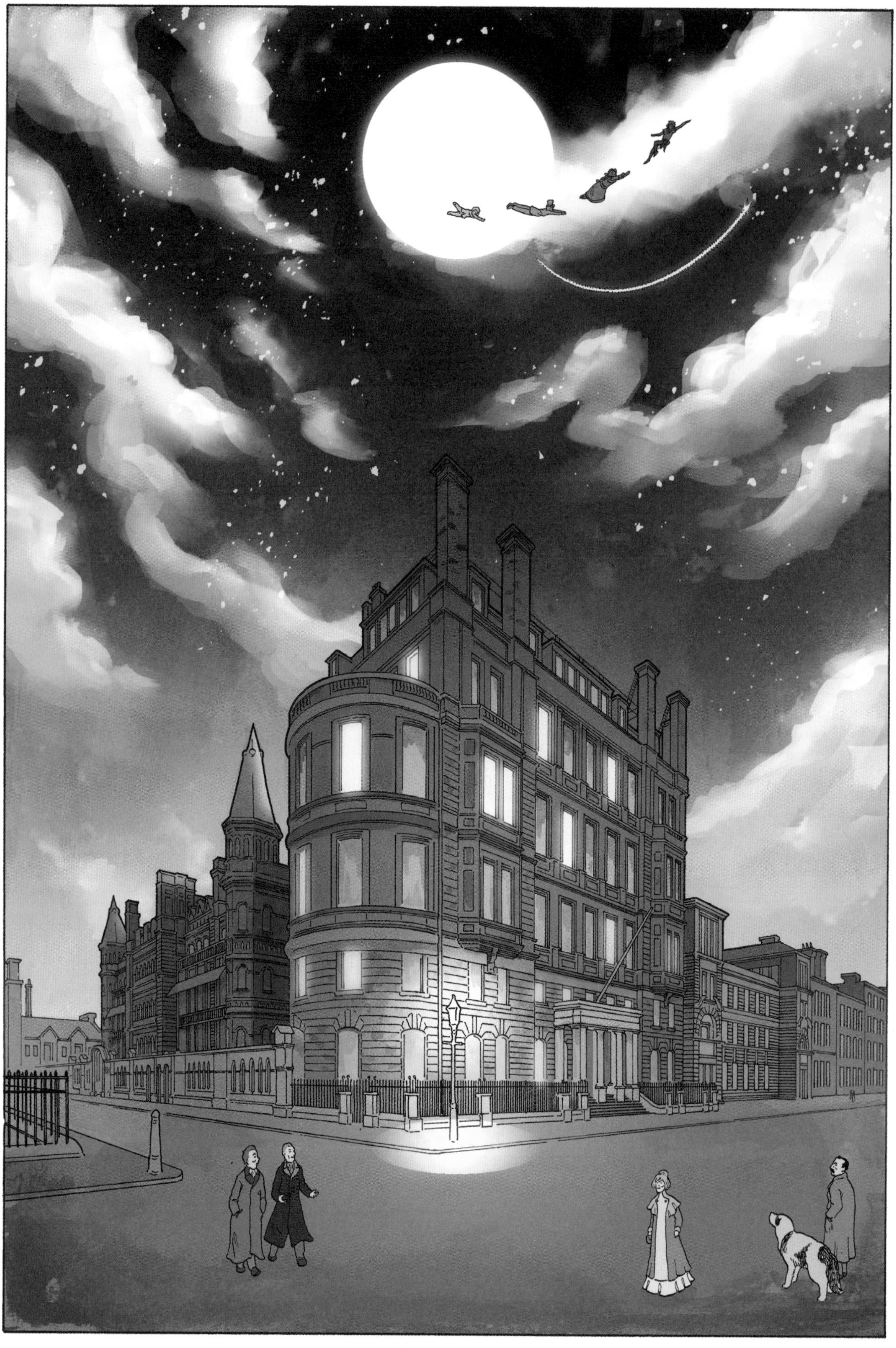

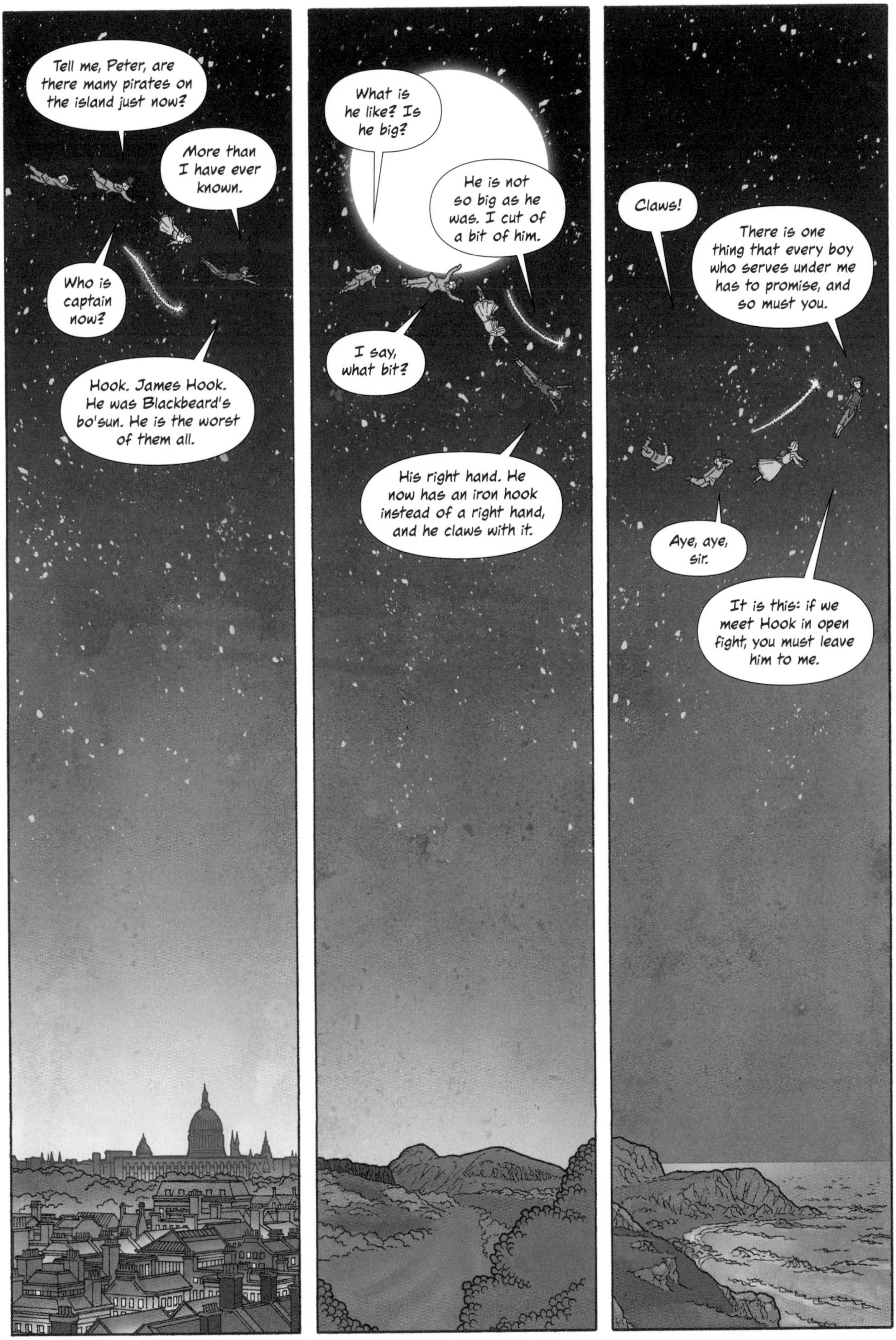

Tell me, Peter, are there many pirates on the island just now?
More than I have ever known.
Who is captain now?
Hook. James Hook. He was Blackbeard's bo'sun. He is the worst of them all.
What is he like? Is he big?
He is not so big as he was. I cut of a bit of him.
I say, what bit?
His right hand. He now has an iron hook instead of a right hand, and he claws with it.
Claws!
There is one thing that every boy who serves under me has to promise, and so must you.
Aye, aye, sir.
It is this: if we meet Hook in open fight, you must leave him to me.

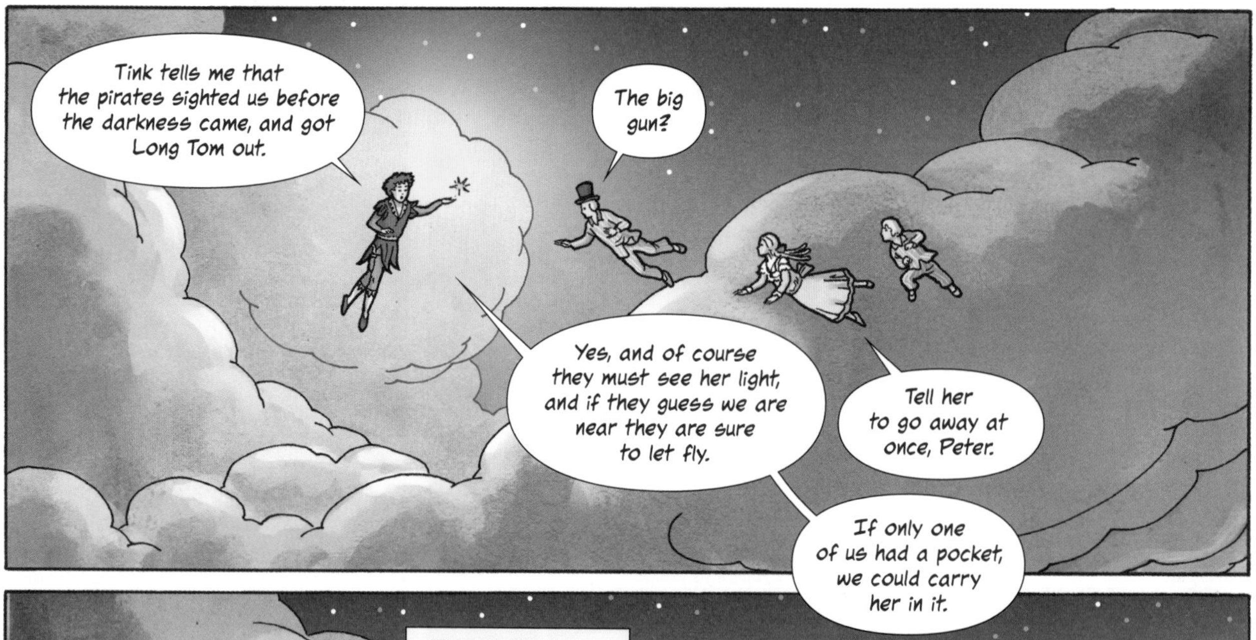
Tink tells me that the pirates sighted us before the darkness came, and got Long Tom out.
The big gun?
Yes, and of course they must see her light, and if they guess we are near they are sure to let fly.
Tell her to go away at once, Peter.
If only one of us had a pocket, we could carry her in it.

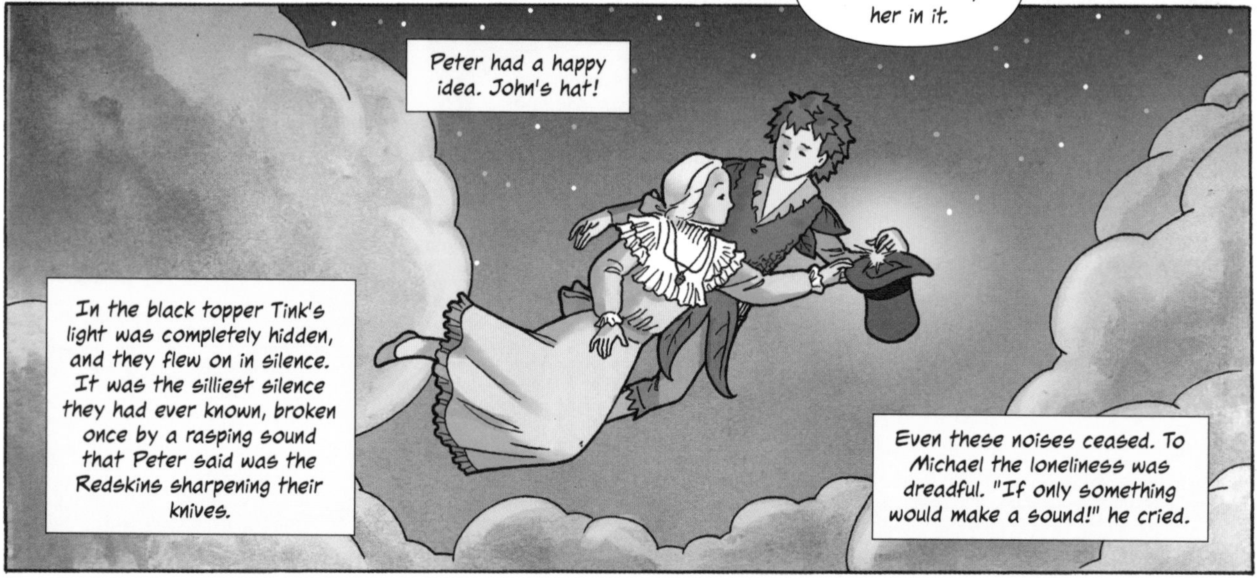
Peter had a happy idea. John's hat!
In the black topper Tink's light was completely hidden, and they flew on in silence. It was the silliest silence they had ever known, broken once by a rasping sound that Peter said was the Redskins sharpening their knives.
Even these noises ceased. To Michael the loneliness was dreadful. "If only something would make a sound!" he cried.

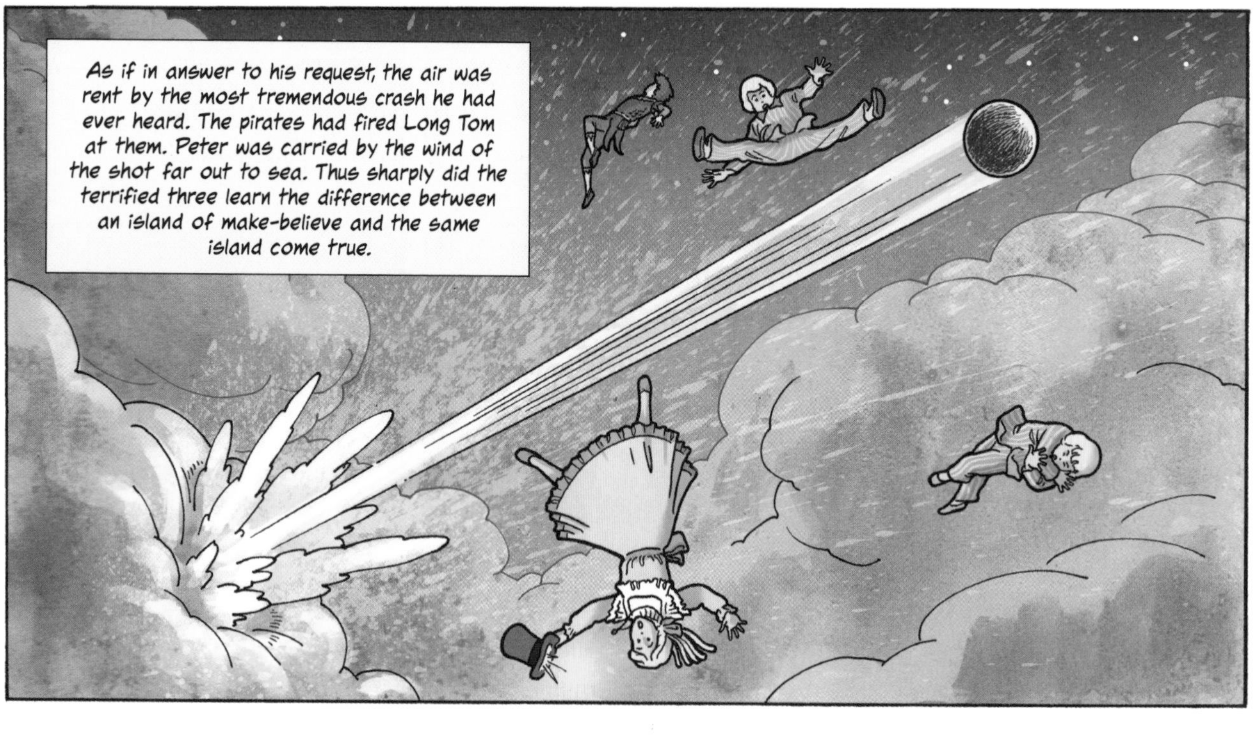
As if in answer to his request, the air was rent by the most tremendous crash he had ever heard. The pirates had fired Long Tom at them. Peter was carried by the wind of the shot far out to sea. Thus sharply did the terrified three learn the difference between an island of make-believe and the same island come true.

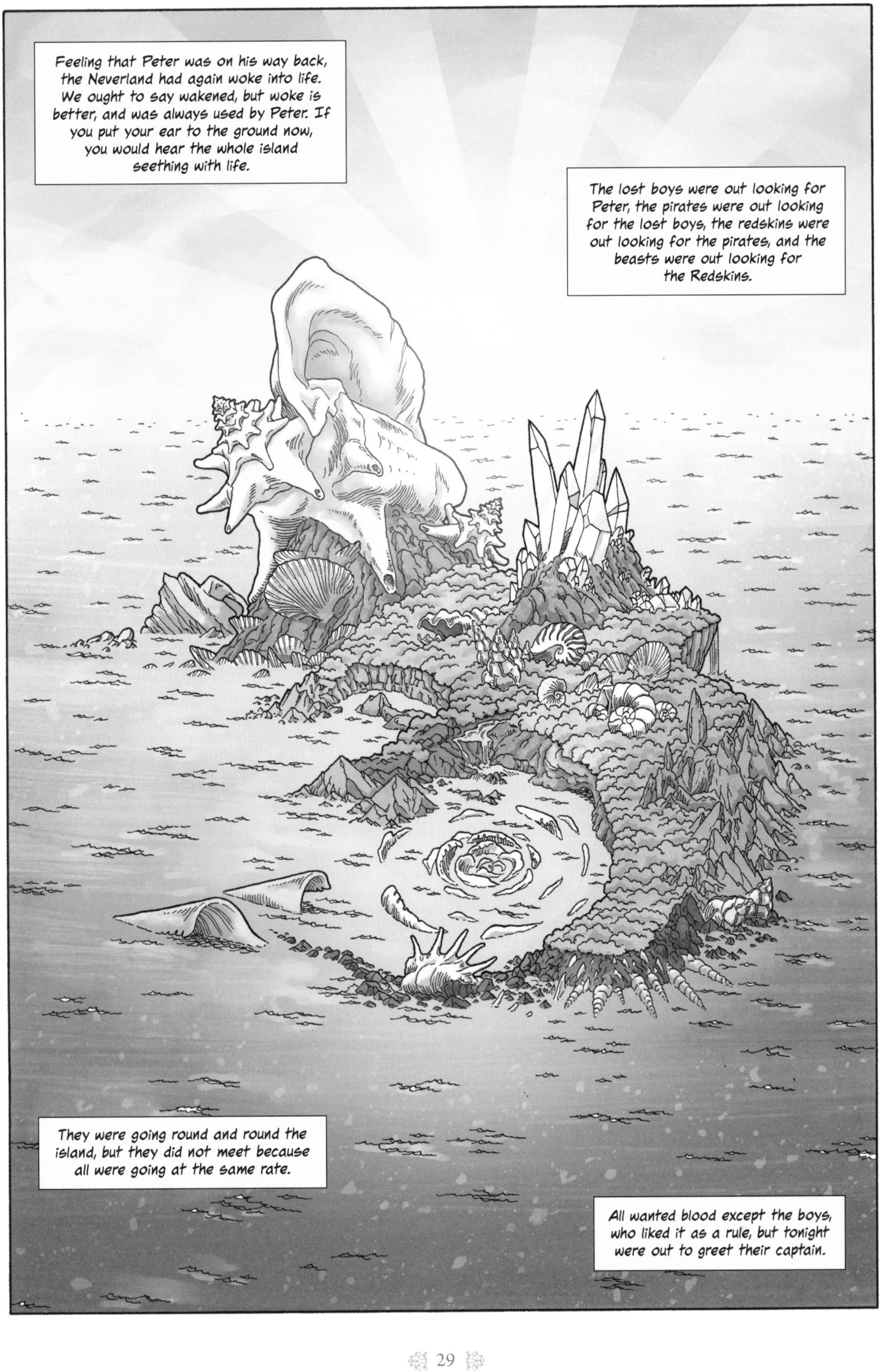
Feeling that Peter was on his way back, the Neverland had again woke into life. We ought to say wakened, but woke is better, and was always used by Peter. If you put your ear to the ground now, you would hear the whole island seething with life.
The lost boys were out looking for Peter, the pirates were out looking for the lost boys, the redskins were out looking for the pirates, and the beasts were out looking for the Redskins.
They were going round and round the island, but they did not meet because all were going at the same rate.
All wanted blood except the boys, who liked it as a rule, but tonight were out to greet their captain.

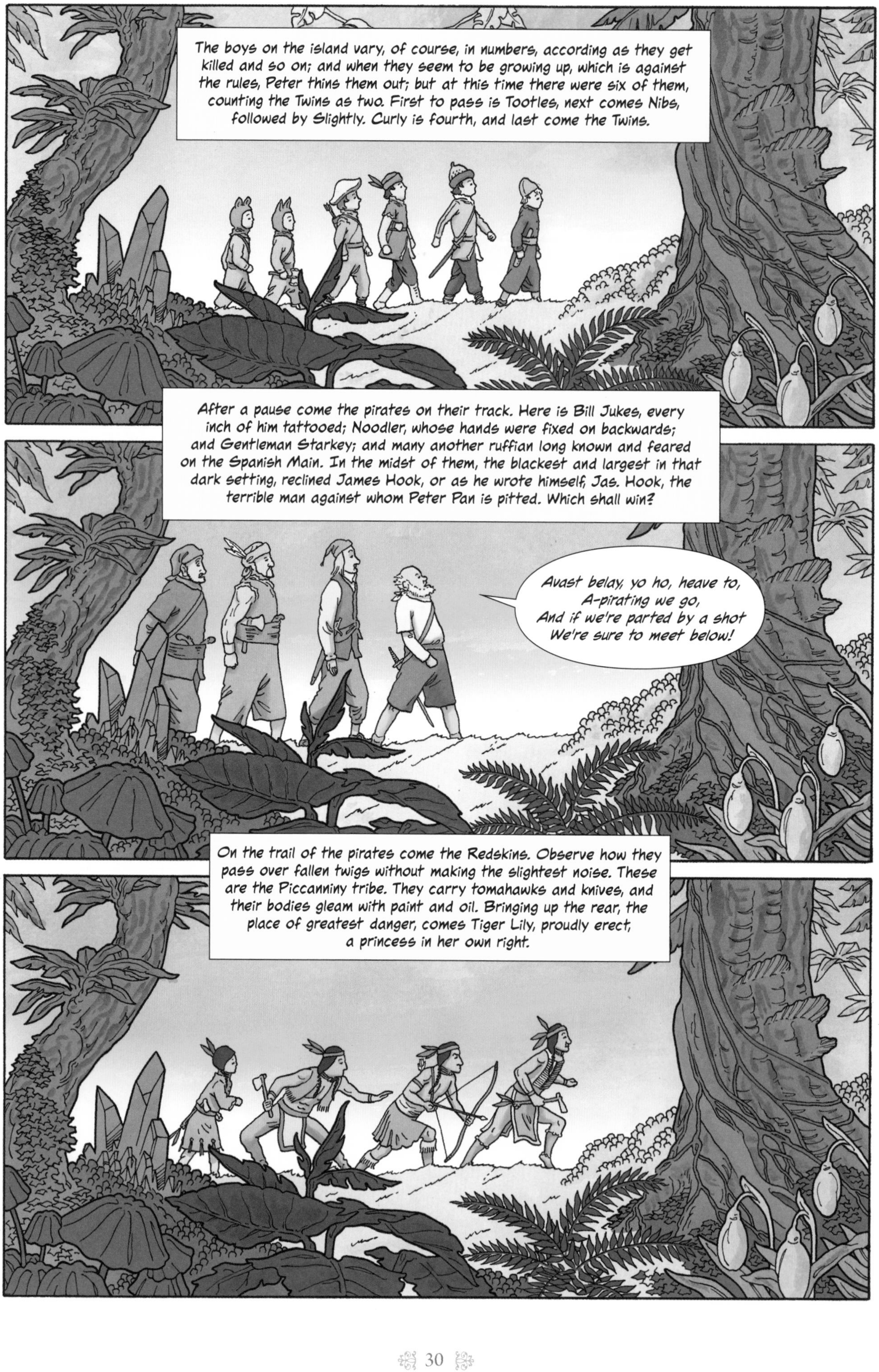

The boys on the island vary, of course, in numbers, according as they get killed and so on; and when they seem to be growing up, which is against the rules, Peter thins them out; but at this time there were six of them, counting the Twins as two. First to pass is Tootles, next comes Nibs, followed by Slightly. Curly is fourth, and last come the Twins.
After a pause come the pirates on their track. Here is Bill Jukes, every inch of him tattooed; Noodler, whose hands were fixed on backwards; and Gentleman Starkey; and many another ruffian long known and feared on the Spanish Main. In the midst of them, the blackest and largest in that dark setting, reclined James Hook, or as he wrote himself, Jas. Hook, the terrible man against whom Peter Pan is pitted. Which shall win?
Avast belay, yo ho, heave to, A-pirating we go, And if we're parted by a shot We're sure to meet below!
On the trail of the pirates come the Redskins. Observe how they pass over fallen twigs without making the slightest noise. These are the Piccanniny tribe. They carry tomahawks and knives, and their bodies gleam with paint and oil. Bringing up the rear, the place of greatest danger, comes Tiger Lily, proudly erect, a princess in her own right.

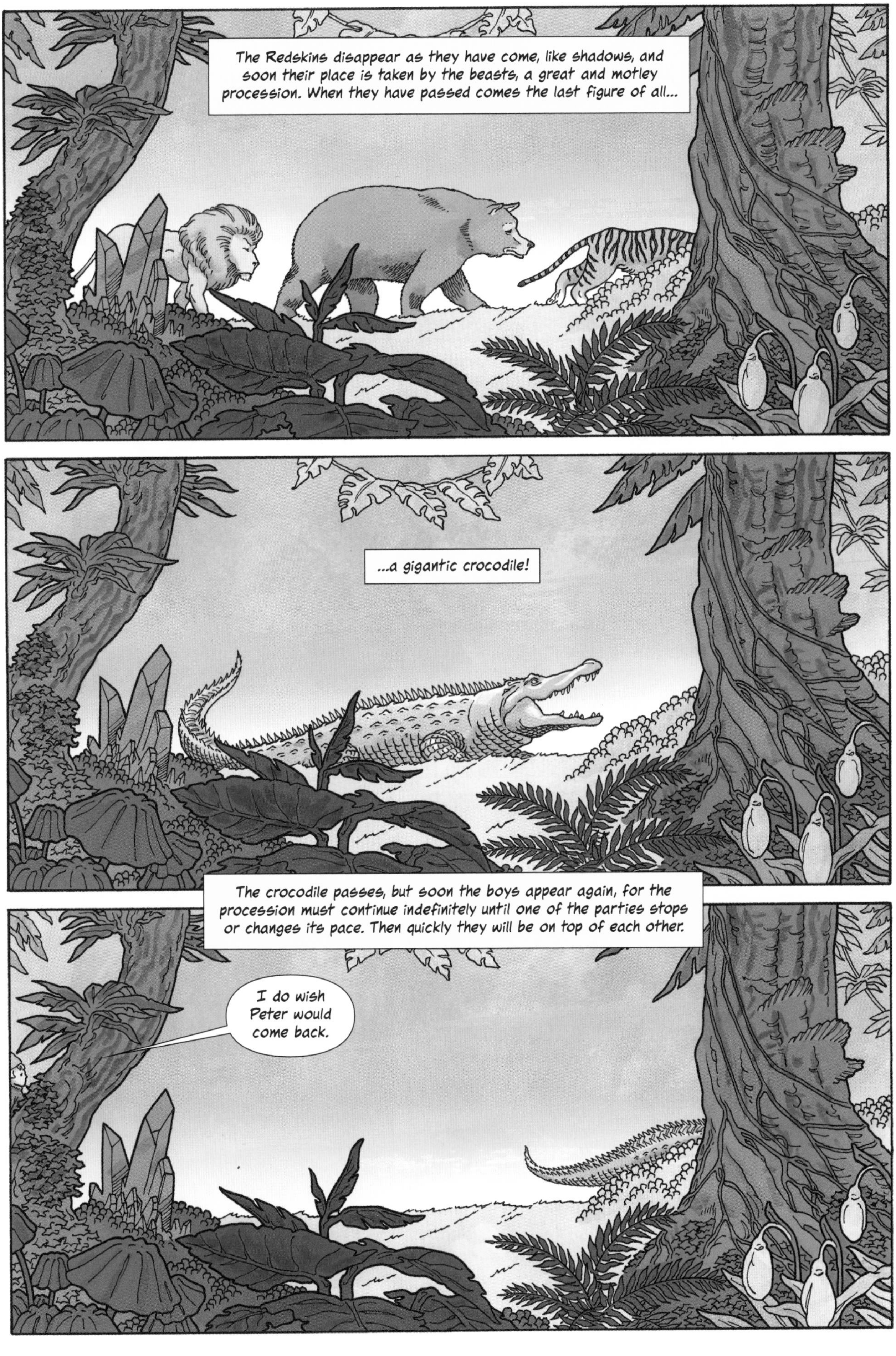
The Redskins disappear as they have come, like shadows, and soon their place is taken by the beasts, a great and motley procession. When they have passed comes the last figure of all...
...a gigantic crocodile!
The crocodile passes, but soon the boys appear again, for the procession must continue indefinitely until one of the parties stops or changes its pace. Then quickly they will be on top of each other.
I do wish Peter would come back.

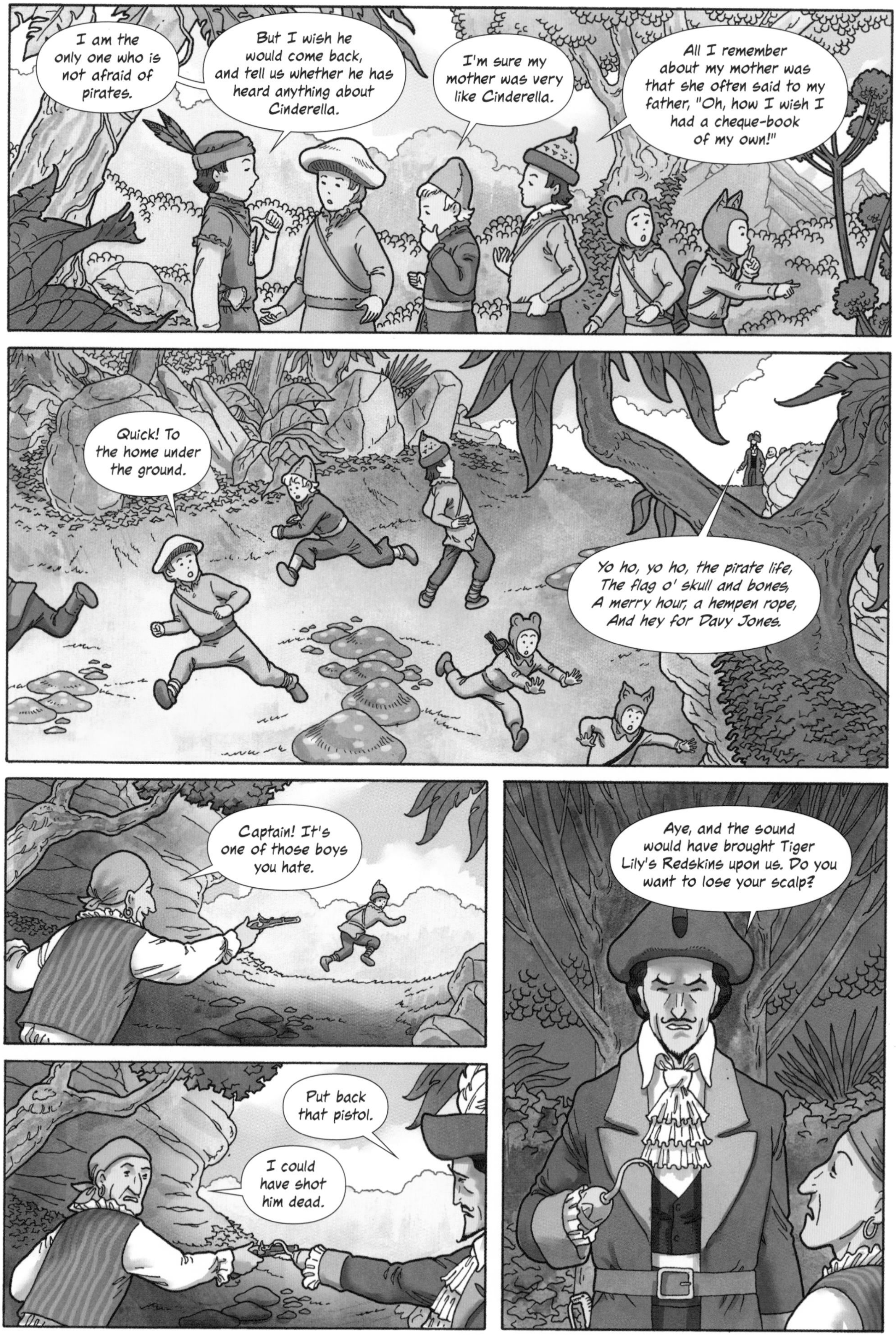

I am the only one who is not afraid of pirates.
But I wish he would come back, and tell us whether he has heard anything about Cinderella.
I'm sure my mother was very like Cinderella.
All I remember about my mother was that she often said to my father, "Oh, how I wish I had a cheque-book of my own!"
Quick! To the home under the ground.
Yo ho, yo ho, the pirate life,
The flag o' skull and bones,
A merry hour, a hempen rope,
And hey for Davy Jones.
Captain! It's one of those boys you hate.
Aye, and the sound would have brought Tiger Lily's Redskins upon us. Do you want to lose your scalp?
Put back that pistol.
I could have shot him dead.

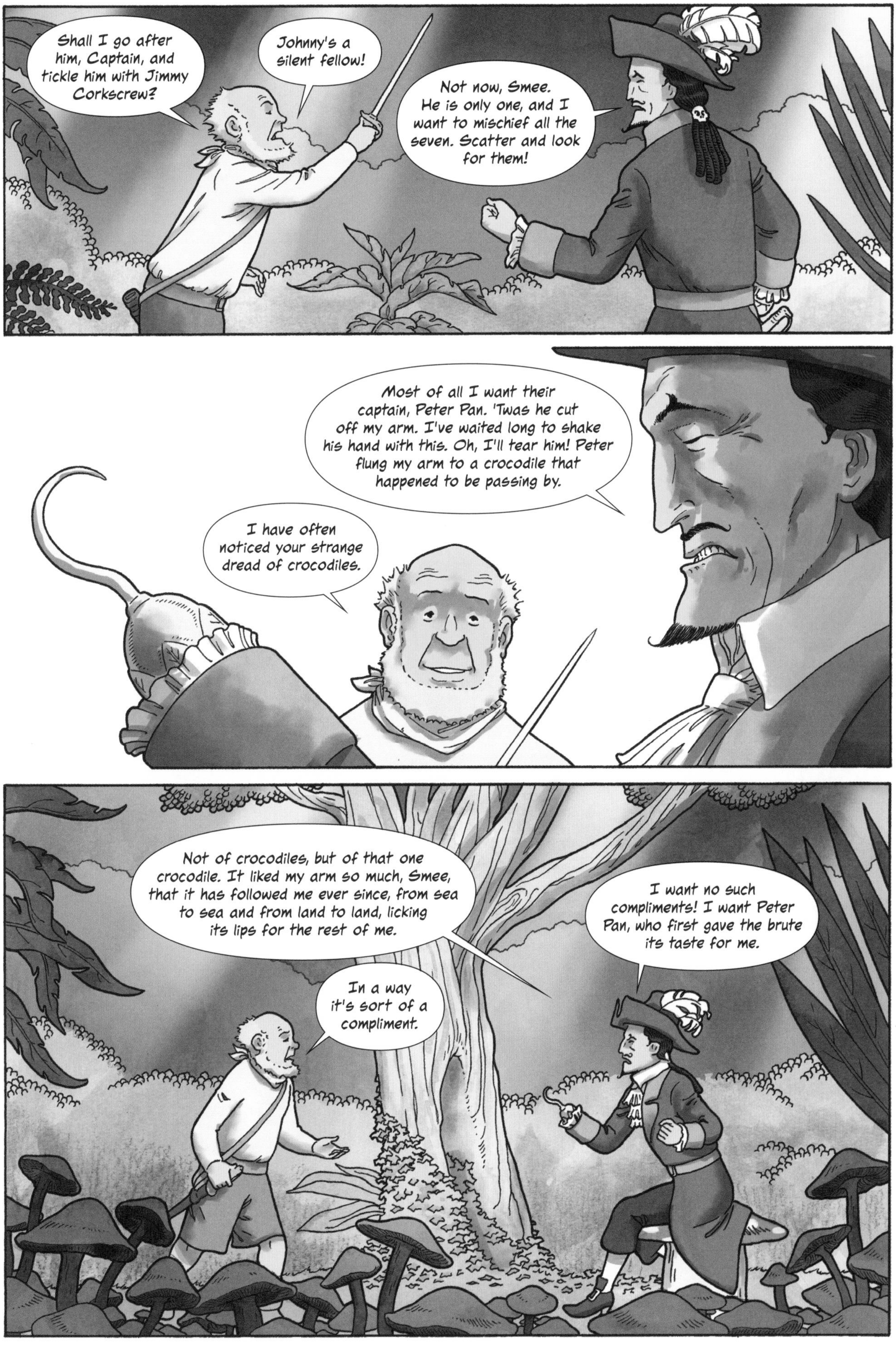
Shall I go after him, Captain, and tickle him with Jimmy Corkscrew?
Johnny's a silent fellow!
Not now, Smee. He is only one, and I want to mischief all the seven. Scatter and look for them!
Most of all I want their captain, Peter Pan. 'Twas he cut off my arm. I've waited long to shake his hand with this. Oh, I'll tear him! Peter flung my arm to a crocodile that happened to be passing by.
I have often noticed your strange dread of crocodiles.
Not of crocodiles, but of that one crocodile. It liked my arm so much, Smee, that it has followed me ever since, from sea to sea and from land to land, licking its lips for the rest of me.
In a way it's sort of a compliment.
I want no such compliments! I want Peter Pan, who first gave the brute its taste for me.

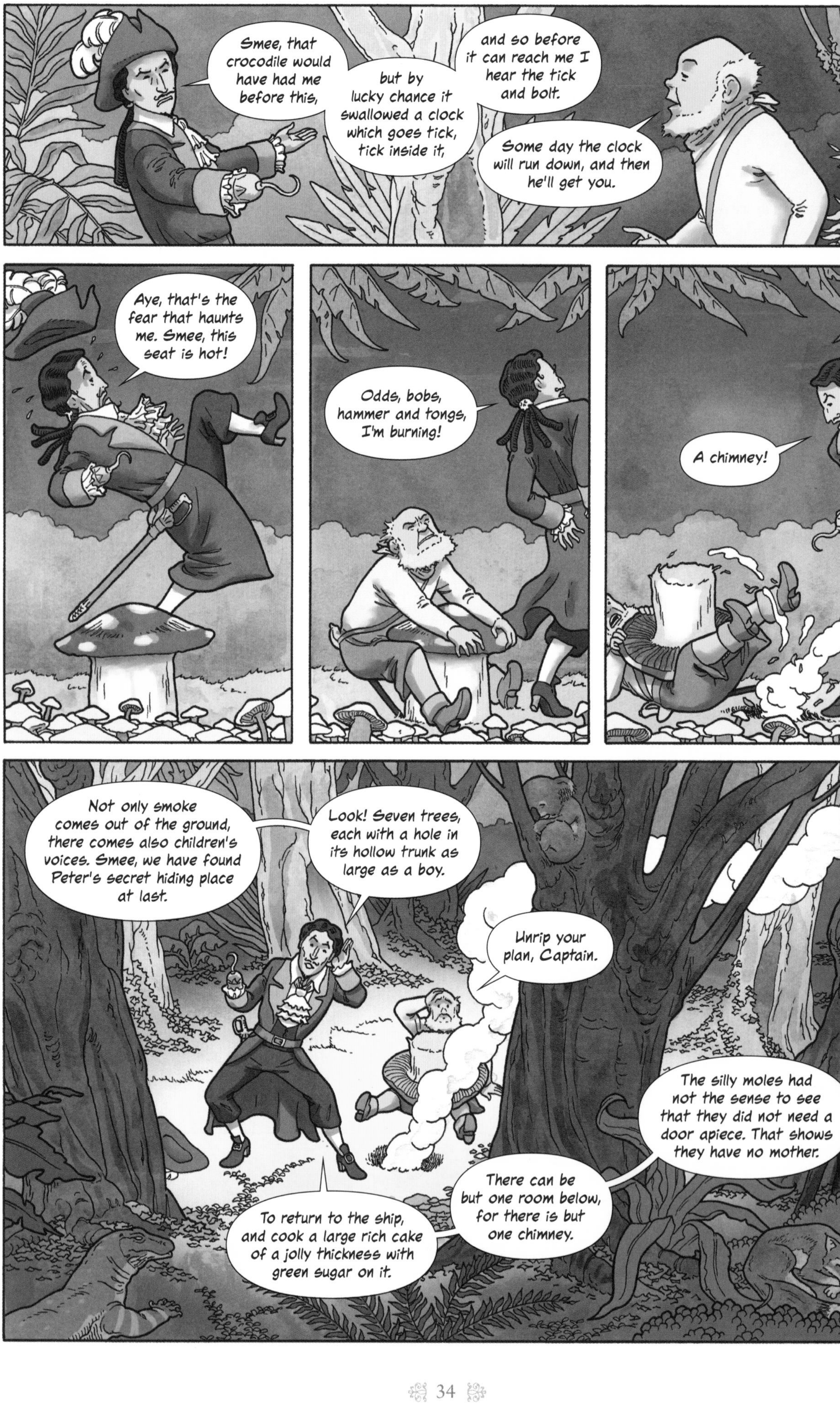
Smee, that crocodile would have had me before this,
but by lucky chance it swallowed a clock which goes tick, tick inside it,
and so before it can reach me I hear the tick and bolt.
Some day the clock will run down, and then he'll get you.
Aye, that's the fear that haunts me. Smee, this seat is hot!
Odds, bobs, hammer and tongs, I'm burning!
A chimney!
Not only smoke comes out of the ground, there comes also children's voices. Smee, we have found Peter's secret hiding place at last.
Look! Seven trees, each with a hole in its hollow trunk as large as a boy.
Unrip your plan, Captain.
To return to the ship, and cook a large rich cake of a jolly thickness with green sugar on it.
There can be but one room below, for there is but one chimney.
The silly moles had not the sense to see that they did not need a door apiece. That shows they have no mother.

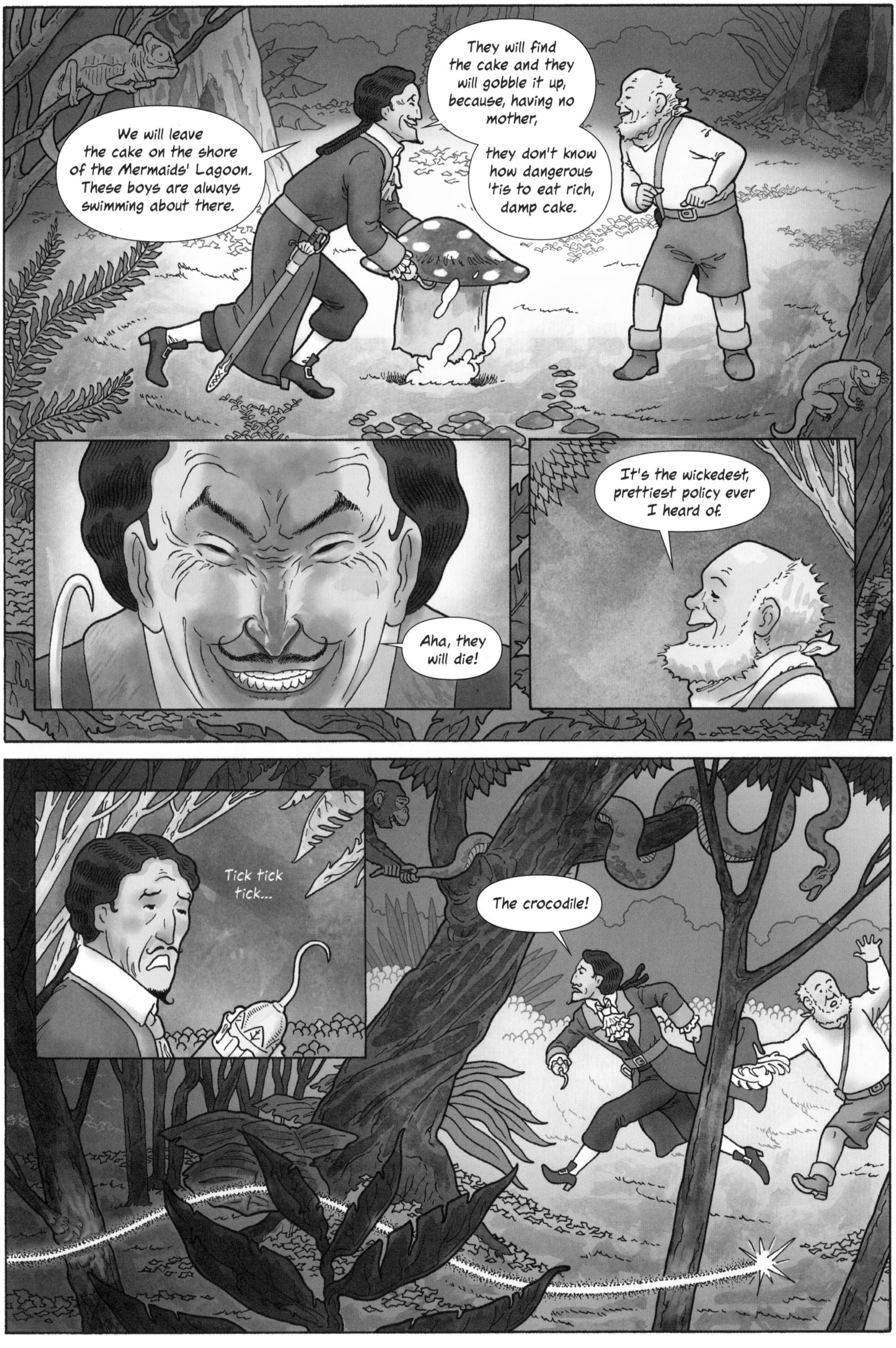
We will leave the cake on the shore of the Mermaids' Lagoon. These boys are always swimming about there.
They will find the cake and they will gobble it up, because, having no mother,
they don't know how dangerous 'tis to eat rich, damp cake.
Aha, they will die!
It's the wickedest, prettiest policy ever I heard of.
Tick tick tick...
The crocodile!

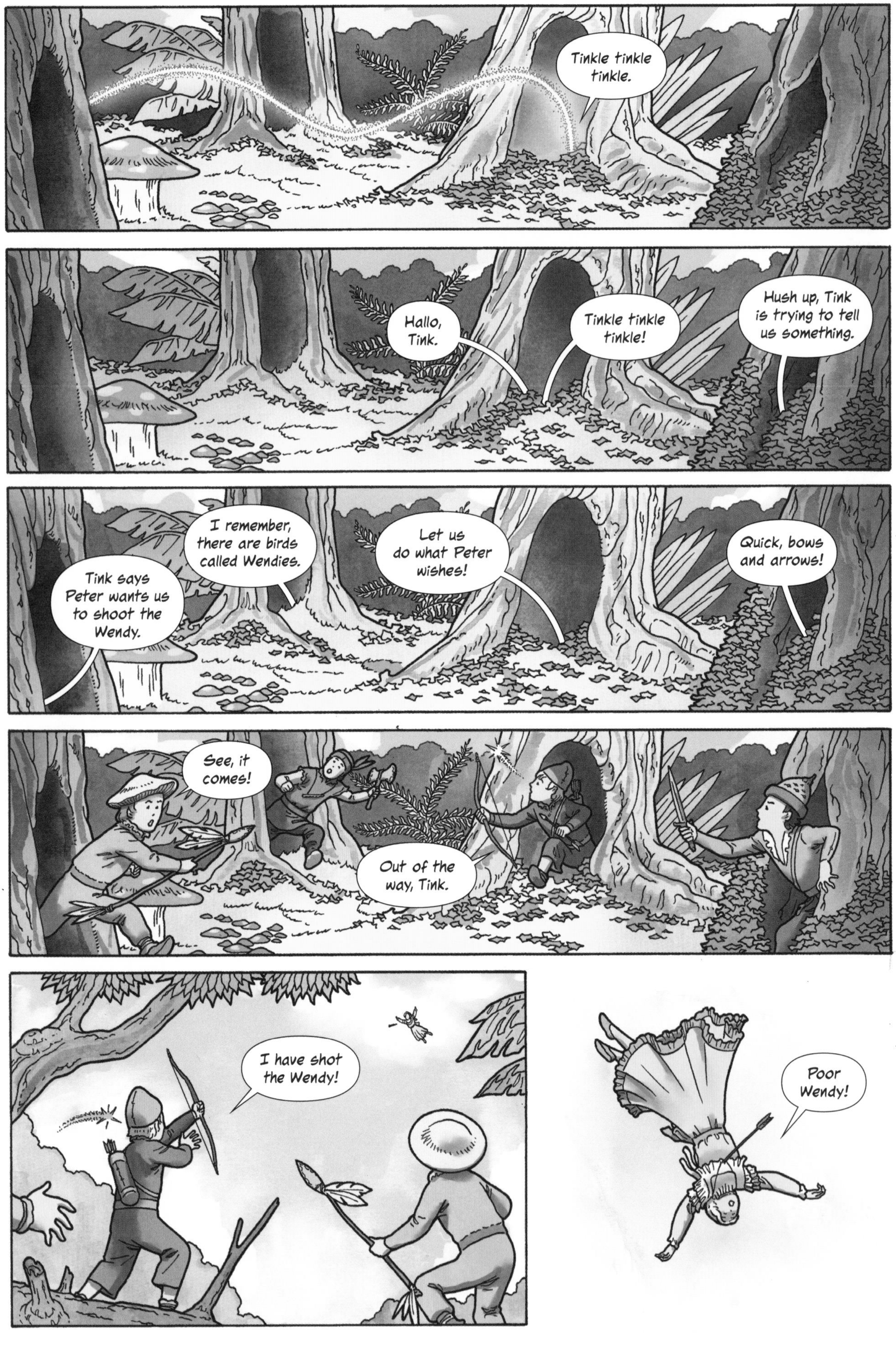
Tinkle tinkle tinkle.
Hallo, Tink.
Tinkle tinkle tinkle!
Hush up, Tink is trying to tell us something.
Tink says Peter wants us to shoot the Wendy.
I remember, there are birds called Wendies.
Let us do what Peter wishes!
Quick, bows and arrows!
See, it comes!
Out of the way, Tink.
I have shot the Wendy!
Poor Wendy!

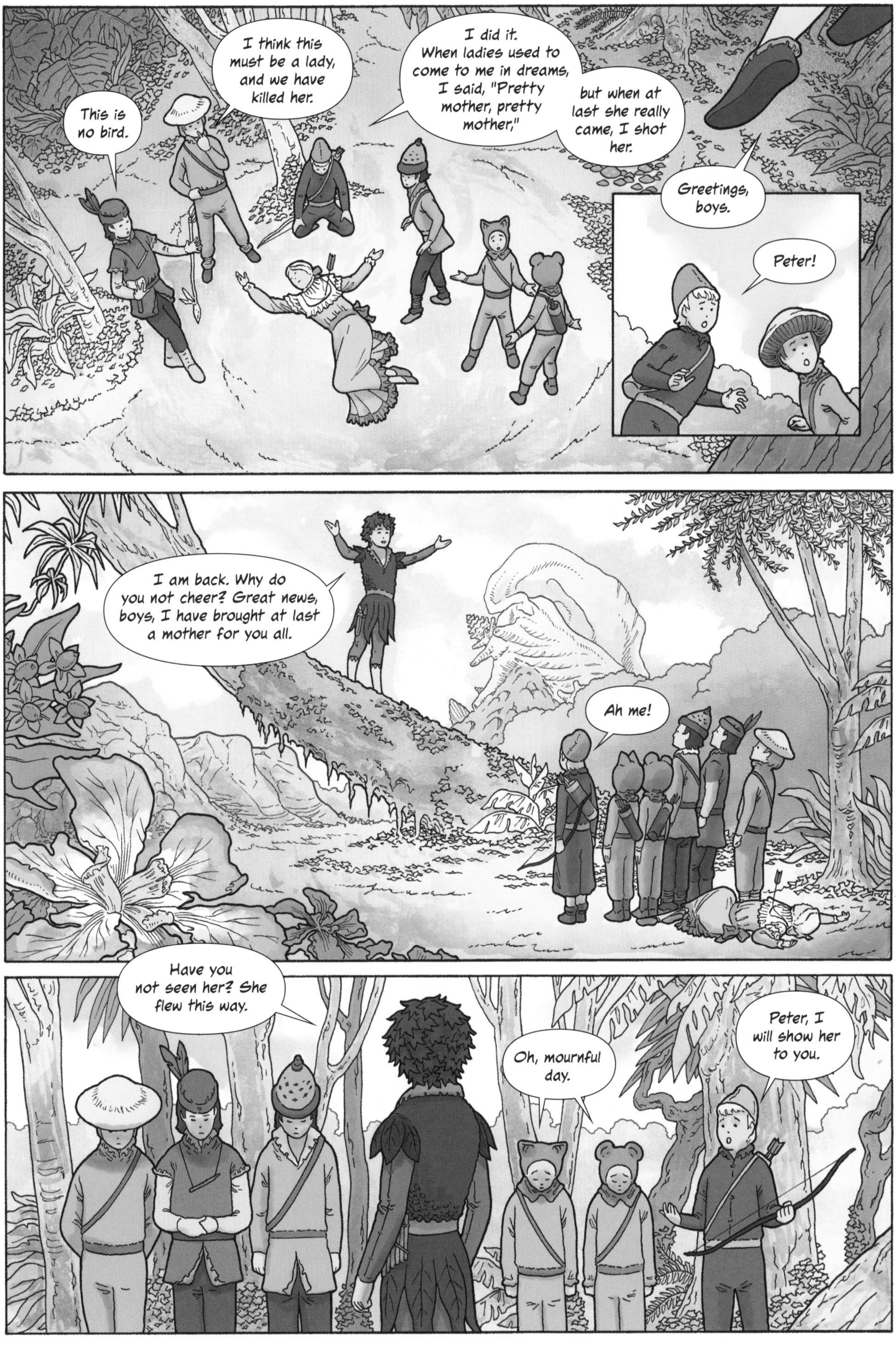
This is no bird.
I think this must be a lady, and we have killed her.
I did it. When ladies used to come to me in dreams, I said, "Pretty mother, pretty mother,"
but when at last she really came, I shot her.
Greetings, boys.
Peter!
I am back. Why do you not cheer? Great news, boys, I have brought at last a mother for you all.
Ah me!
Have you not seen her? She flew this way.
Oh, mournful day.
Peter, I will show her to you.

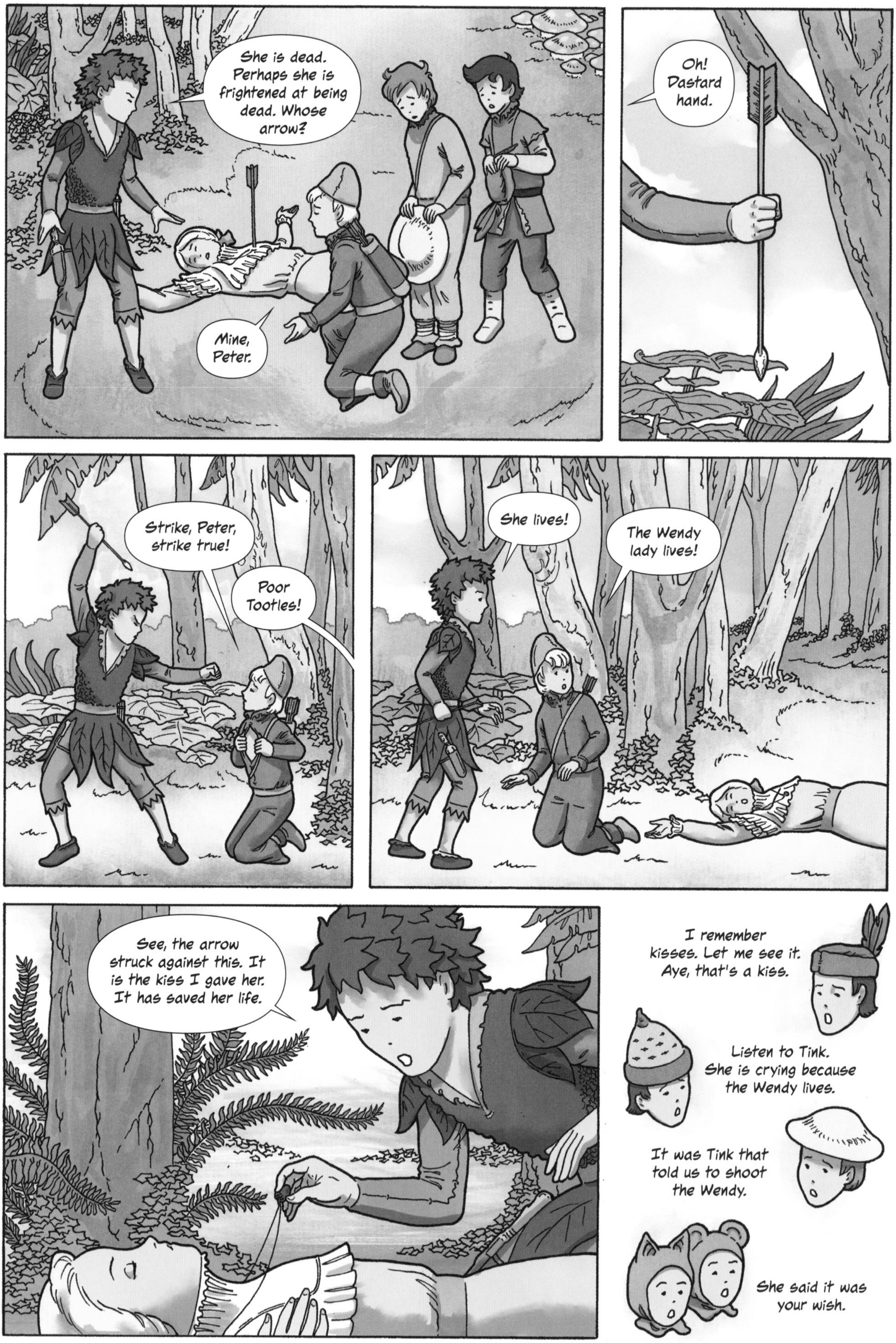
She is dead. Perhaps she is frightened at being dead. Whose arrow?
Mine, Peter.
Oh! Dastard hand.
Strike, Peter, strike true!
Poor Tootles!
She lives!
The Wendy lady lives!
See, the arrow struck against this. It is the kiss I gave her. It has saved her life.
I remember kisses. Let me see it. Aye, that's a kiss.
Listen to Tink. She is crying because the Wendy lives.
It was Tink that told us to shoot the Wendy.
She said it was your wish.

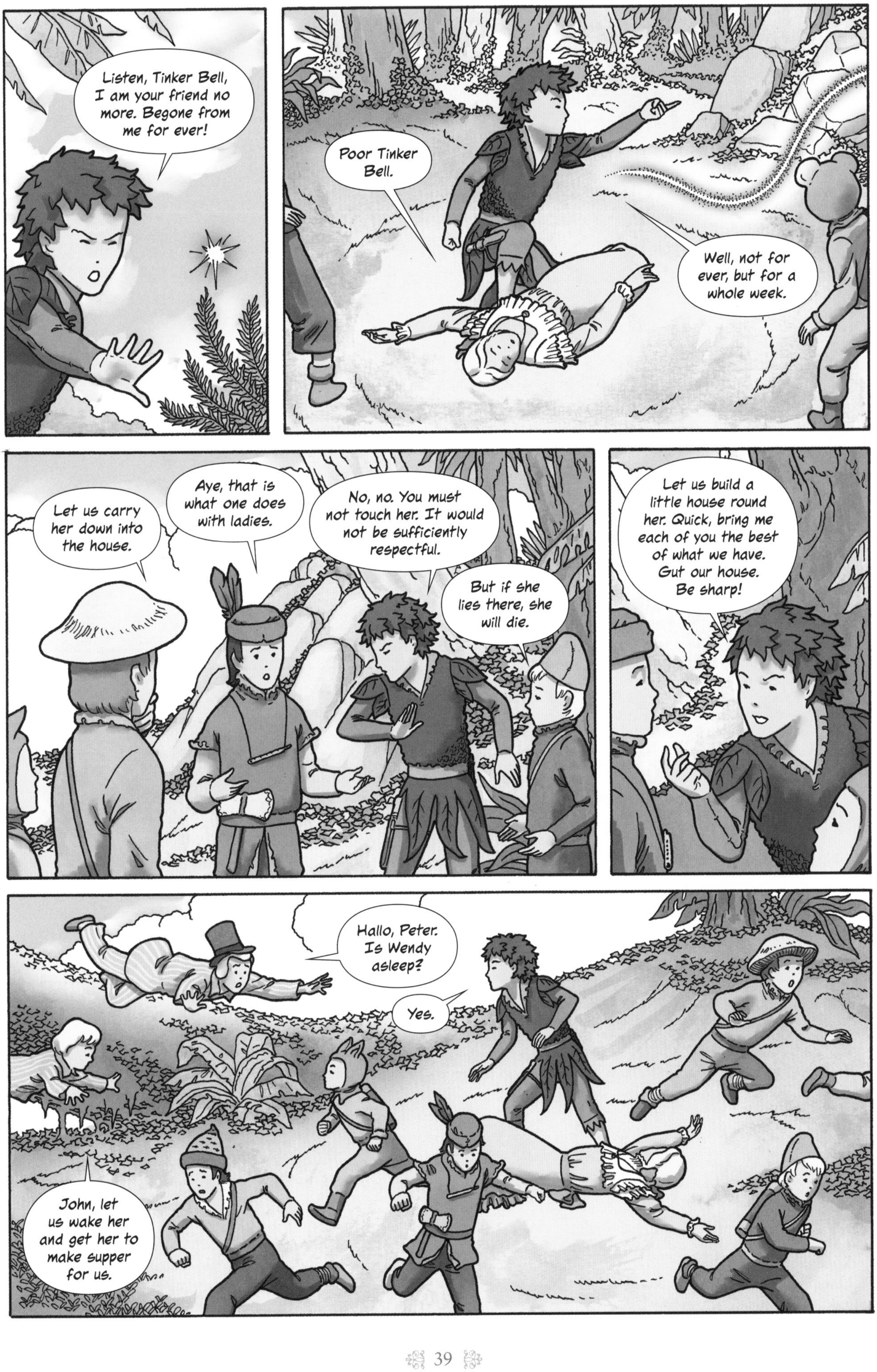
Listen, Tinker Bell, I am your friend no more. Begone from me for ever!
Poor Tinker Bell.
Well, not for ever, but for a whole week.
Let us carry her down into the house.
Aye, that is what one does with ladies.
No, no. You must not touch her. It would not be sufficiently respectful.
But if she lies there, she will die.
Let us build a little house round her. Quick, bring me each of you the best of what we have. Gut our house. Be sharp!
Hallo, Peter. Is Wendy asleep?
Yes.
John, let us wake her and get her to make supper for us.

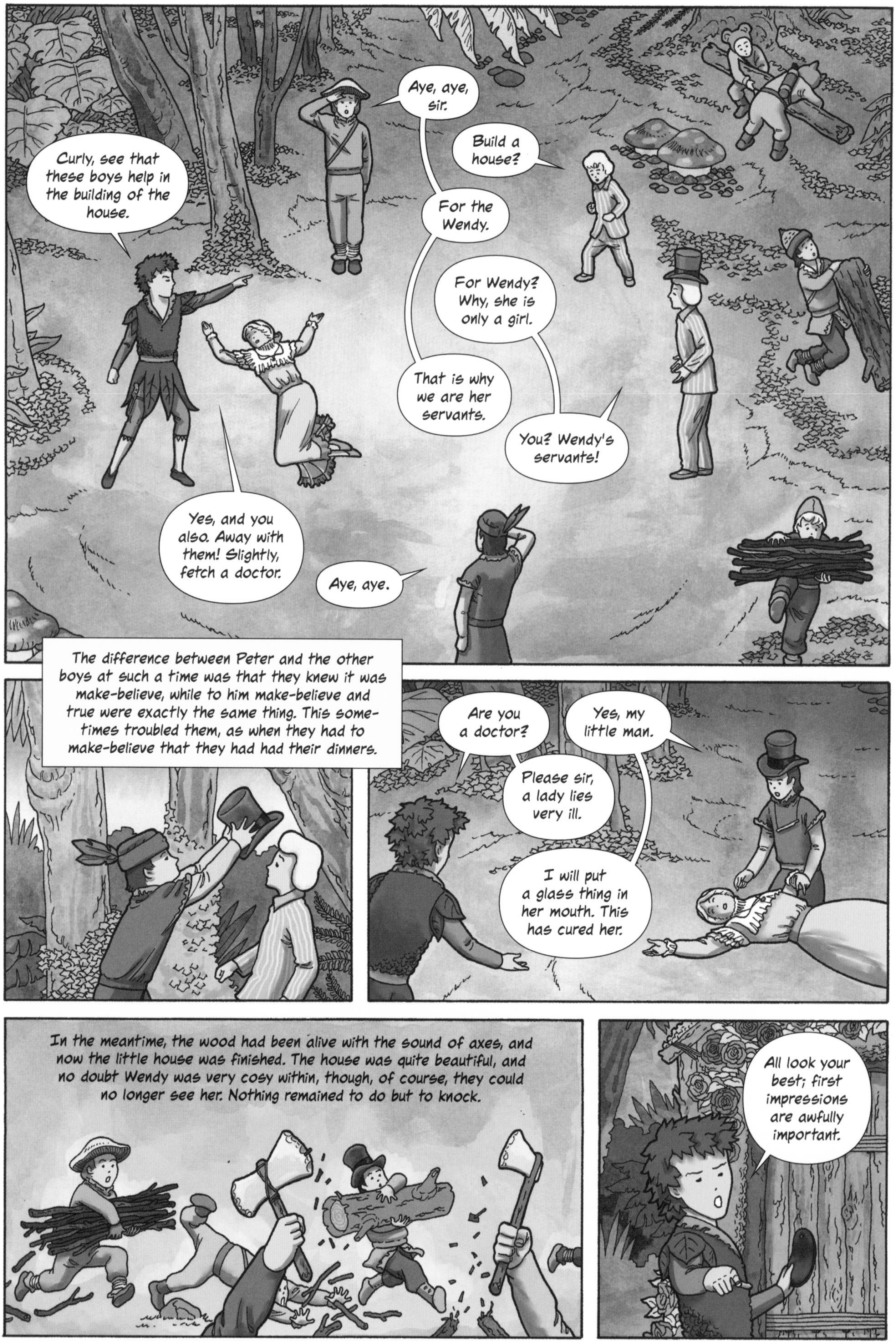
Curly, see that these boys help in the building of the house.
Aye, aye, sir.
Build a house?
For the Wendy.
For Wendy? Why, she is only a girl.
That is why we are her servants.
You? Wendy's servants!
Yes, and you also. Away with them! Slightly, fetch a doctor.
Aye, aye.
The difference between Peter and the other boys at such a time was that they knew it was make-believe, while to him make-believe and true were exactly the same thing. This sometimes troubled them, as when they had to make-believe that they had had their dinners.
Are you a doctor?
Yes, my little man.
Please sir, a lady lies very ill.
I will put a glass thing in her mouth. This has cured her.
In the meantime, the wood had been alive with the sound of axes, and now the little house was finished. The house was quite beautiful, and no doubt Wendy was very cosy within, though, of course, they could no longer see her. Nothing remained to do but to knock.
All look your best; first impressions are awfully important.

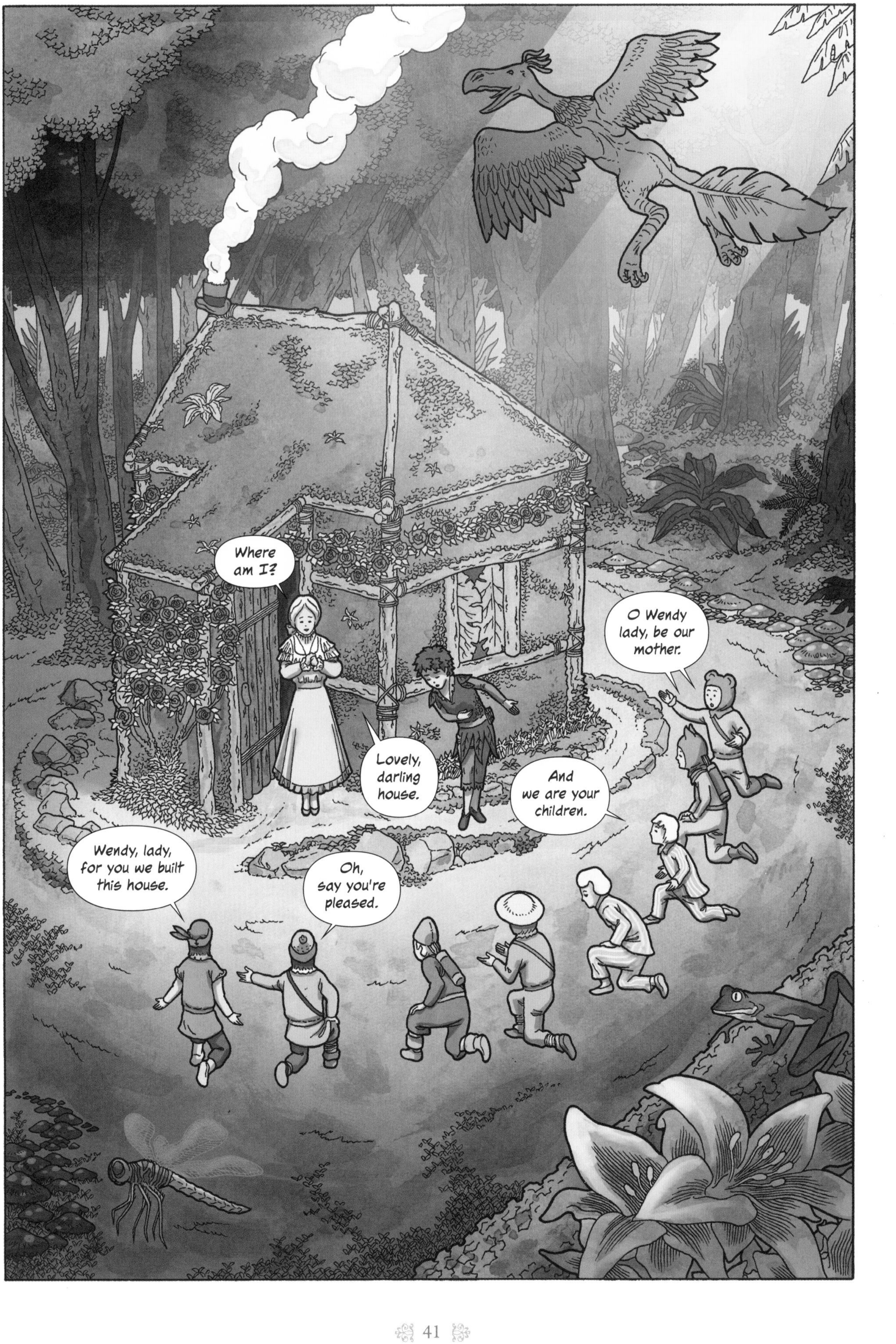
Where am I?
Lovely, darling house.
O Wendy lady, be our mother.
And we are your children.
Wendy, lady, for you we built this house.
Oh, say you're pleased.

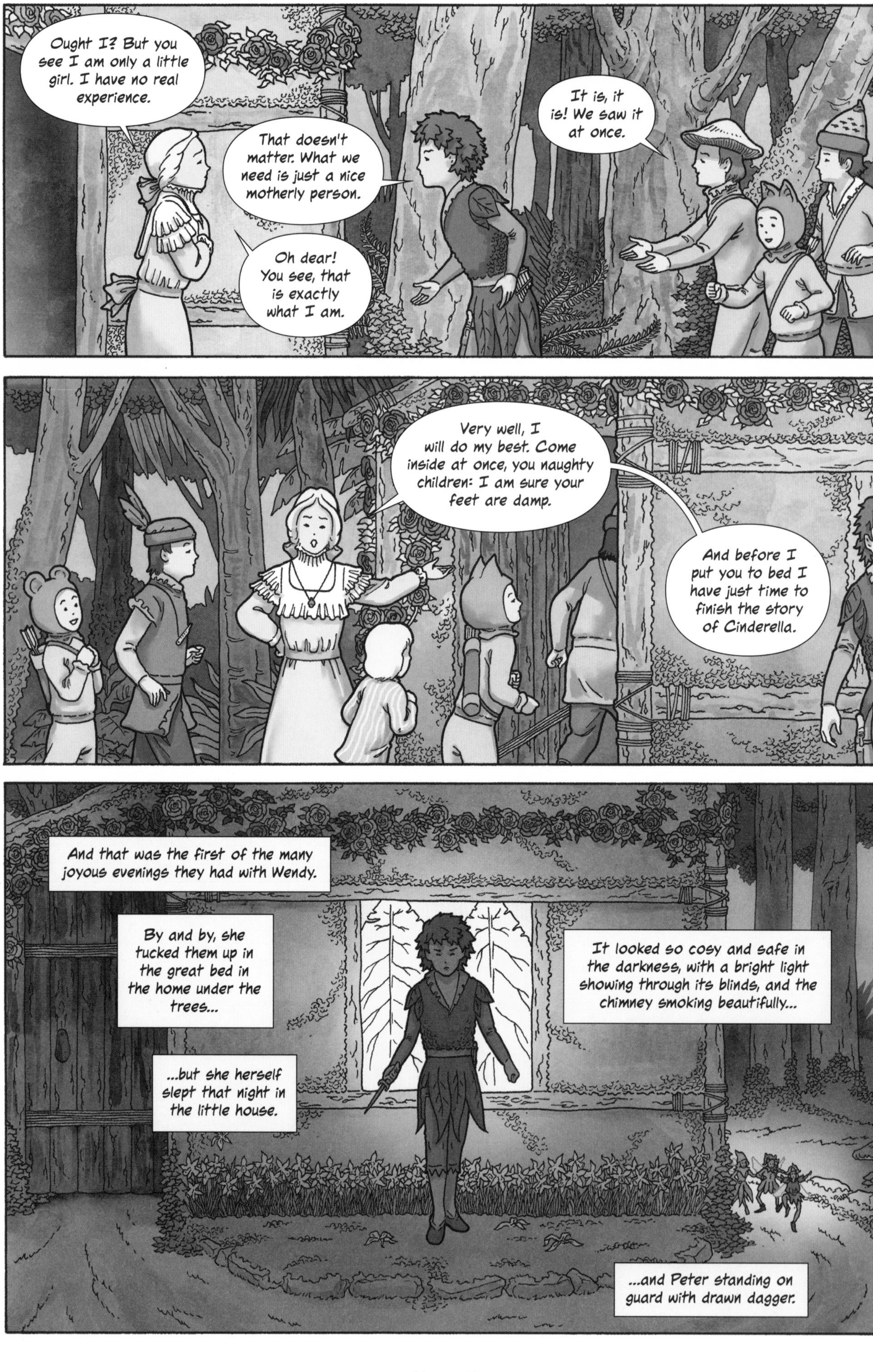

Ought I? But you see I am only a little girl. I have no real experience.
That doesn't matter. What we need is just a nice motherly person.
Oh dear! You see, that is exactly what I am.
It is, it is! We saw it at once.
Very well, I will do my best. Come inside at once, you naughty children: I am sure your feet are damp.
And before I put you to bed I have just time to finish the story of Cinderella.
And that was the first of the many joyous evenings they had with Wendy.
By and by, she tucked them up in the great bed in the home under the trees...
...but she herself slept that night in the little house.
It looked so cosy and safe in the darkness, with a bright light showing through its blinds, and the chimney smoking beautifully...
...and Peter standing on guard with drawn dagger.

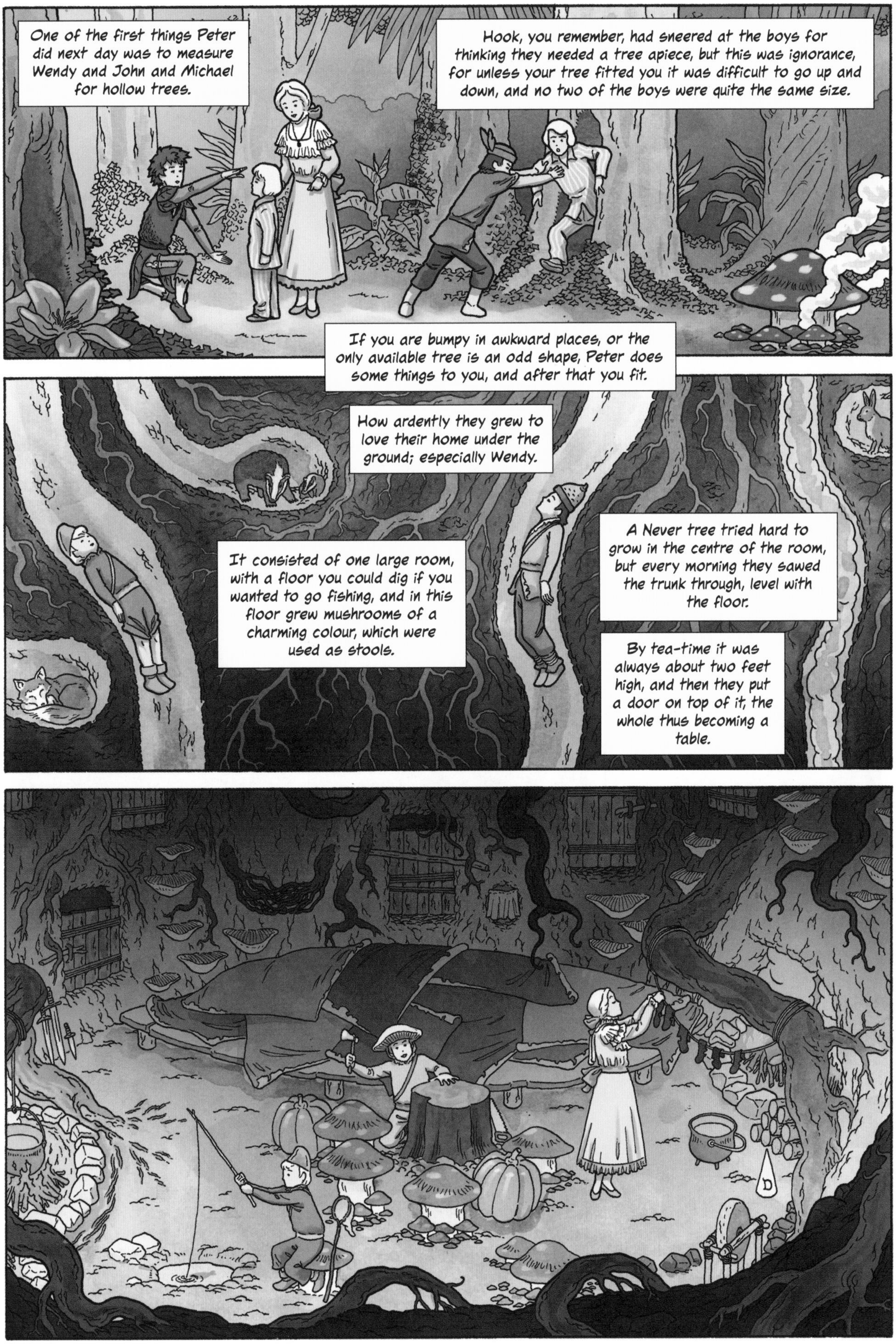
One of the first things Peter did next day was to measure Wendy and John and Michael for hollow trees.
Hook, you remember, had sneered at the boys for thinking they needed a tree apiece, but this was ignorance, for unless your tree fitted you it was difficult to go up and down, and no two of the boys were quite the same size.
If you are bumpy in awkward places, or the only available tree is an odd shape, Peter does some things to you, and after that you fit.
How ardently they grew to love their home under the ground; especially Wendy.
It consisted of one large room, with a floor you could dig if you wanted to go fishing, and in this floor grew mushrooms of a charming colour, which were used as stools.
A Never tree tried hard to grow in the centre of the room, but every morning they sawed the trunk through, level with the floor.
By tea-time it was always about two feet high, and then they put a door on top of it, the whole thus becoming a table.
D

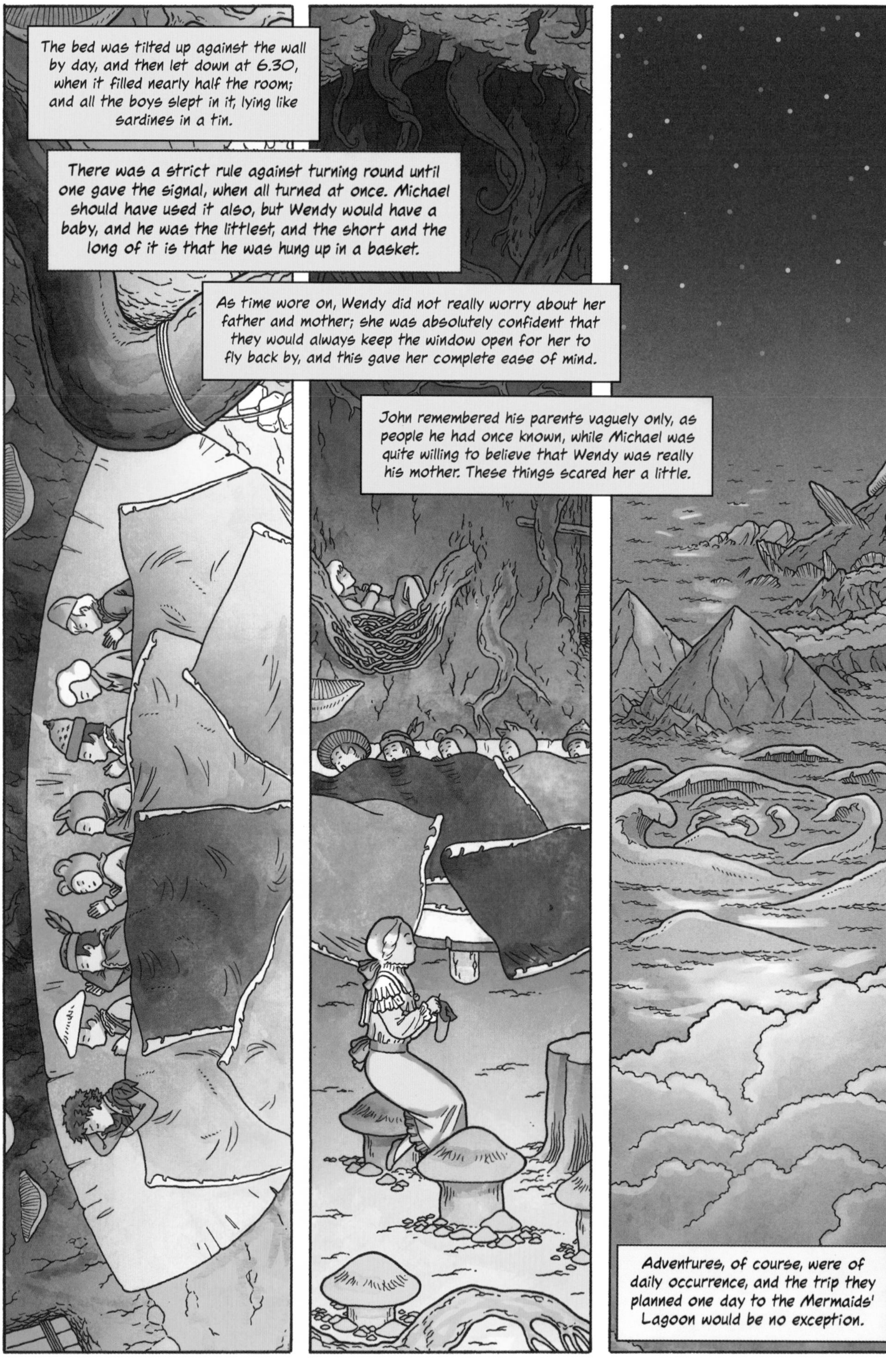
The bed was tilted up against the wall by day, and then let down at 6.30, when it filled nearly half the room; and all the boys slept in it, lying like sardines in a tin.
There was a strict rule against turning round until one gave the signal, when all turned at once. Michael should have used it also, but Wendy would have a baby, and he was the littlest, and the short and the long of it is that he was hung up in a basket.
As time wore on, Wendy did not really worry about her father and mother; she was absolutely confident that they would always keep the window open for her to fly back by, and this gave her complete ease of mind.
John remembered his parents vaguely only, as people he had once known, while Michael was quite willing to believe that Wendy was really his mother. These things scared her a little.
Adventures, of course, were of daily occurrence, and the trip they planned one day to the Mermaids' Lagoon would be no exception.

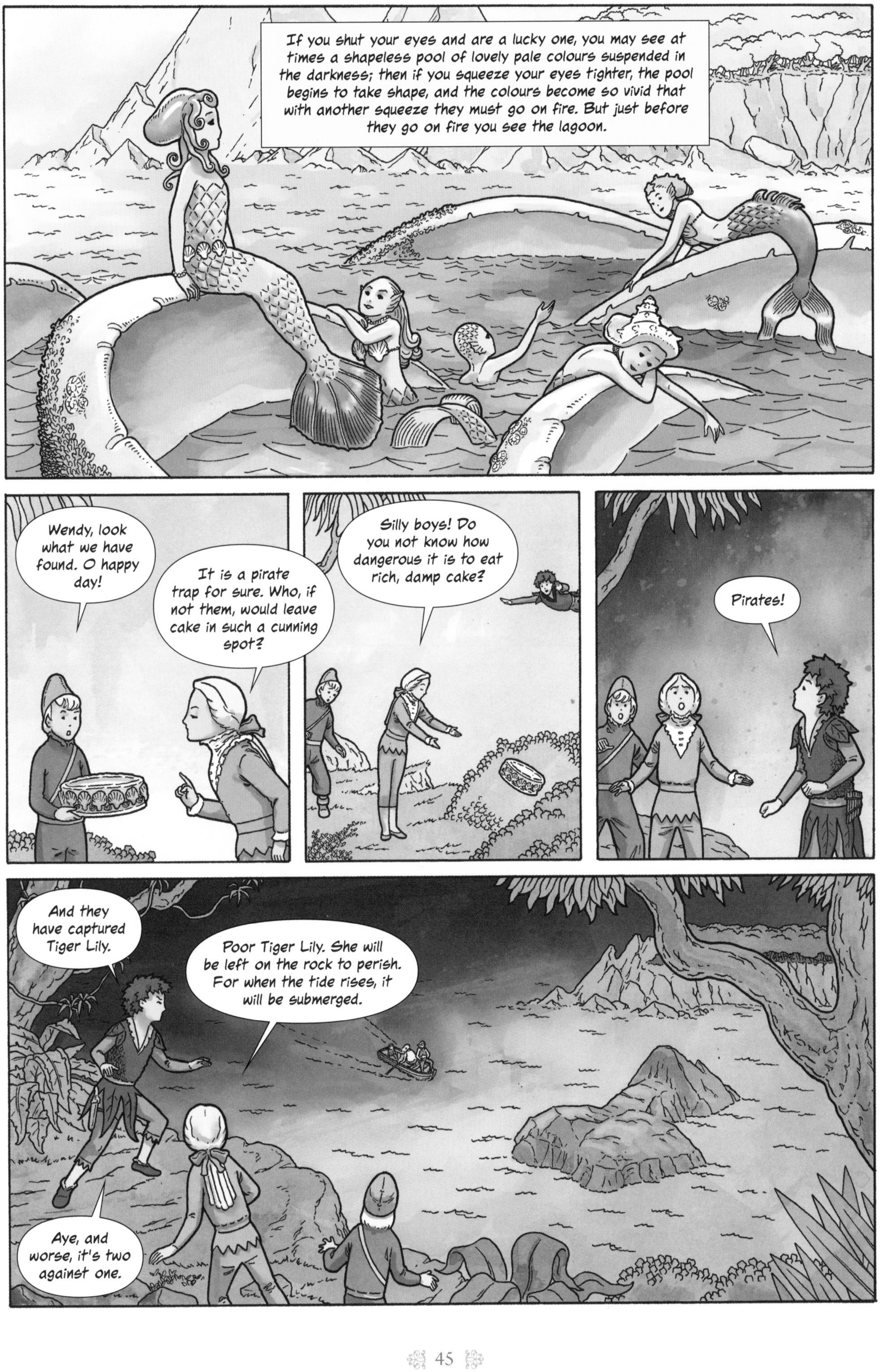
If you shut your eyes and are a lucky one, you may see at times a shapeless pool of lovely pale colours suspended in the darkness; then if you squeeze your eyes tighter, the pool begins to take shape, and the colours become so vivid that with another squeeze they must go on fire. But just before they go on fire you see the lagoon.
Wendy, look what we have found. O happy day!
It is a pirate trap for sure. Who, if not them, would leave cake in such a cunning spot?
Silly boys! Do you not know how dangerous it is to eat rich, damp cake?
Pirates!
And they have captured Tiger Lily.
Poor Tiger Lily. She will be left on the rock to perish. For when the tide rises, it will be submerged.
Aye, and worse, it's two against one.

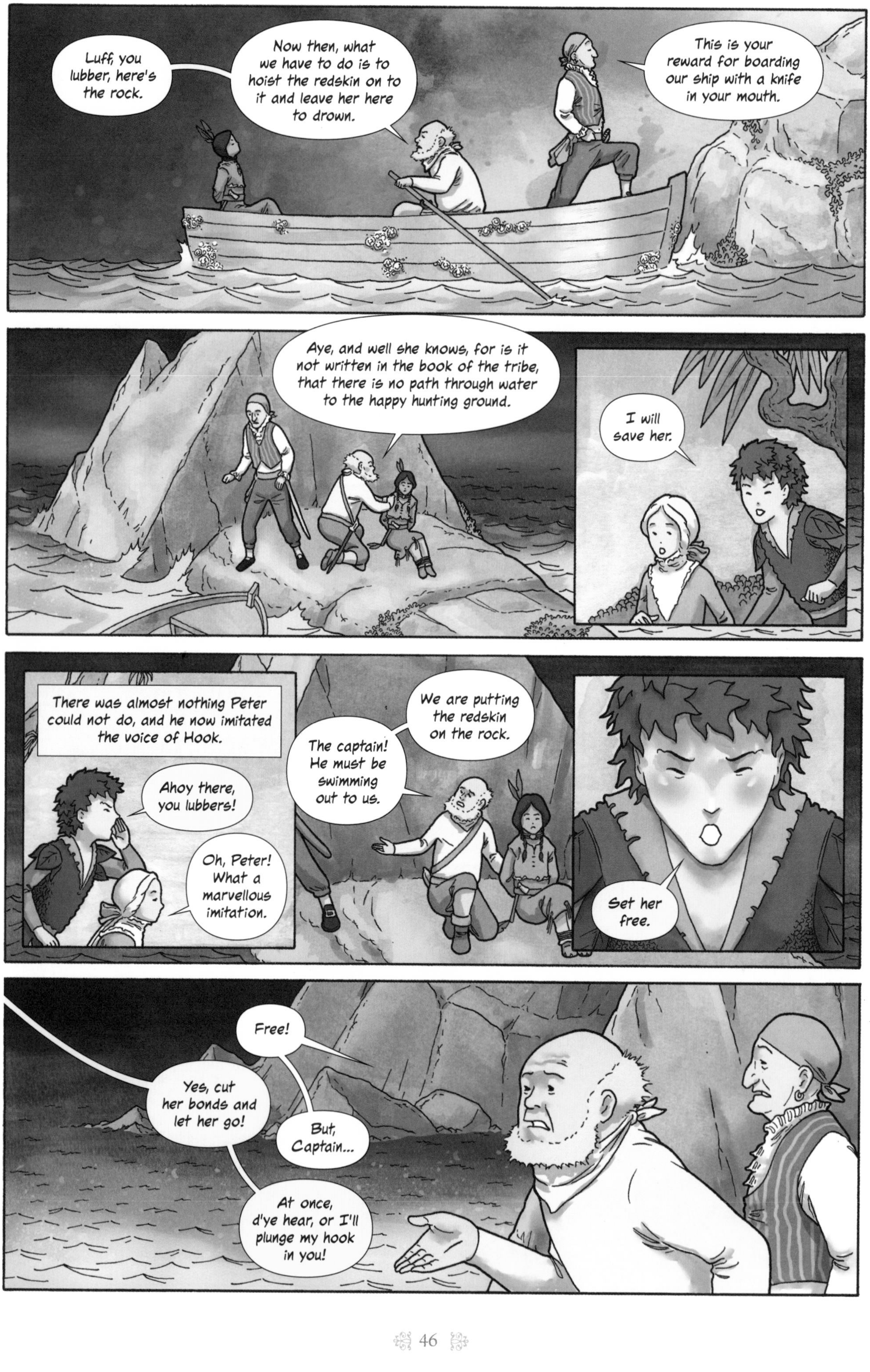
Luff, you lubber, here's the rock.
Now then, what we have to do is to hoist the redskin on to it and leave her here to drown.
This is your reward for boarding our ship with a knife in your mouth.
Aye, and well she knows, for is it not written in the book of the tribe, that there is no path through water to the happy hunting ground.
I will save her.
There was almost nothing Peter could not do, and he now imitated the voice of Hook.
Ahoy there, you lubbers!
Oh, Peter! What a marvellous imitation.
The captain! He must be swimming out to us.
We are putting the redskin on the rock.
Set her free.
Free!
Yes, cut her bonds and let her go!
But, Captain...
At once, d'ye hear, or I'll plunge my hook in you!

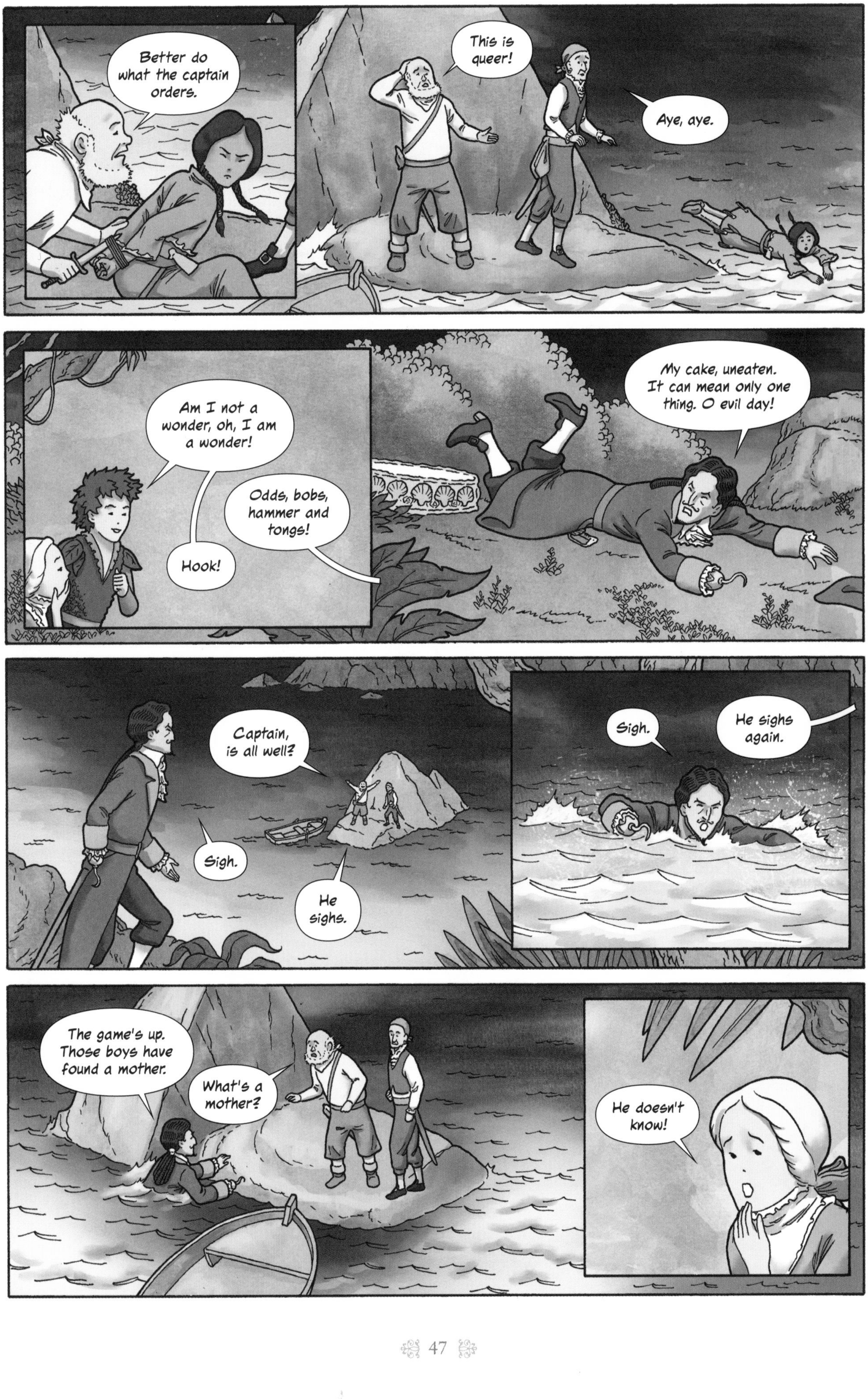
Better do what the captain orders.
This is queer!
Aye, aye.
Am I not a wonder, oh, I am a wonder!
Hook!
Odds, bobs, hammer and tongs!
My cake, uneaten. It can mean only one thing. O evil day!
Captain, is all well?
Sigh.
He sighs.
Sigh.
He sighs again.
The game's up. Those boys have found a mother.
What's a mother?
He doesn't know!

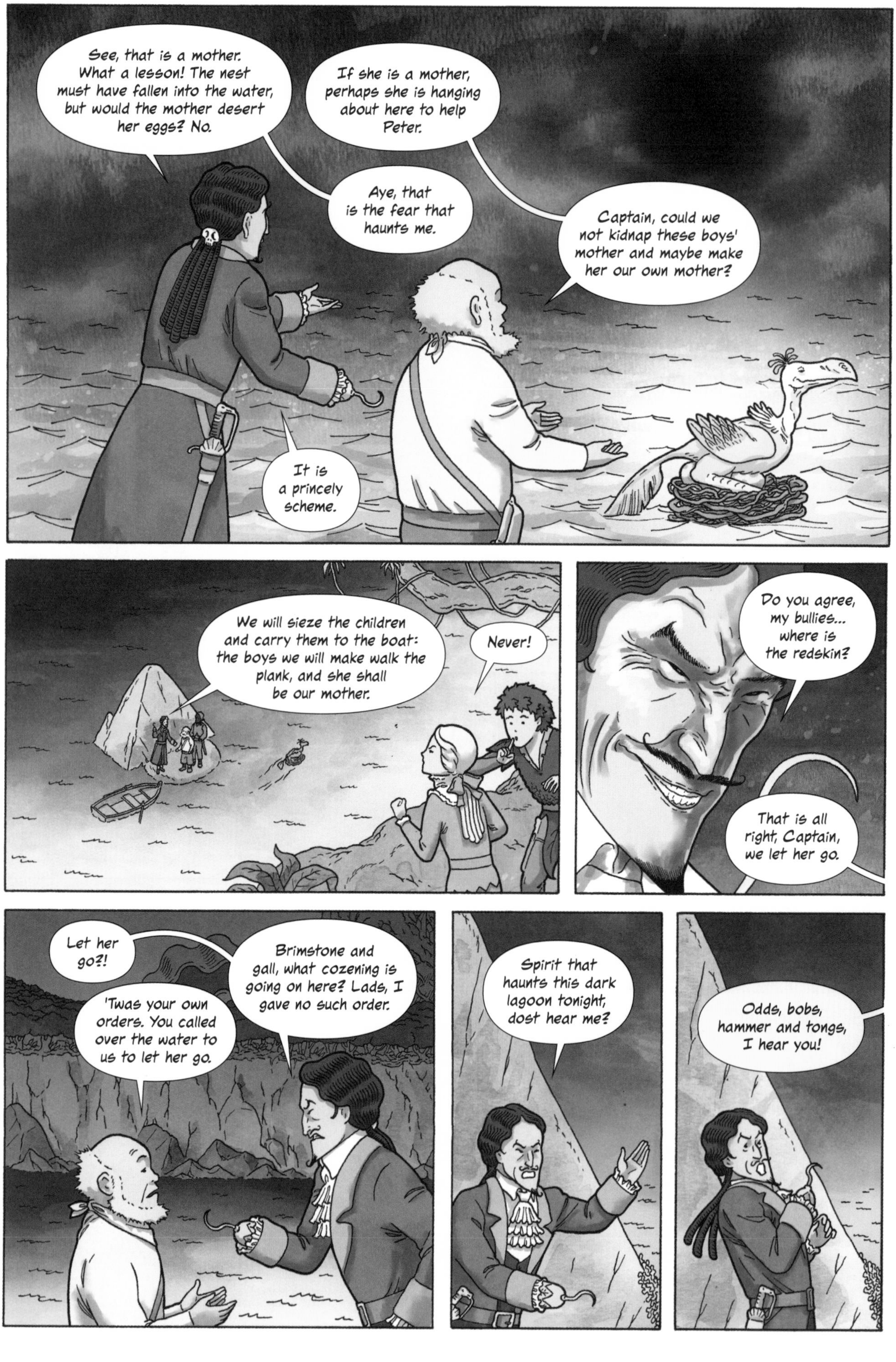
See, that is a mother. What a lesson! The nest must have fallen into the water, but would the mother desert her eggs? No.
If she is a mother, perhaps she is hanging about here to help Peter.
Aye, that is the fear that haunts me.
Captain, could we not kidnap these boys' mother and maybe make her our own mother?
It is a princely scheme.
We will sieze the children and carry them to the boat: the boys we will make walk the plank, and she shall be our mother.
Never!
Do you agree, my bullies... where is the redskin?
That is all right, Captain, we let her go.
Let her go?!
Brimstone and gall, what cozening is going on here? Lads, I gave no such order.
'Twas your own orders. You called over the water to us to let her go.
Spirit that haunts this dark lagoon tonight, dost hear me?
Odds, bobs, hammer and tongs, I hear you!

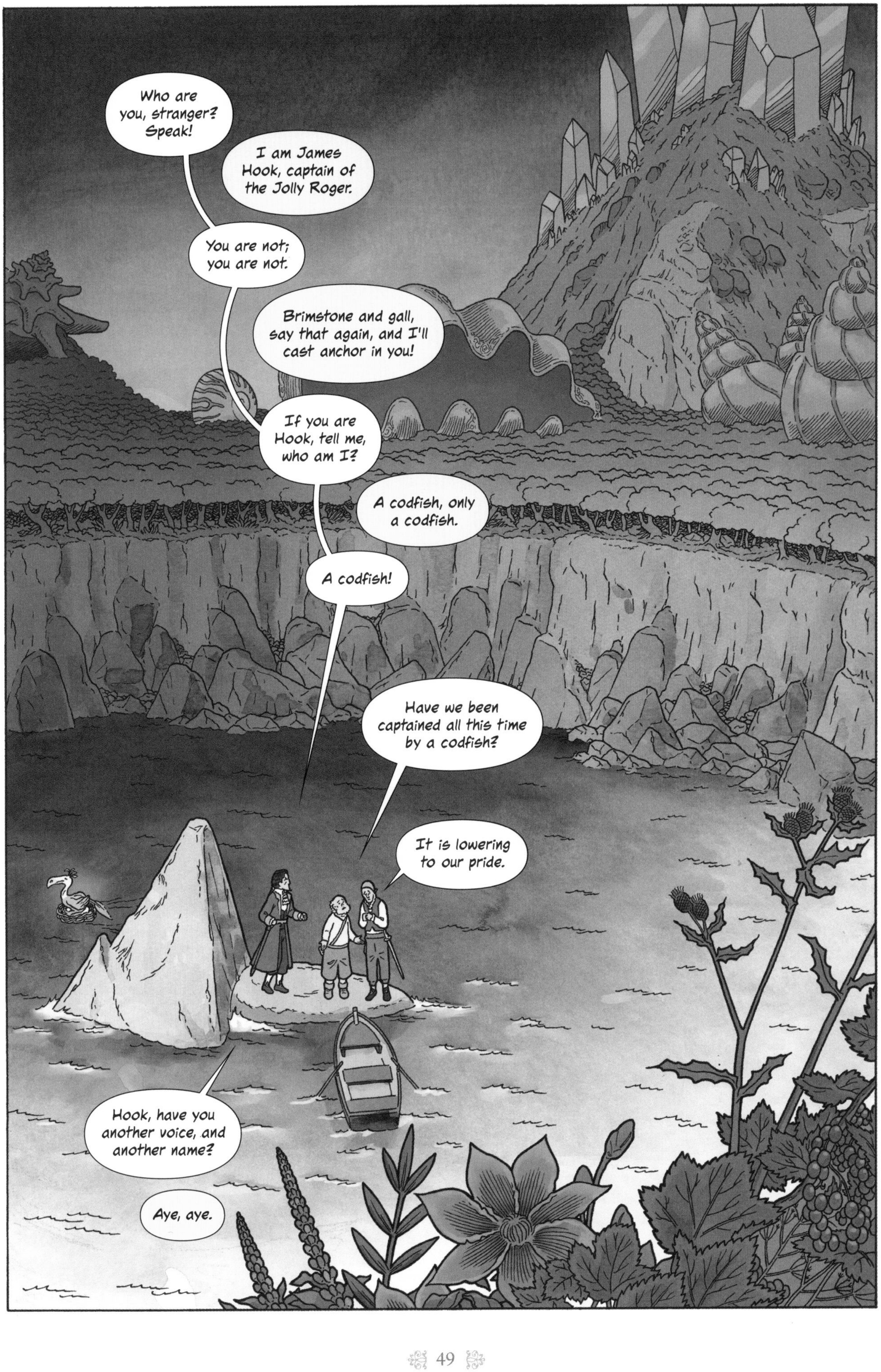
Who are you, stranger? Speak!
I am James Hook, captain of the Jolly Roger.
You are not; you are not.
Brimstone and gall, say that again, and I'll cast anchor in you!
If you are Hook, tell me, who am I?
A codfish, only a codfish.
A codfish!
Have we been captained all this time by a codfish?
It is lowering to our pride.
Hook, have you another voice, and another name?
Aye, aye.

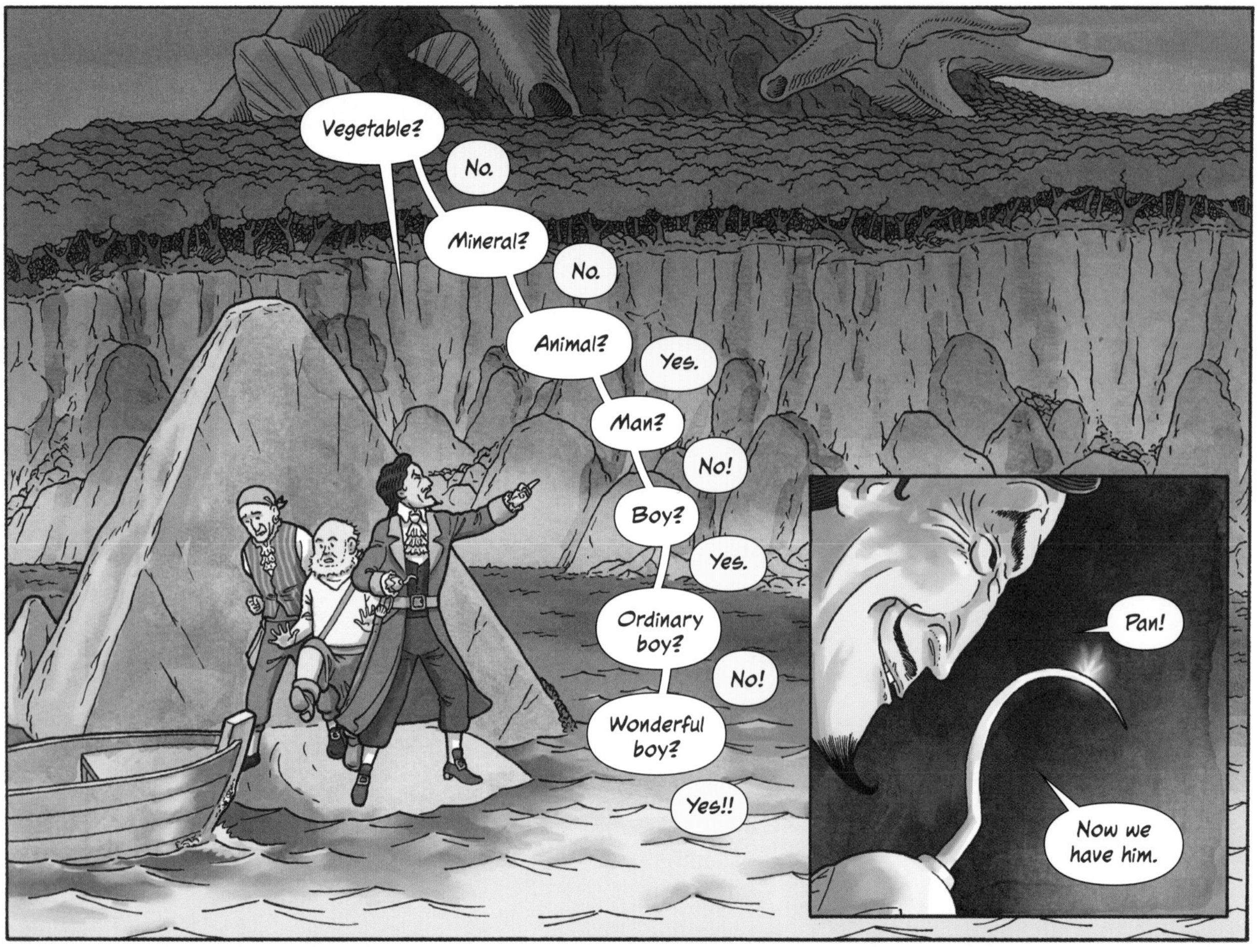
Vegetable?
No.
Mineral?
No.
Animal?
Yes.
Man?
No!
Boy?
Yes.
Ordinary boy?
No!
Wonderful boy?
Yes!!
Pan!
Now we have him.

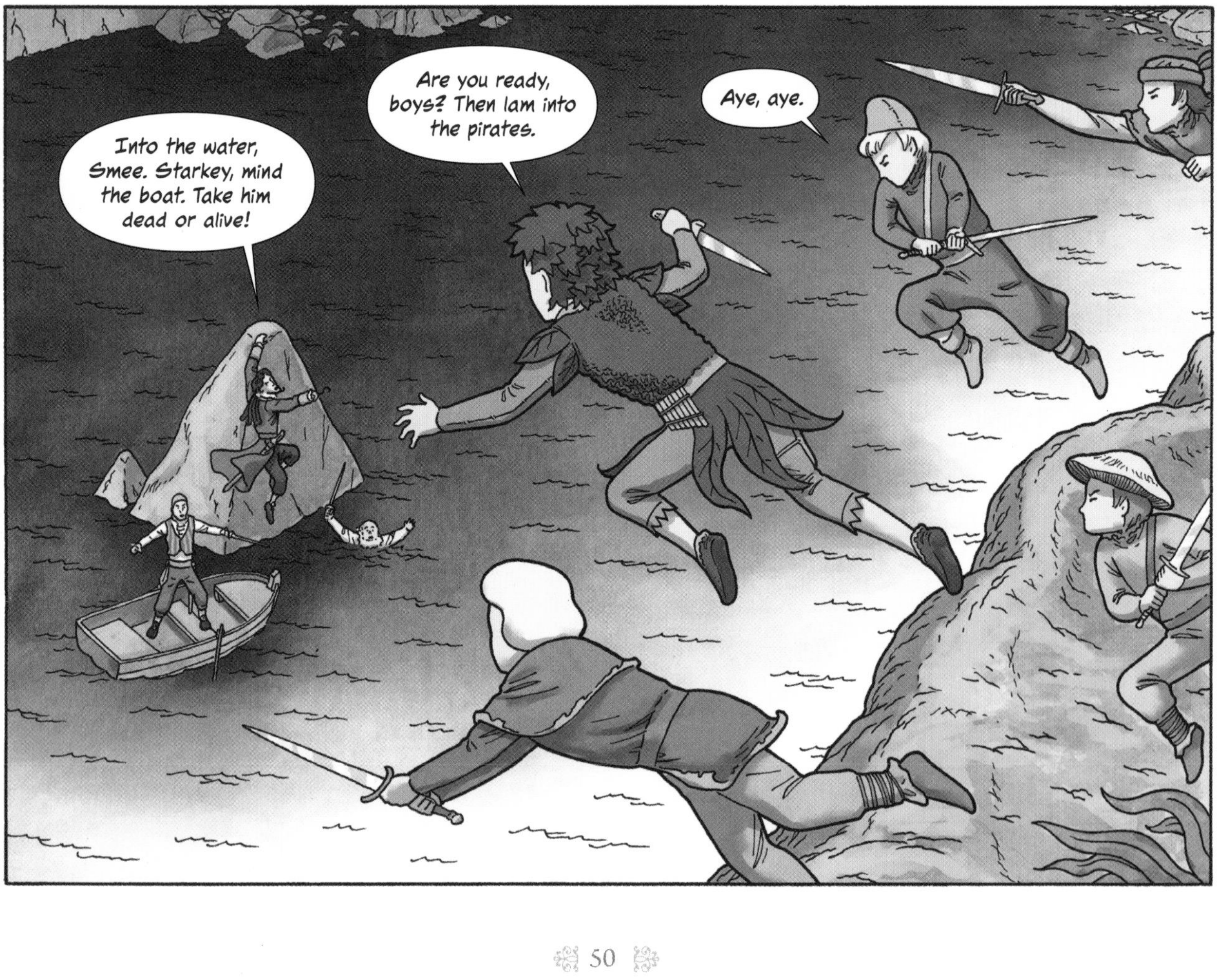
Into the water, Smee. Starkey, mind the boat. Take him dead or alive!
Are you ready, boys? Then lam into the pirates.
Aye, aye.

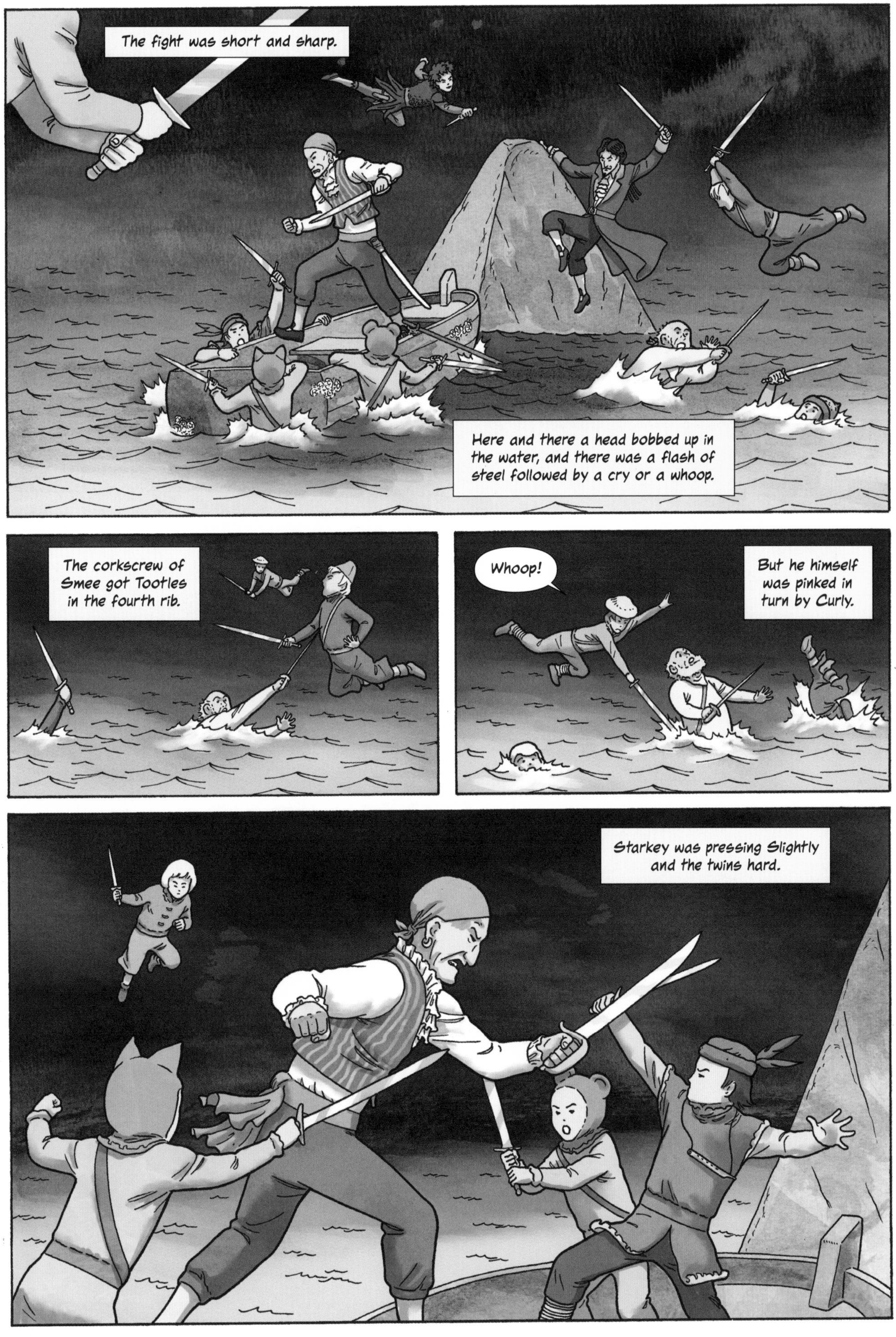
The fight was short and sharp.
Here and there a head bobbed up in the water, and there was a flash of steel followed by a cry or a whoop.
The corkscrew of Smee got Tootles in the fourth rib.
Whoop!
But he himself was pinked in turn by Curly.
Starkey was pressing Slightly and the twins hard.

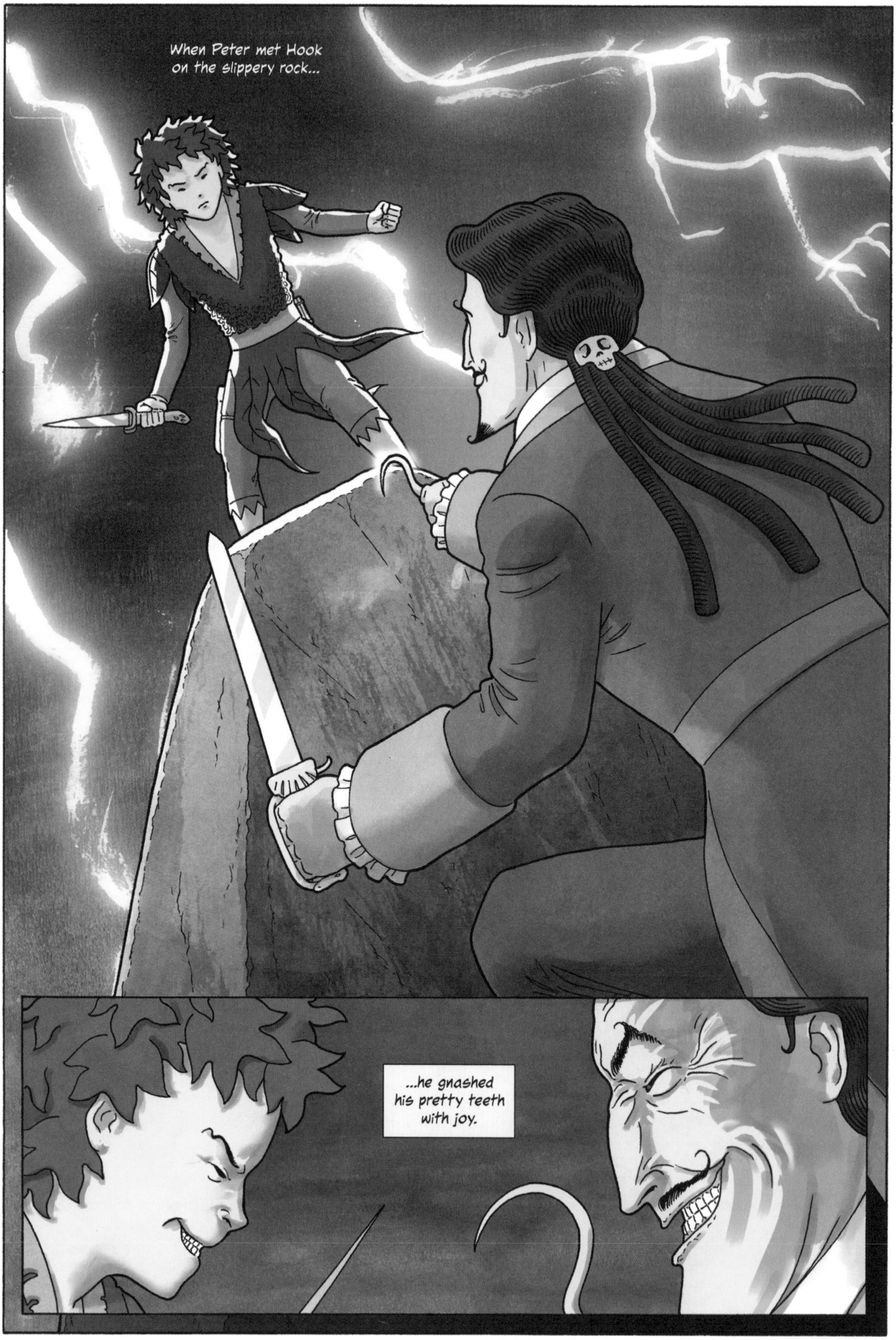
When Peter met Hook
on the slippery rock...
...he gnashed
his pretty teeth
with joy.

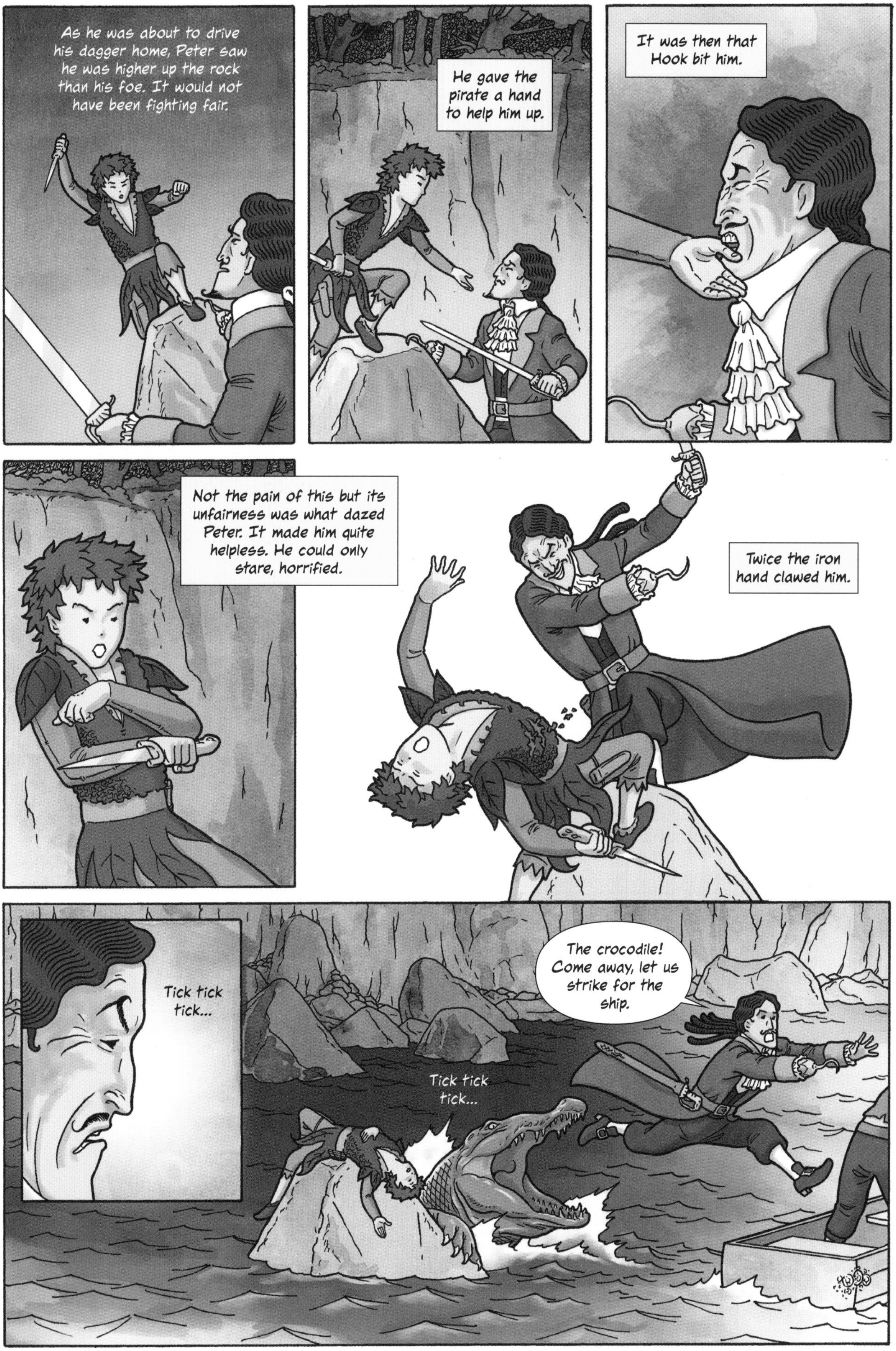
As he was about to drive his dagger home, Peter saw he was higher up the rock than his foe. It would not have been fighting fair.
He gave the pirate a hand to help him up.
It was then that Hook bit him.
Not the pain of this but its unfairness was what dazed Peter. It made him quite helpless. He could only stare, horrified.
Twice the iron hand clawed him.
Tick tick tick...
Tick tick tick...
The crocodile! Come away, let us strike for the ship.

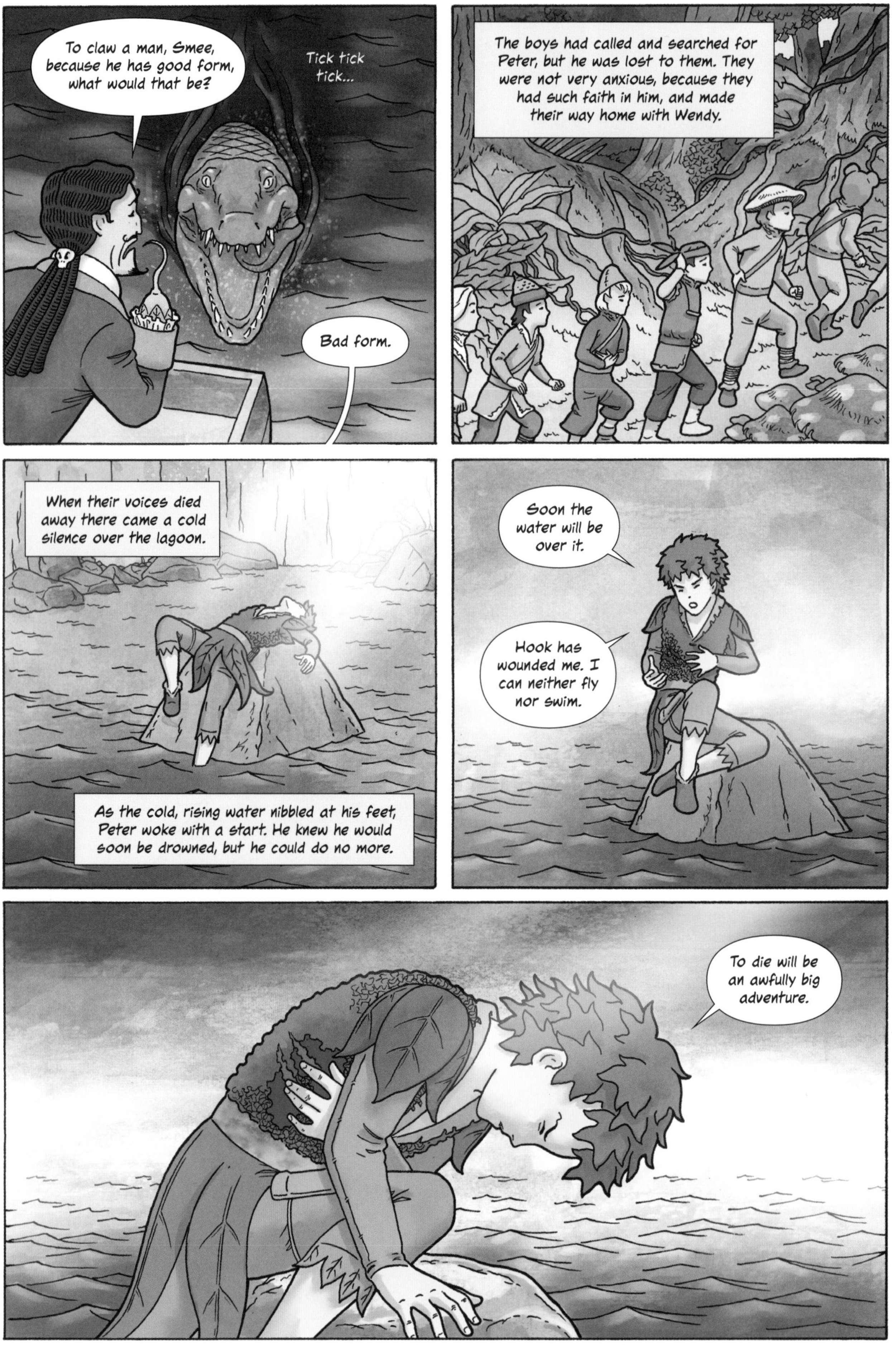
To claw a man, Smee, because he has good form, what would that be?
Tick tick tick...
Bad form.
The boys had called and searched for Peter, but he was lost to them. They were not very anxious, because they had such faith in him, and made their way home with Wendy.
When their voices died away there came a cold silence over the lagoon.
As the cold, rising water nibbled at his feet, Peter woke with a start. He knew he would soon be drowned, but he could do no more.
Soon the water will be over it.
Hook has wounded me. I can neither fly nor swim.
To die will be an awfully big adventure.

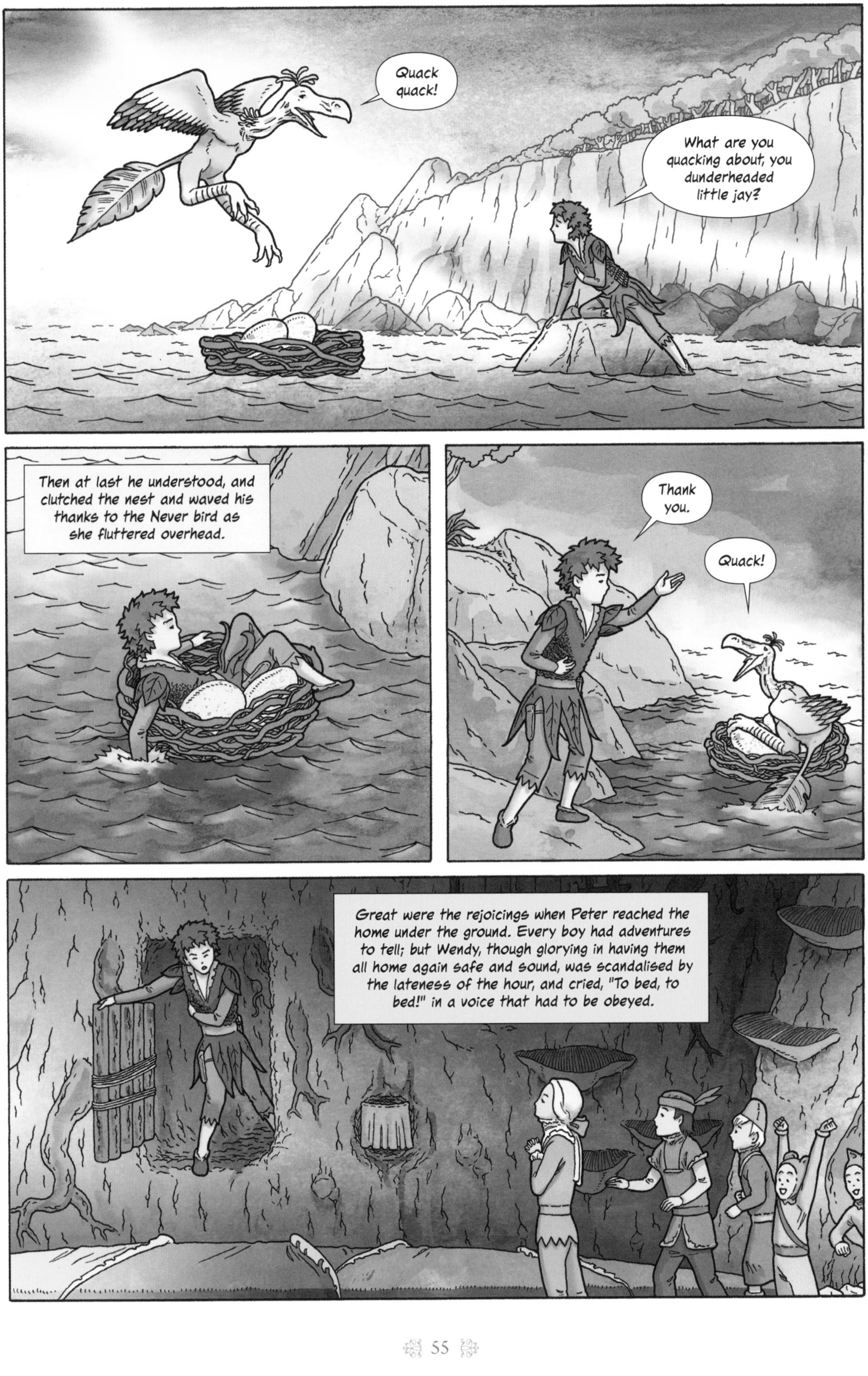
Quack quack!
What are you quacking about, you dunderheaded little jay?
Then at last he understood, and clutched the nest and waved his thanks to the Never bird as she fluttered overhead.
Thank you.
Quack!
Great were the rejoicings when Peter reached the home under the ground. Every boy had adventures to tell; but Wendy, though glorying in having them all home again safe and sound, was scandalised by the lateness of the hour, and cried, "To bed, to bed!" in a voice that had to be obeyed.

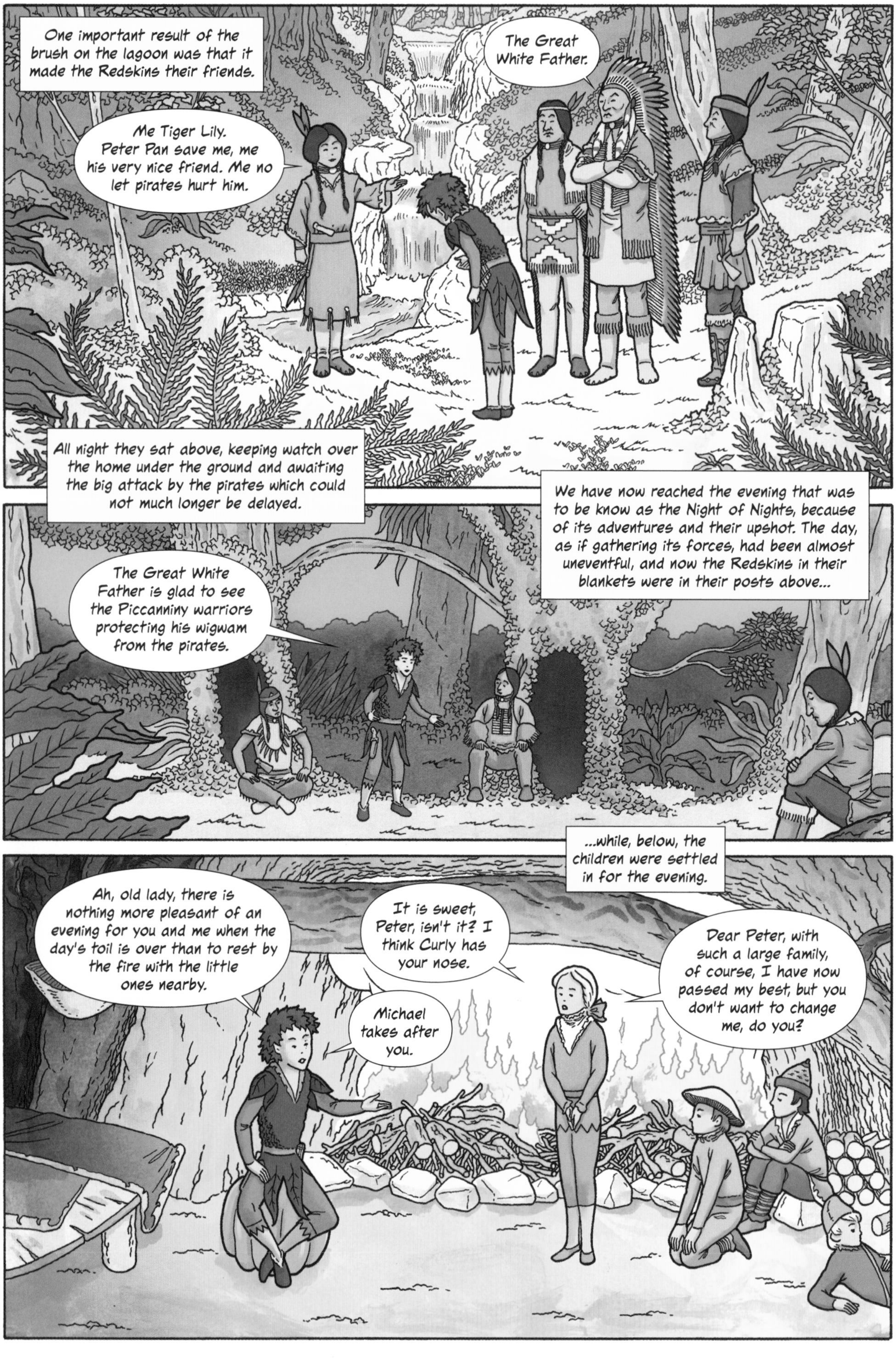
One important result of the brush on the lagoon was that it made the Redskins their friends.
The Great White Father.
Me Tiger Lily. Peter Pan save me, me his very nice friend. Me no let pirates hurt him.
All night they sat above, keeping watch over the home under the ground and awaiting the big attack by the pirates which could not much longer be delayed.
We have now reached the evening that was to be know as the Night of Nights, because of its adventures and their upshot. The day, as if gathering its forces, had been almost uneventful, and now the Redskins in their blankets were in their posts above...
The Great White Father is glad to see the Piccanniny warriors protecting his wigwam from the pirates.
...while, below, the children were settled in for the evening.
Ah, old lady, there is nothing more pleasant of an evening for you and me when the day's toil is over than to rest by the fire with the little ones nearby.
It is sweet, Peter, isn't it? I think Curly has your nose.
Michael takes after you.
Dear Peter, with such a large family, of course, I have now passed my best, but you don't want to change me, do you?

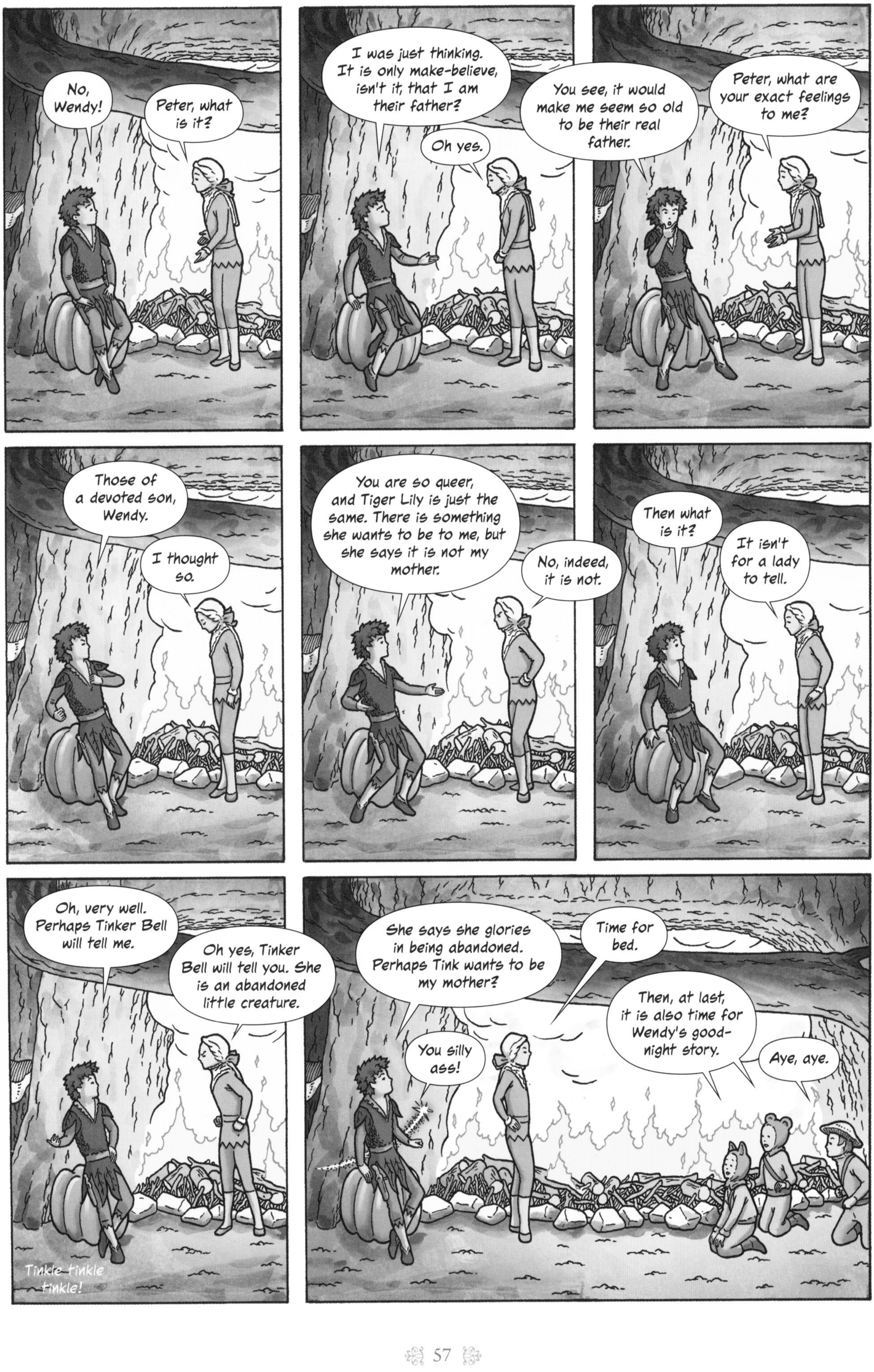
No, Wendy!
Peter, what is it?
I was just thinking. It is only make-believe, isn't it, that I am their father?
Oh yes.
You see, it would make me seem so old to be their real father.
Peter, what are your exact feelings to me?
Those of a devoted son, Wendy.
I thought so.
You are so queer, and Tiger Lily is just the same. There is something she wants to be to me, but she says it is not my mother.
No, indeed, it is not.
Then what is it?
It isn't for a lady to tell.
Oh, very well. Perhaps Tinker Bell will tell me.
Oh yes, Tinker Bell will tell you. She is an abandoned little creature.
Tinkle tinkle tinkle!
She says she glories in being abandoned. Perhaps Tink wants to be my mother?
You silly ass!
Time for bed.
Then, at last, it is also time for Wendy's good-night story.
Aye, aye.

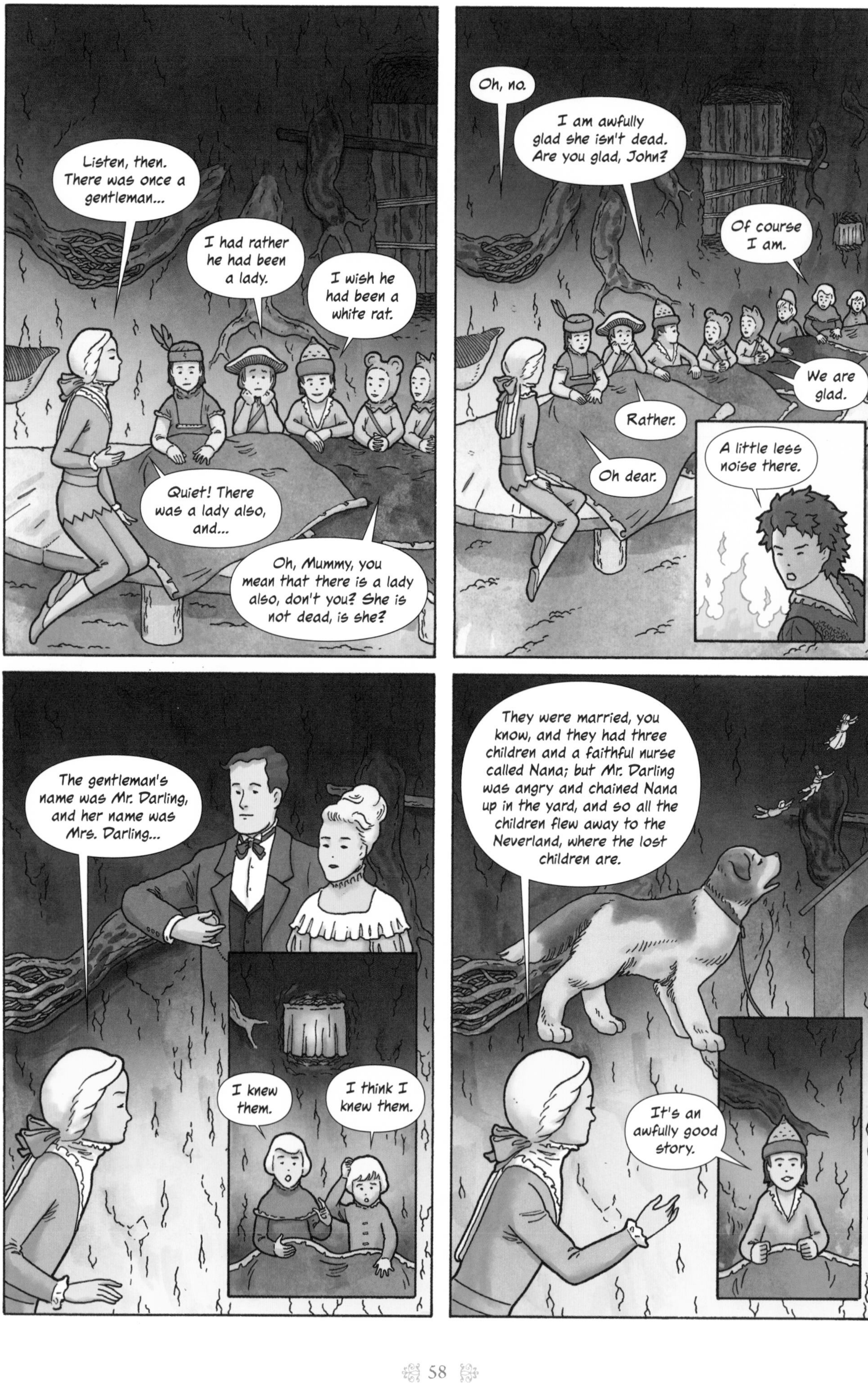

Listen, then. There was once a gentleman...
I had rather he had been a lady.
I wish he had been a white rat.
Quiet! There was a lady also, and...
Oh, Mummy, you mean that there is a lady also, don't you? She is not dead, is she?
Oh, no.
I am awfully glad she isn't dead. Are you glad, John?
Of course I am.
We are glad.
Rather.
Oh dear.
A little less noise there.
The gentleman's name was Mr. Darling, and her name was Mrs. Darling...
I knew them.
I think I knew them.
They were married, you know, and they had three children and a faithful nurse called Nana; but Mr. Darling was angry and chained Nana up in the yard, and so all the children flew away to the Neverland, where the lost children are.
It's an awfully good story.

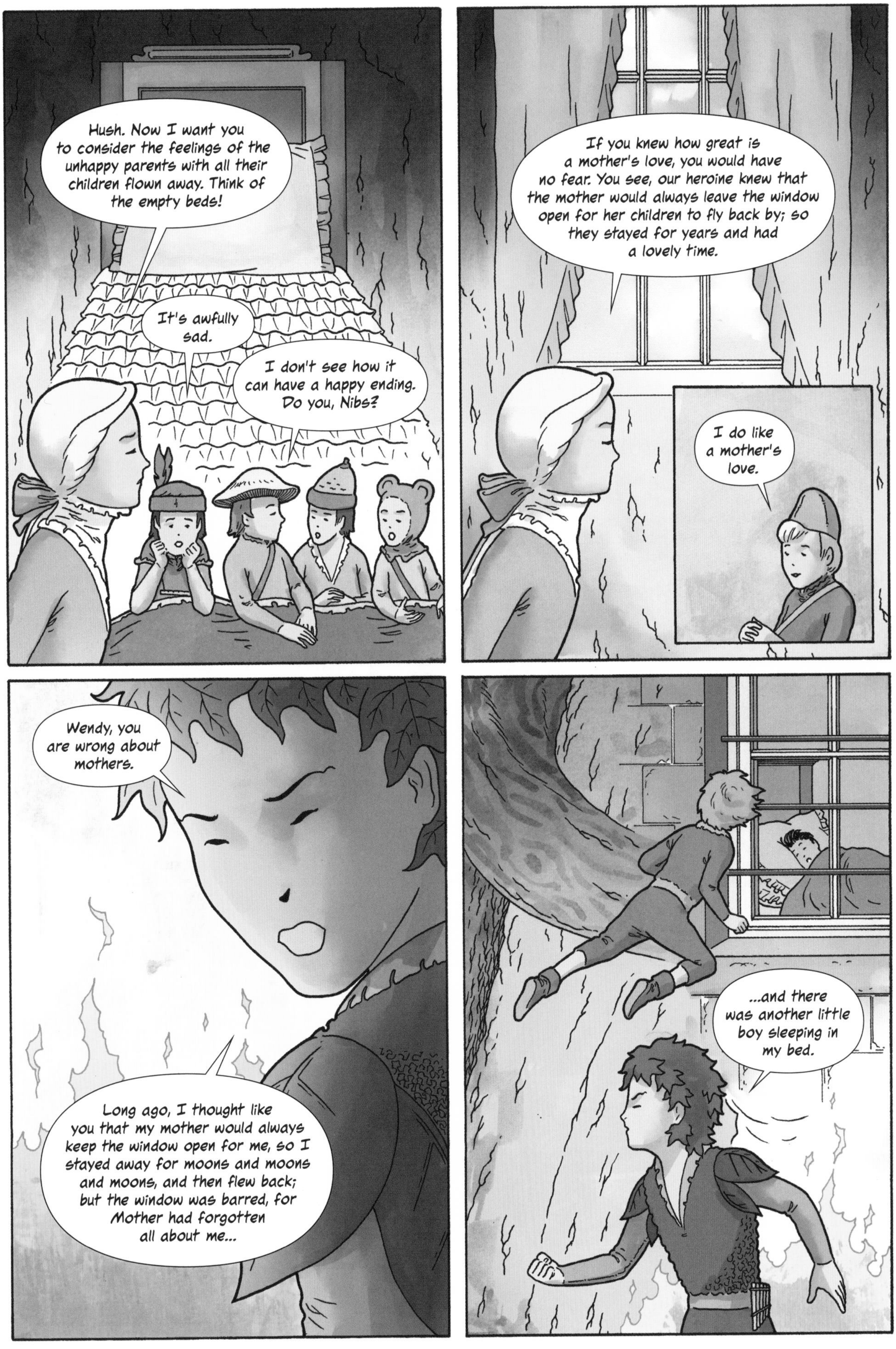
Hush. Now I want you to consider the feelings of the unhappy parents with all their children flown away. Think of the empty beds!
It's awfully sad.
I don't see how it can have a happy ending. Do you, Nibs?
If you knew how great is a mother's love, you would have no fear. You see, our heroine knew that the mother would always leave the window open for her children to fly back by; so they stayed for years and had a lovely time.
I do like a mother's love.
Wendy, you are wrong about mothers.
Long ago, I thought like you that my mother would always keep the window open for me, so I stayed away for moons and moons and moons, and then flew back; but the window was barred, for Mother had forgotten all about me...
...and there was another little boy sleeping in my bed.

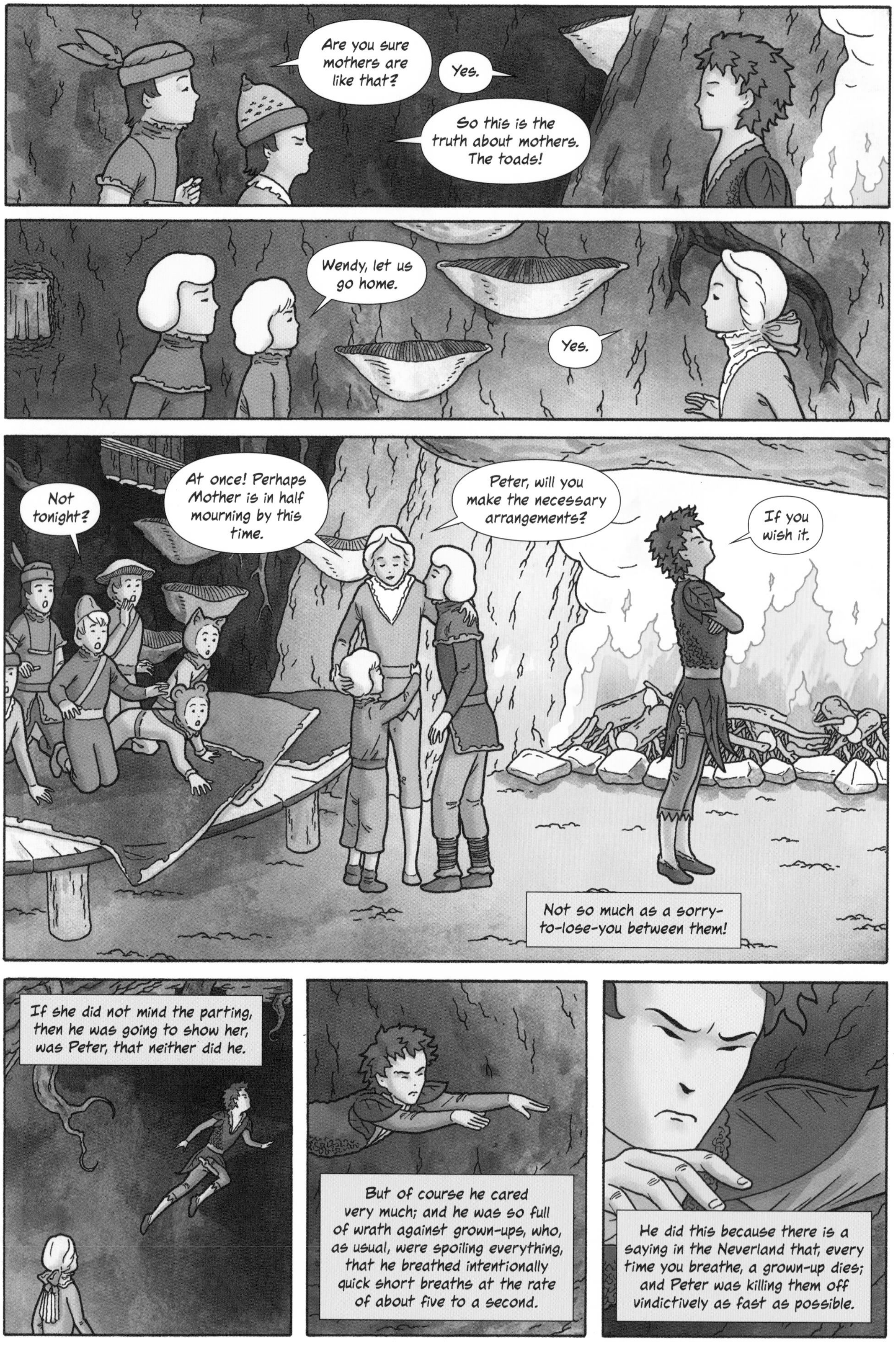
Are you sure mothers are like that?
Yes.
So this is the truth about mothers. The toads!
Wendy, let us go home.
Yes.
Not tonight?
At once! Perhaps Mother is in half mourning by this time.
Peter, will you make the necessary arrangements?
If you wish it.
Not so much as a sorry-to-lose-you between them!
If she did not mind the parting, then he was going to show her, was Peter, that neither did he.
But of course he cared very much; and he was so full of wrath against grown-ups, who, as usual, were spoiling everything, that he breathed intentionally quick short breaths at the rate of about five to a second.
He did this because there is a saying in the Neverland that, every time you breathe, a grown-up dies; and Peter was killing them off vindictively as fast as possible.

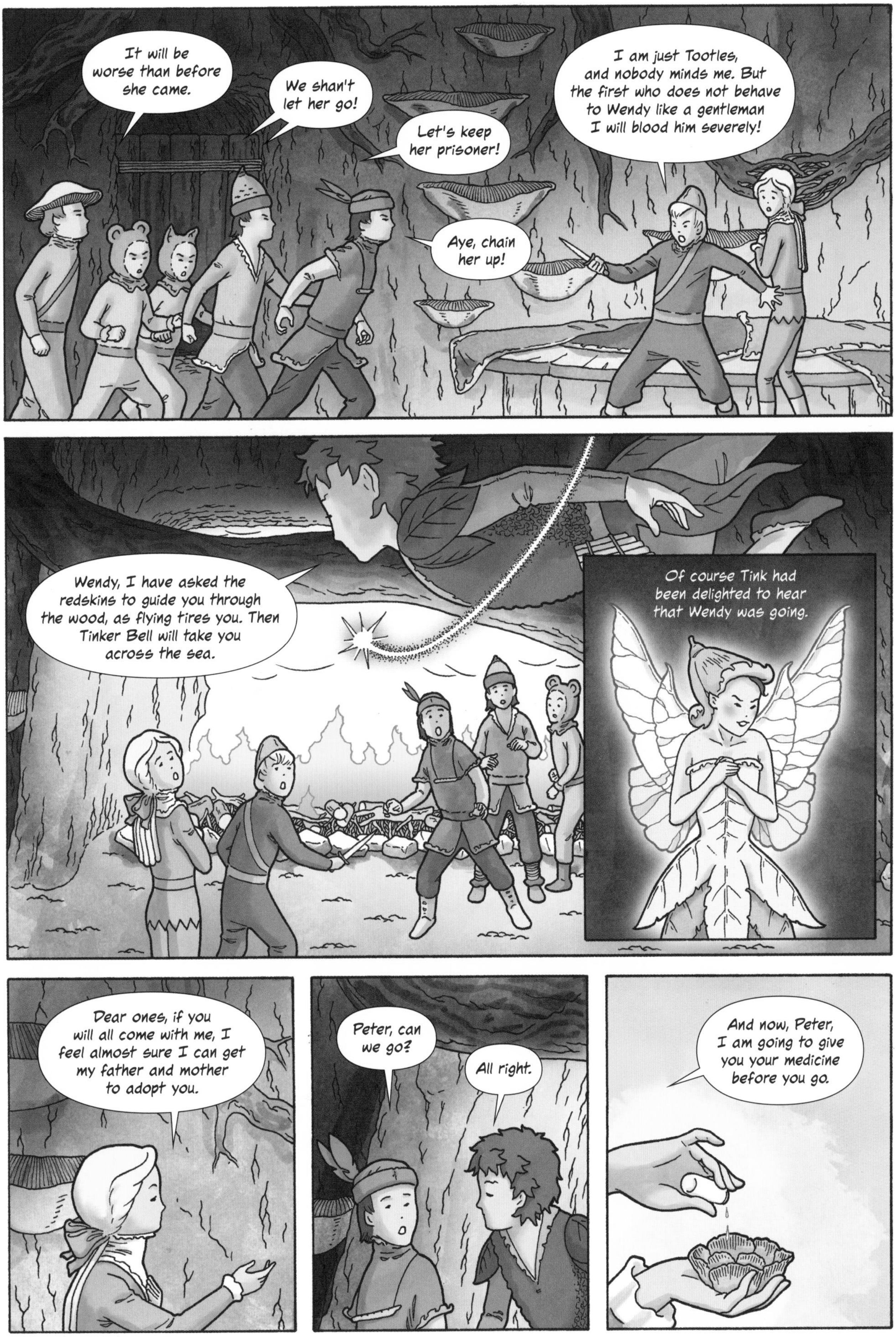
It will be worse than before she came.
We shan't let her go!
Let's keep her prisoner!
Aye, chain her up!
I am just Tootles, and nobody minds me. But the first who does not behave to Wendy like a gentleman I will blood him severely!
Wendy, I have asked the redskins to guide you through the wood, as flying tires you. Then Tinker Bell will take you across the sea.
Of course Tink had been delighted to hear that Wendy was going.
Dear ones, if you will all come with me, I feel almost sure I can get my father and mother to adopt you.
Peter, can we go?
All right.
And now, Peter, I am going to give you your medicine before you go.

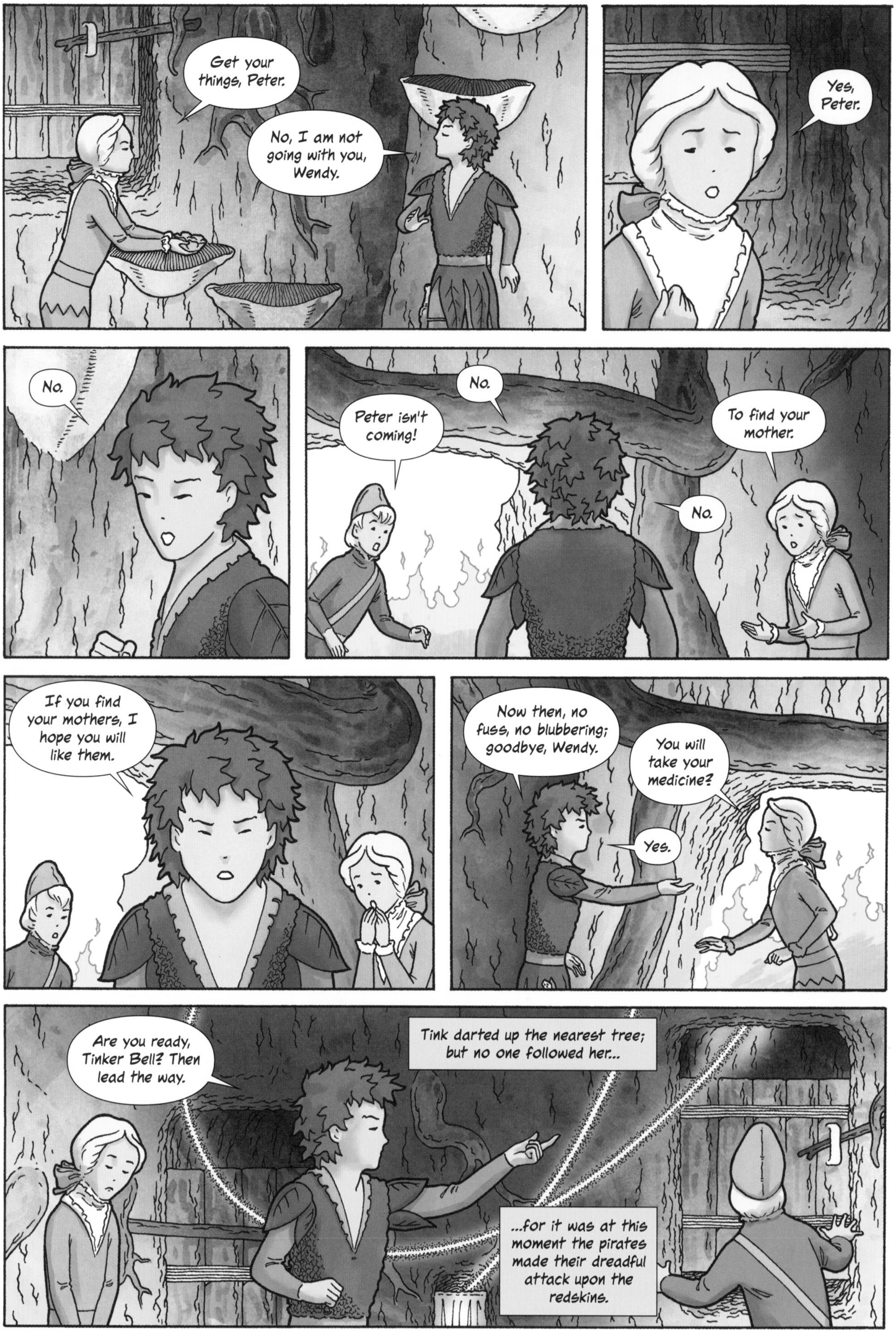
Get your things, Peter.
No, I am not going with you, Wendy.
Yes, Peter.
No.
Peter isn't coming!
No.
To find your mother.
No.
If you find your mothers, I hope you will like them.
Now then, no fuss, no blubbering; goodbye, Wendy.
You will take your medicine?
Yes.
Are you ready, Tinker Bell? Then lead the way.
Tink darted up the nearest tree; but no one followed her...
...for it was at this moment the pirates made their dreadful attack upon the redskins.

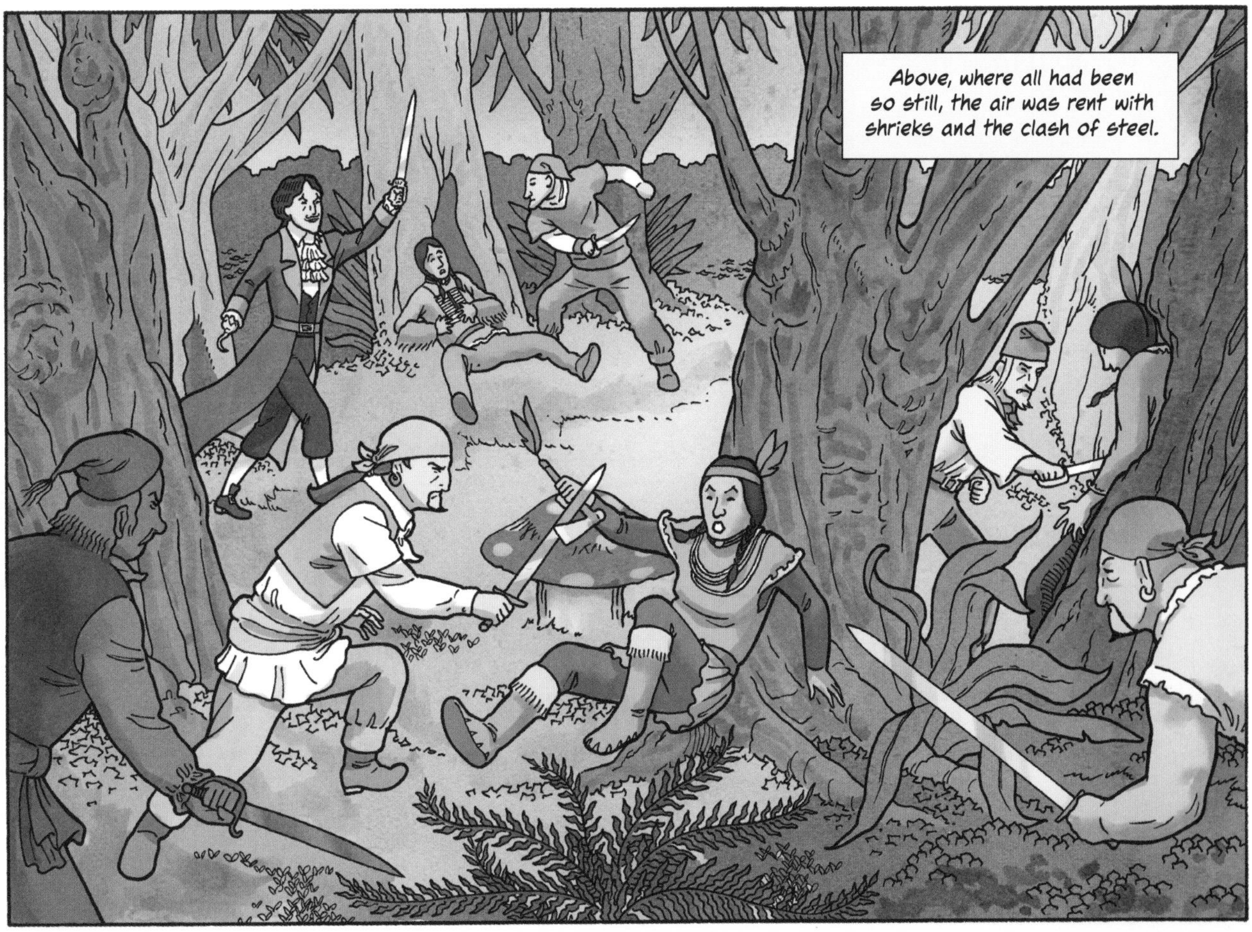
Above, where all had been so still, the air was rent with shrieks and the clash of steel.

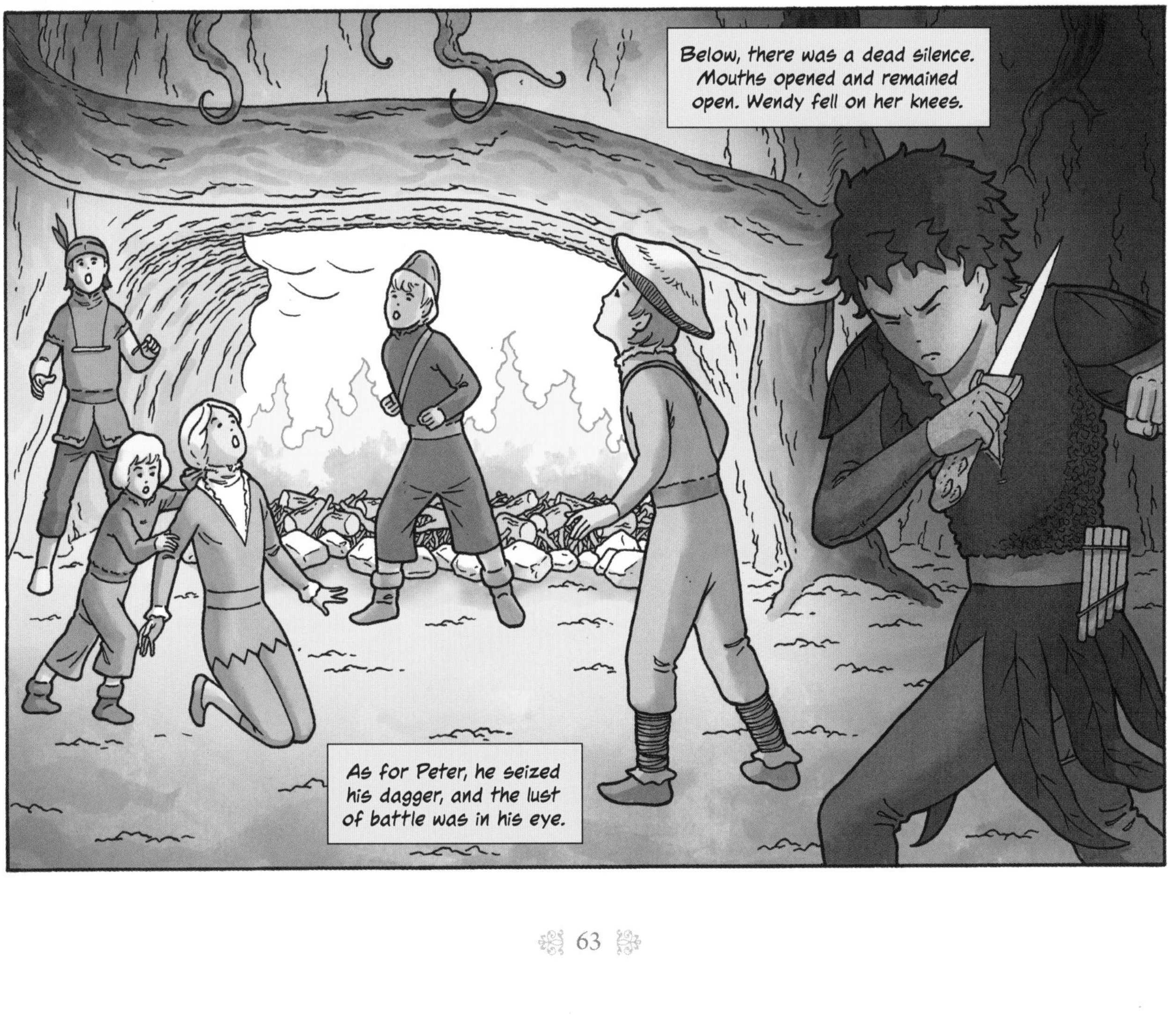
Below, there was a dead silence. Mouths opened and remained open. Wendy fell on her knees.
As for Peter, he seized his dagger, and the lust of battle was in his eye.

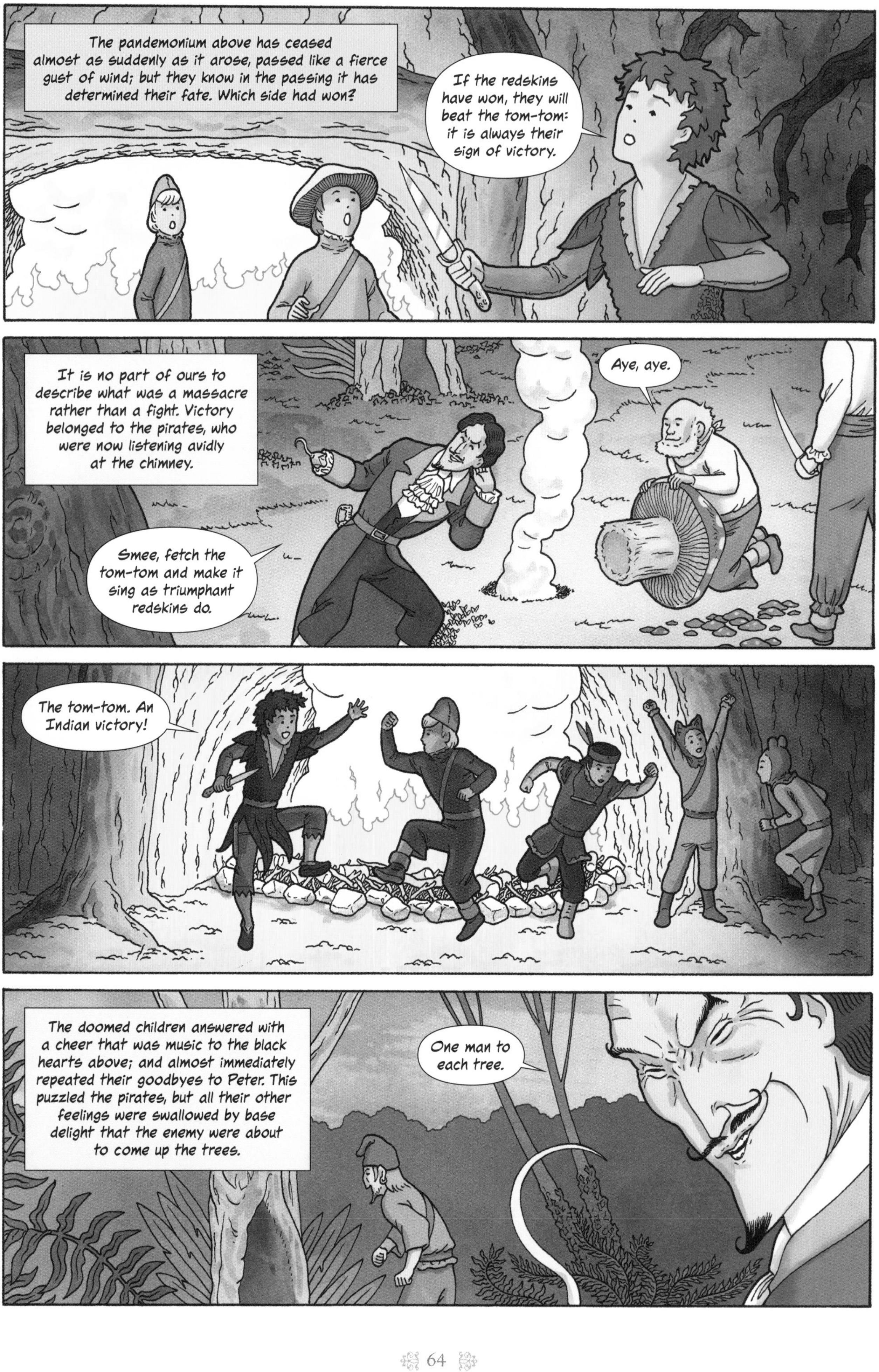
The pandemonium above has ceased almost as suddenly as it arose, passed like a fierce gust of wind; but they know in the passing it has determined their fate. Which side had won?
If the redskins have won, they will beat the tom-tom: it is always their sign of victory.
It is no part of ours to describe what was a massacre rather than a fight. Victory belonged to the pirates, who were now listening avidly at the chimney.
Aye, aye.
Smee, fetch the tom-tom and make it sing as triumphant redskins do.
The tom-tom. An Indian victory!
The doomed children answered with a cheer that was music to the black hearts above; and almost immediately repeated their goodbyes to Peter. This puzzled the pirates, but all their other feelings were swallowed by base delight that the enemy were about to come up the trees.
One man to each tree.

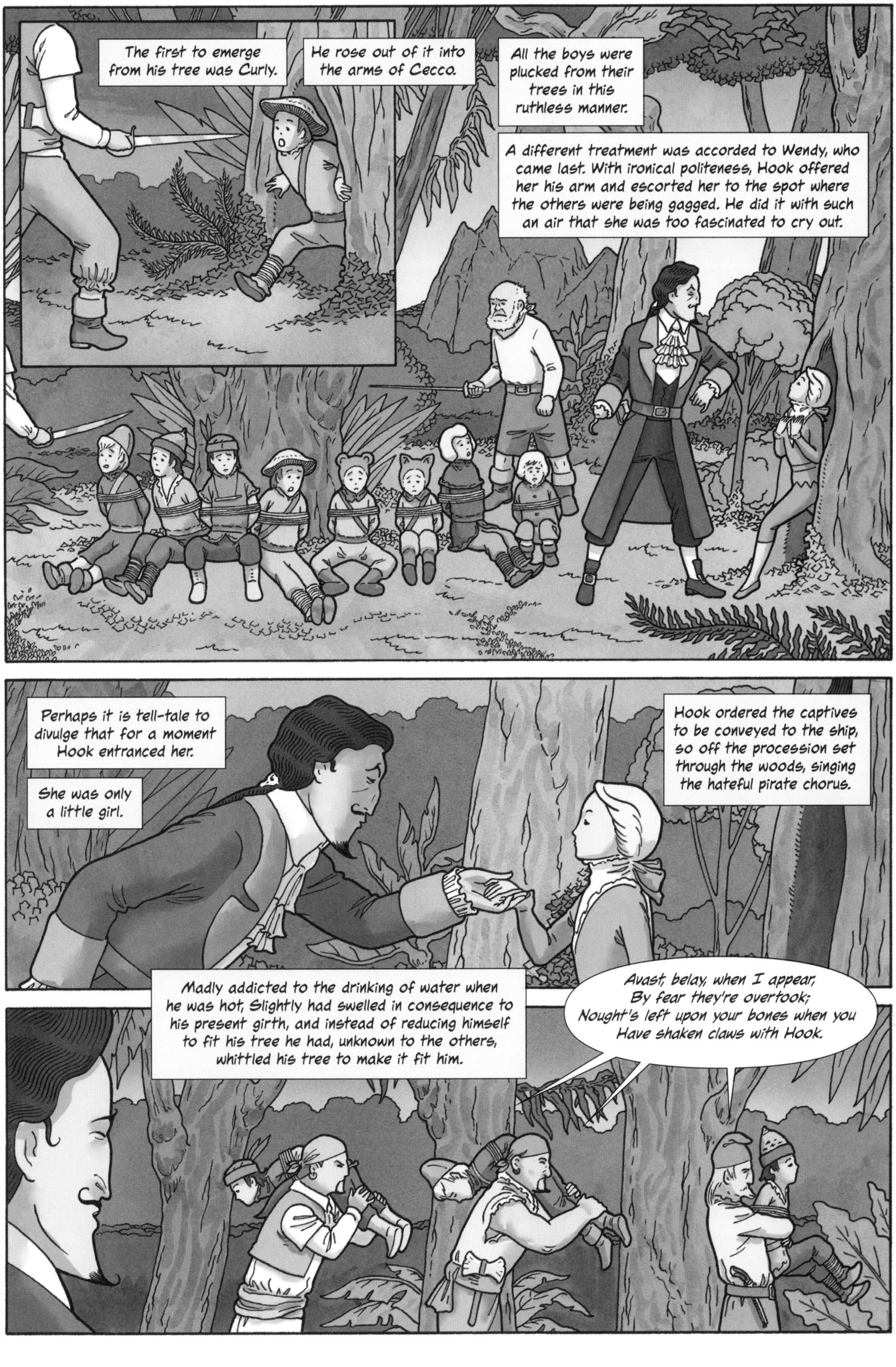
The first to emerge from his tree was Curly.
He rose out of it into the arms of Cecco.
All the boys were plucked from their trees in this ruthless manner.
A different treatment was accorded to Wendy, who came last. With ironical politeness, Hook offered her his arm and escorted her to the spot where the others were being gagged. He did it with such an air that she was too fascinated to cry out.
Perhaps it is tell-tale to divulge that for a moment Hook entranced her.
She was only a little girl.
Hook ordered the captives to be conveyed to the ship, so off the procession set through the woods, singing the hateful pirate chorus.
Madly addicted to the drinking of water when he was hot, Slightly had swelled in consequence to his present girth, and instead of reducing himself to fit his tree he had, unknown to the others, whittled his tree to make it fit him.
Avast, belay, when I appear,
By fear they're overtook;
Nought's left upon your bones when you
Have shaken claws with Hook.

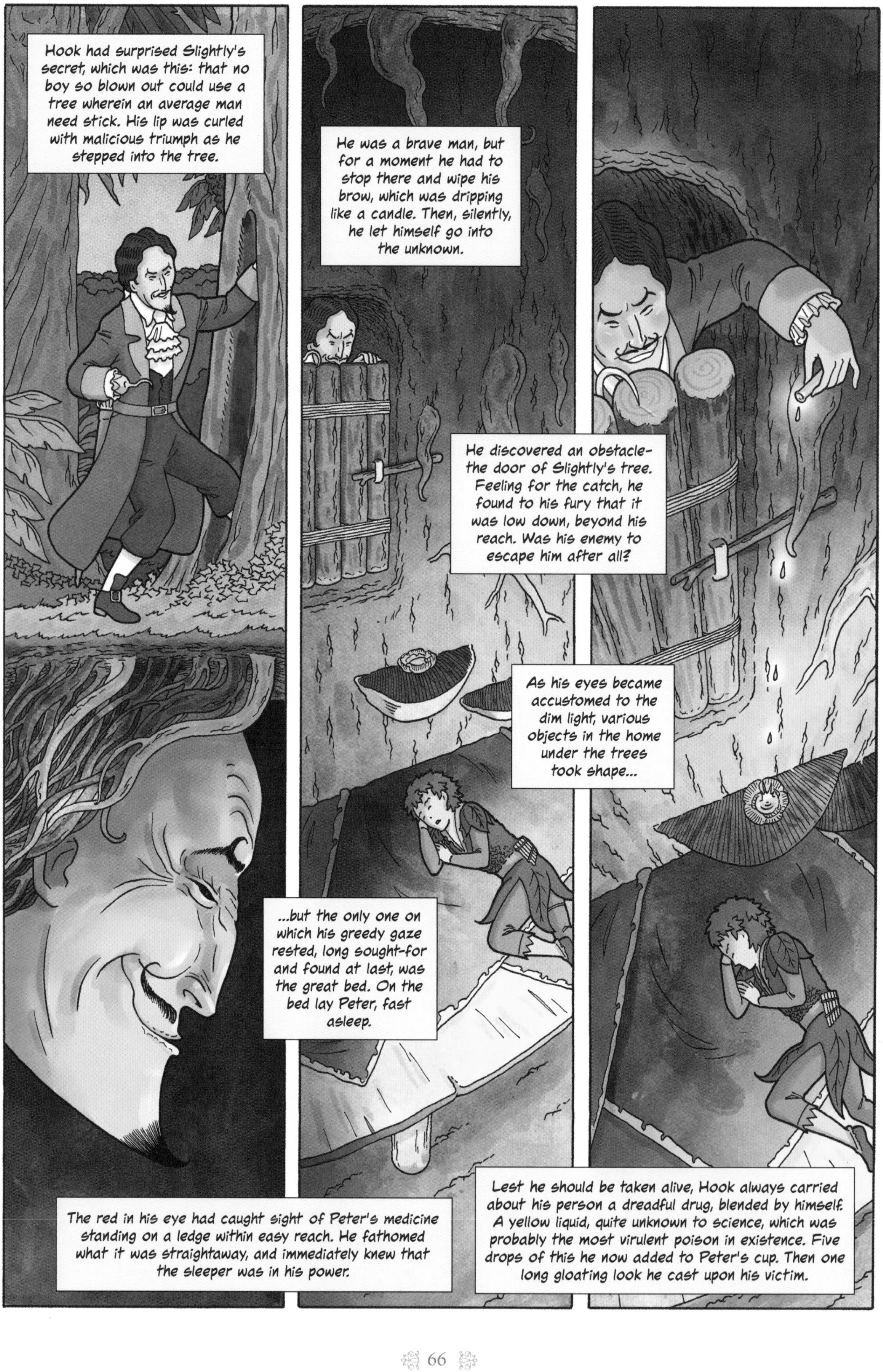
Hook had surprised Slightly's secret, which was this: that no boy so blown out could use a tree wherein an average man need stick. His lip was curled with malicious triumph as he stepped into the tree.
He was a brave man, but for a moment he had to stop there and wipe his brow, which was dripping like a candle. Then, silently, he let himself go into the unknown.
He discovered an obstacle- the door of Slightly's tree. Feeling for the catch, he found to his fury that it was low down, beyond his reach. Was his enemy to escape him after all?
As his eyes became accustomed to the dim light, various objects in the home under the trees took shape...
...but the only one on which his greedy gaze rested, long sought-for and found at last, was the great bed. On the bed lay Peter, fast asleep.
The red in his eye had caught sight of Peter's medicine standing on a ledge within easy reach. He fathomed what it was straightaway, and immediately knew that the sleeper was in his power.
Lest he should be taken alive, Hook always carried about his person a dreadful drug, blended by himself. A yellow liquid, quite unknown to science, which was probably the most virulent poison in existence. Five drops of this he now added to Peter's cup. Then one long gloating look he cast upon his victim.

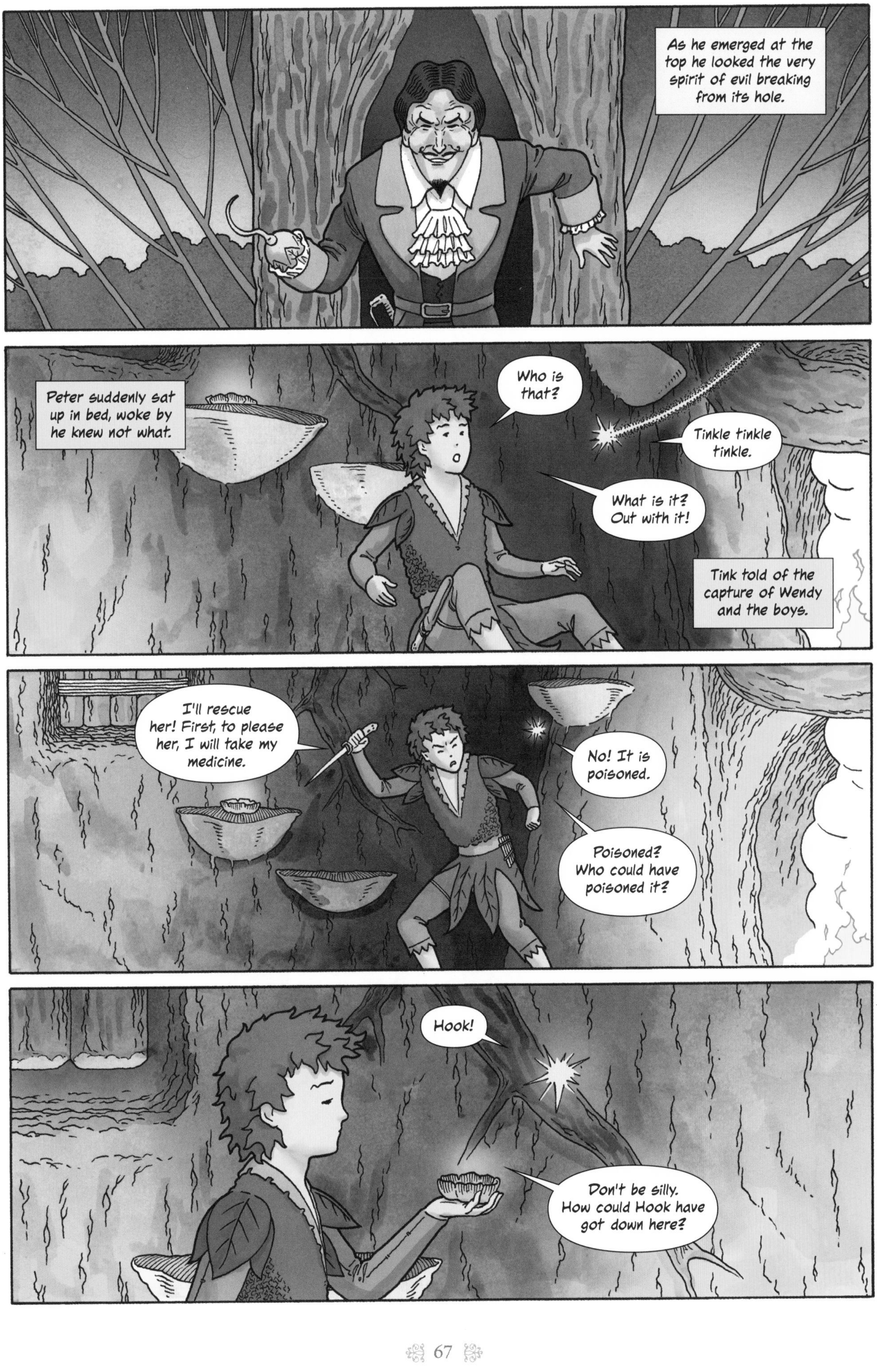
As he emerged at the top he looked the very spirit of evil breaking from its hole.
Peter suddenly sat up in bed, woke by he knew not what.
Who is that?
Tinkle tinkle tinkle.
What is it? Out with it!
Tink told of the capture of Wendy and the boys.
I'll rescue her! First, to please her, I will take my medicine.
No! It is poisoned.
Poisoned? Who could have poisoned it?
Hook!
Don't be silly. How could Hook have got down here?

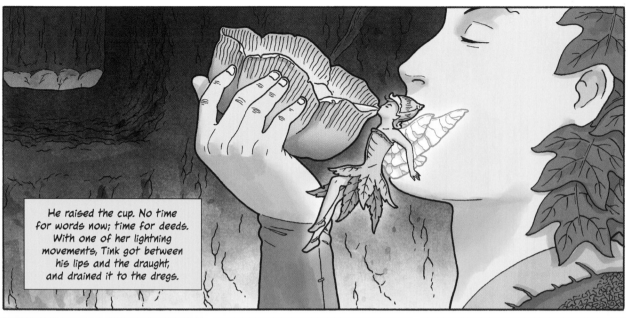

He raised the cup. No time for words now; time for deeds. With one of her lightning movements, Tink got between his lips and the draught, and drained it to the dregs.

Why, Tink, how dare you drink my medicine? What is the matter with you?

It was poisoned, Peter, and now I am going to be dead.

O Tink, did you drink it to save me?

Yes.

But why, Tink?

You silly ass!

Every moment her light is growing fainter. If it goes out she will be no more.

I think I could get well again if children believed in fairies.

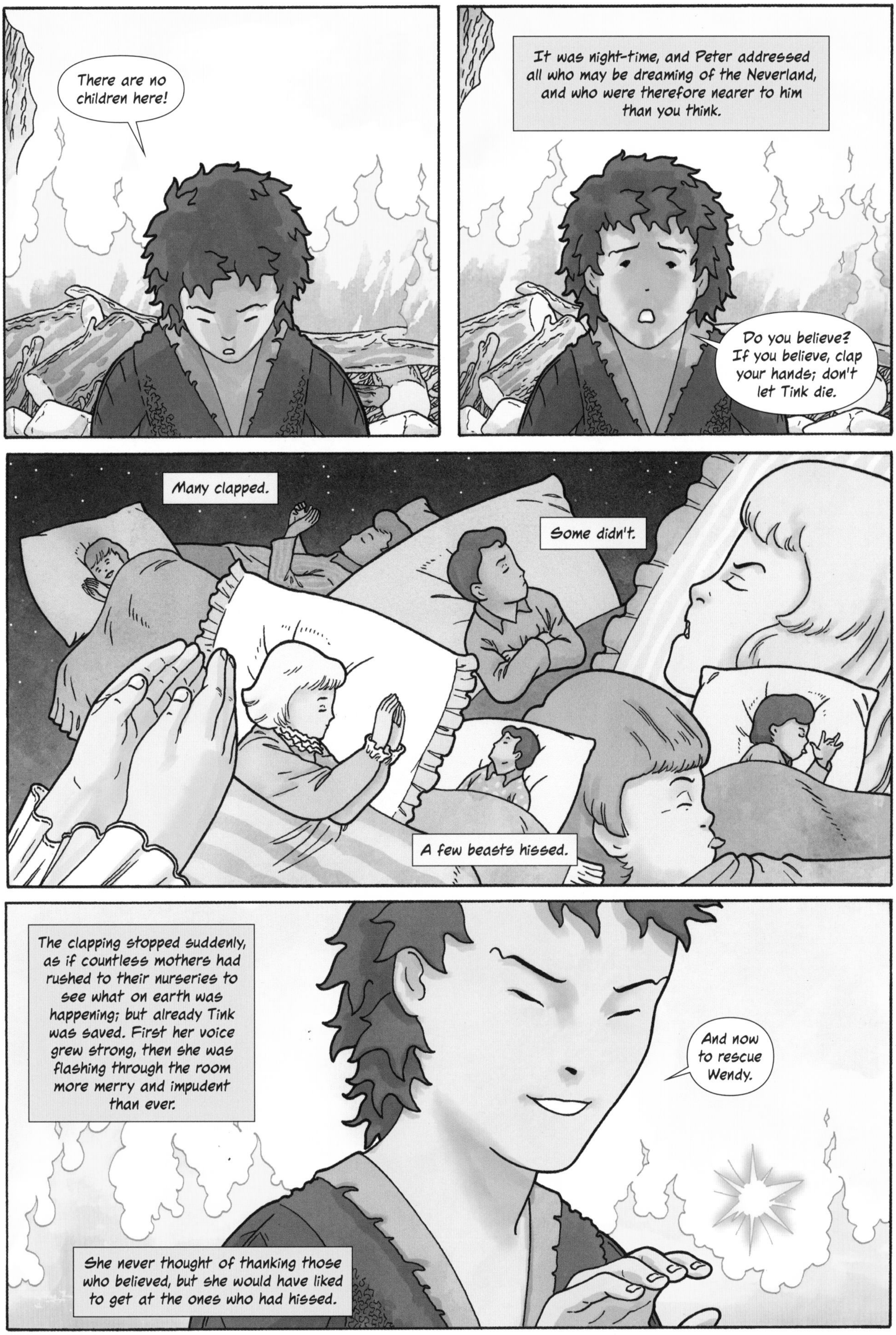

There are no children here!
It was night-time, and Peter addressed all who may be dreaming of the Neverland, and who were therefore nearer to him than you think.
Do you believe? If you believe, clap your hands; don't let Tink die.
Many clapped.
Some didn't.
A few beasts hissed.
The clapping stopped suddenly, as if countless mothers had rushed to their nurseries to see what on earth was happening; but already Tink was saved. First her voice grew strong, then she was flashing through the room more merry and impudent than ever.
And now to rescue Wendy.
She never thought of thanking those who believed, but she would have liked to get at the ones who had hissed.

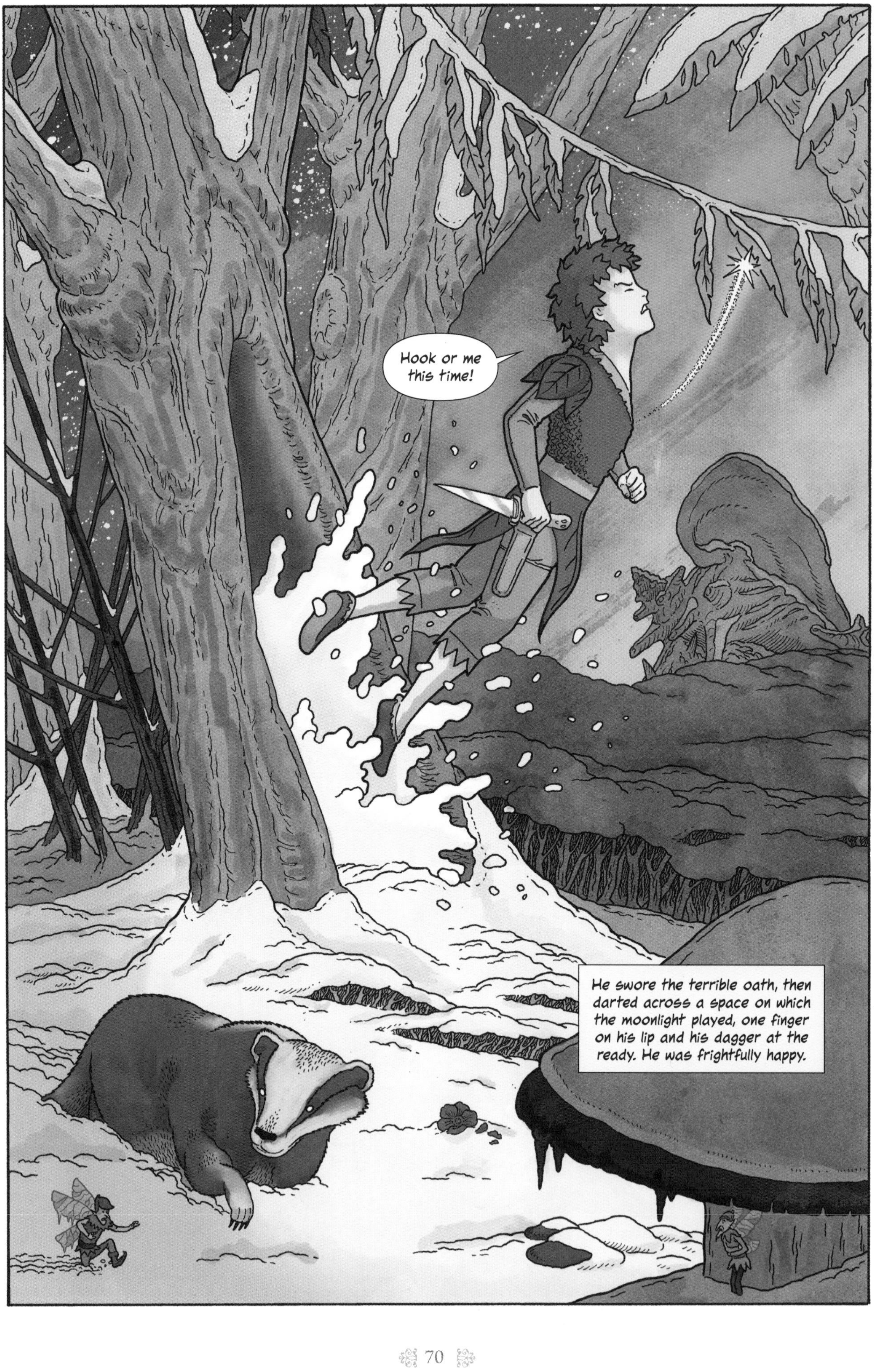
Hook or me this time!
He swore the terrible oath, then darted across a space on which the moonlight played, one finger on his lip and his dagger at the ready. He was frightfully happy.

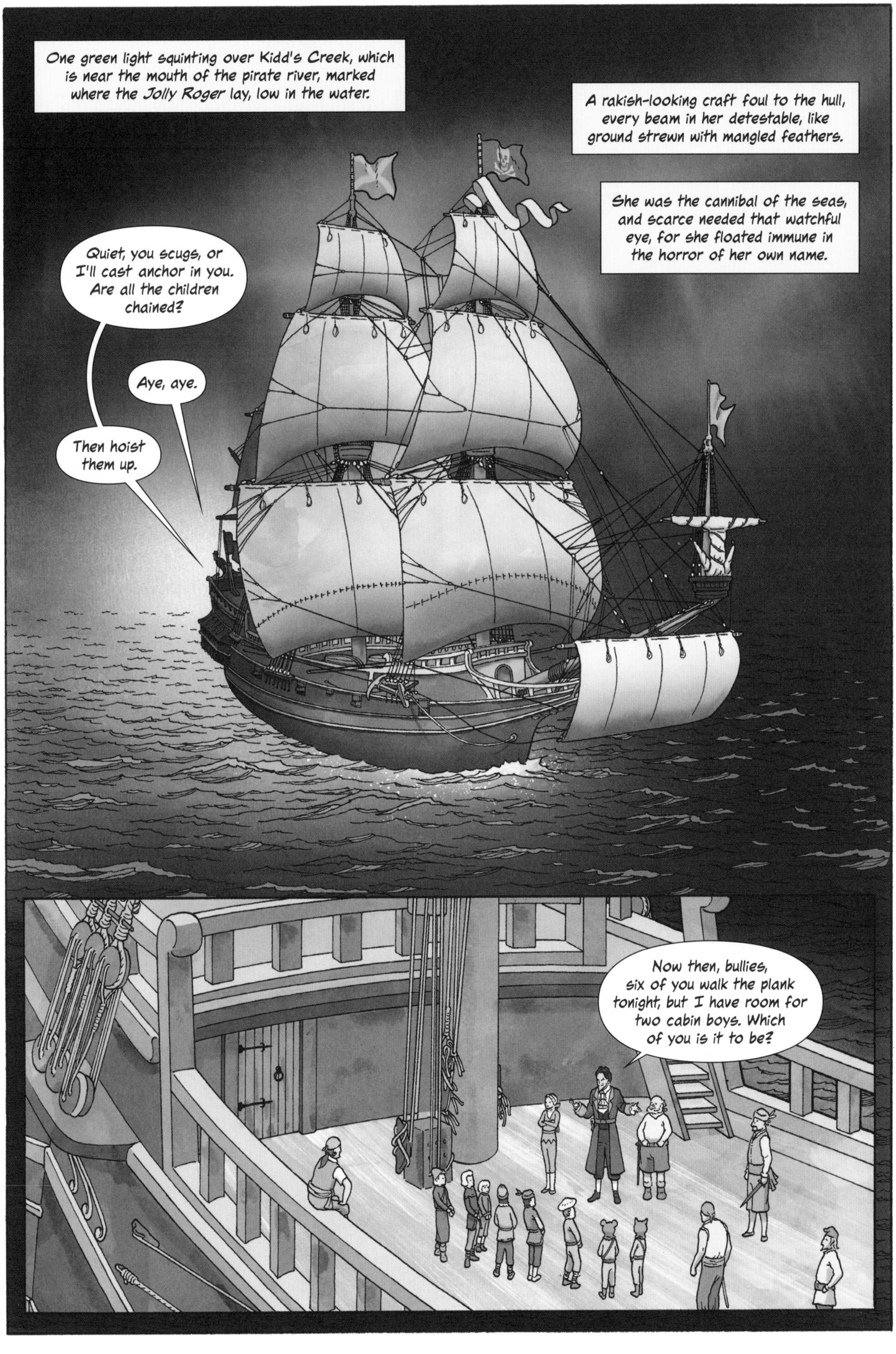

One green light squinting over Kidd's Creek, which is near the mouth of the pirate river, marked where the *Jolly Roger* lay, low in the water.
A rakish-looking craft foul to the hull, every beam in her detestable, like ground strewn with mangled feathers.
She was the cannibal of the seas, and scarce needed that watchful eye, for she floated immune in the horror of her own name.
Quiet, you scugs, or I'll cast anchor in you. Are all the children chained?
Aye, aye.
Then hoist them up.
Now then, bullies, six of you walk the plank tonight, but I have room for two cabin boys. Which of you is it to be?

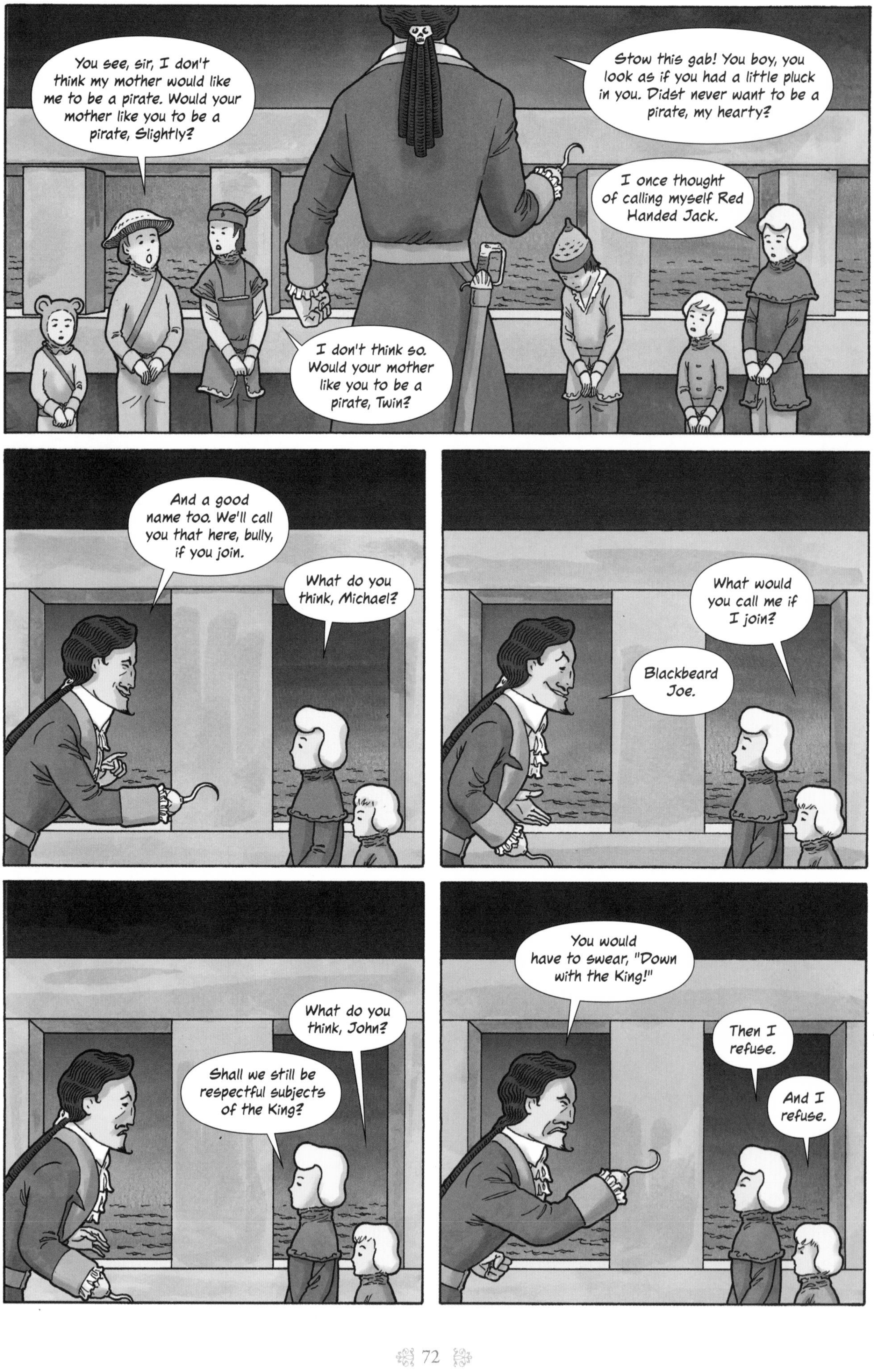
You see, sir, I don't think my mother would like me to be a pirate. Would your mother like you to be a pirate, Slightly?
I don't think so. Would your mother like you to be a pirate, Twin?
Stow this gab! You boy, you look as if you had a little pluck in you. Didst never want to be a pirate, my hearty?
I once thought of calling myself Red Handed Jack.
And a good name too. We'll call you that here, bully, if you join.
What do you think, Michael?
What would you call me if I join?
Blackbeard Joe.
What do you think, John?
Shall we still be respectful subjects of the King?
You would have to swear, "Down with the King!"
Then I refuse.
And I refuse.

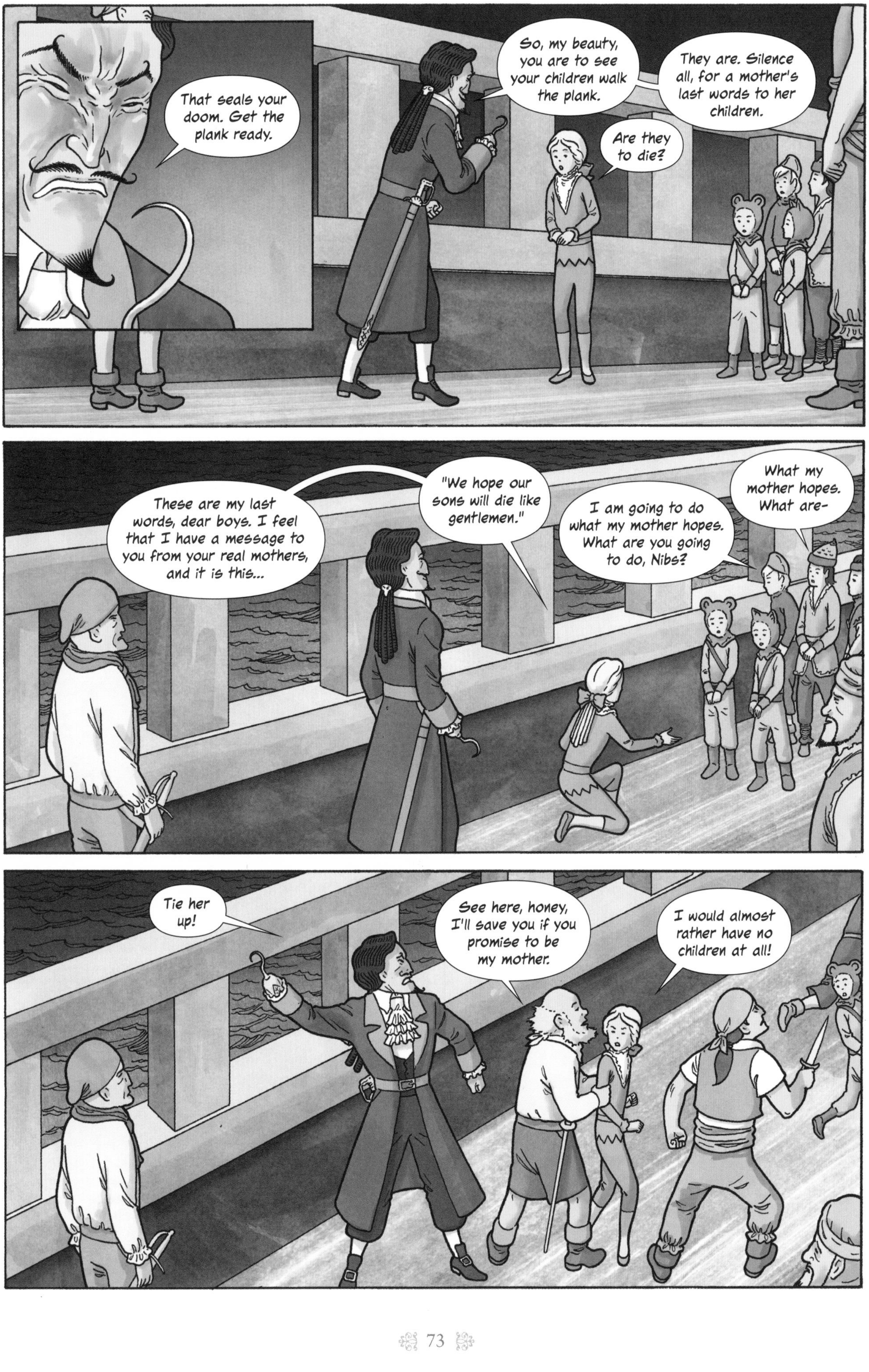
That seals your doom. Get the plank ready.
So, my beauty, you are to see your children walk the plank.
Are they to die?
They are. Silence all, for a mother's last words to her children.
These are my last words, dear boys. I feel that I have a message to you from your real mothers, and it is this...
"We hope our sons will die like gentlemen."
I am going to do what my mother hopes. What are you going to do, Nibs?
What my mother hopes. What are-
Tie her up!
See here, honey, I'll save you if you promise to be my mother.
I would almost rather have no children at all!

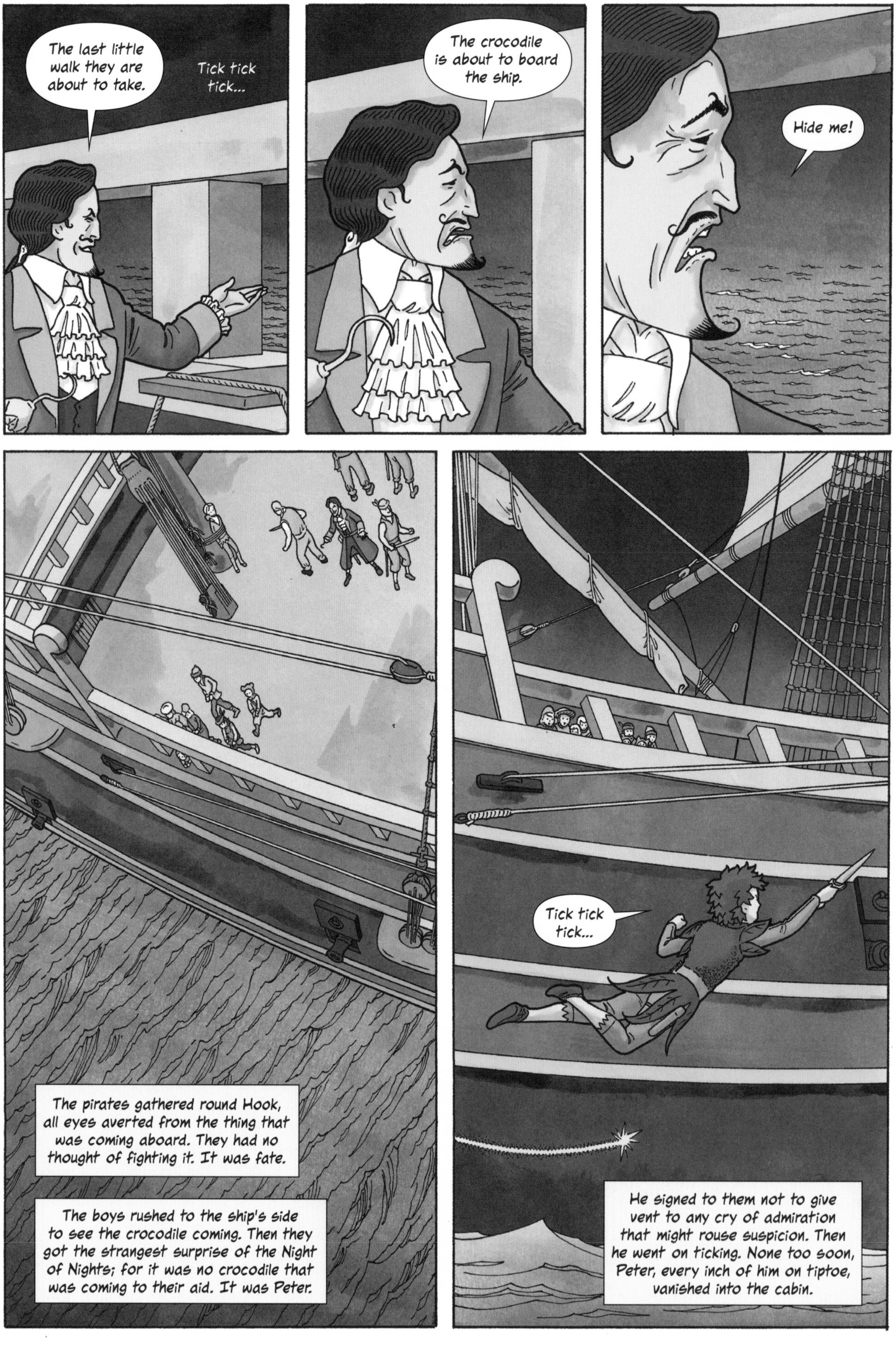
The last little walk they are about to take.
Tick tick tick...
The crocodile is about to board the ship.
Hide me!
The pirates gathered round Hook, all eyes averted from the thing that was coming aboard. They had no thought of fighting it. It was fate.
The boys rushed to the ship's side to see the crocodile coming. Then they got the strangest surprise of the Night of Nights; for it was no crocodile that was coming to their aid. It was Peter.
Tick tick tick...
He signed to them not to give vent to any cry of admiration that might rouse suspicion. Then he went on ticking. None too soon, Peter, every inch of him on tiptoe, vanished into the cabin.

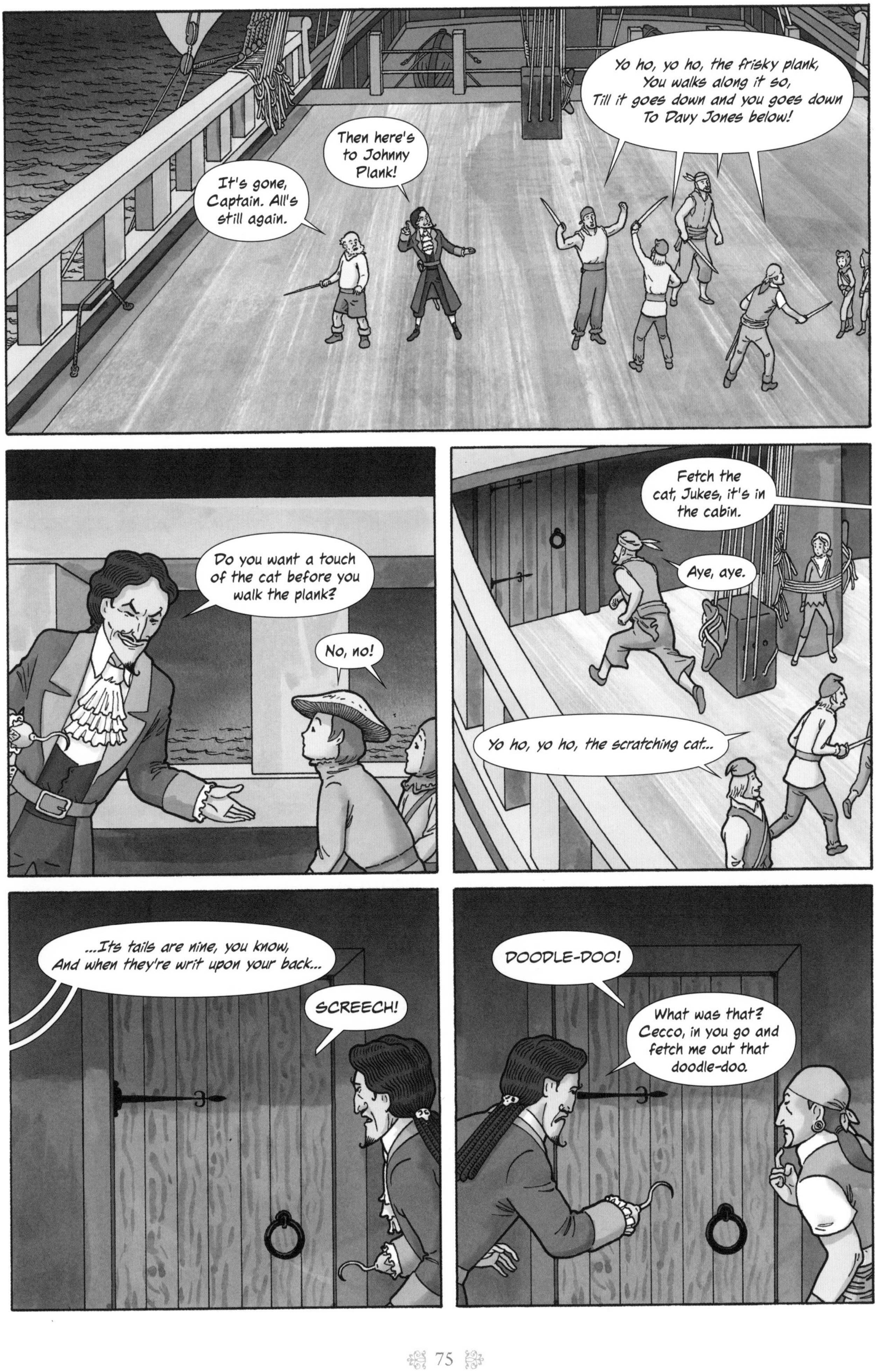
It's gone, Captain. All's still again.
Then here's to Johnny Plank!
Yo ho, yo ho, the frisky plank, You walks along it so, Till it goes down and you goes down To Davy Jones below!
Do you want a touch of the cat before you walk the plank?
No, no!
Fetch the cat, Jukes, it's in the cabin.
Aye, aye.
Yo ho, yo ho, the scratching cat...
...Its tails are nine, you know, And when they're writ upon your back...
SCREECH!
DOODLE-DOO!
What was that? Cecco, in you go and fetch me out that doodle-doo.

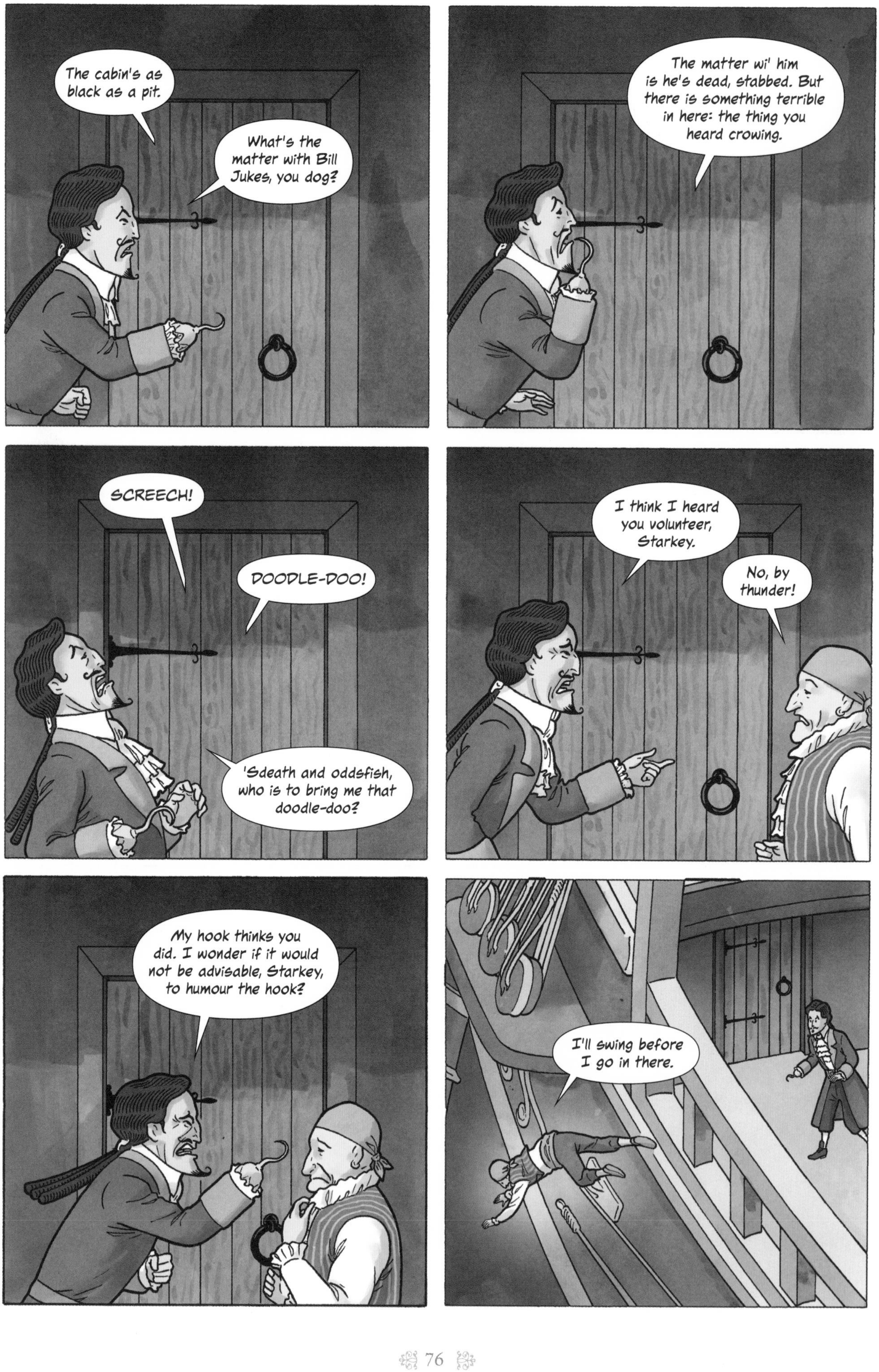
The cabin's as black as a pit.
What's the matter with Bill Jukes, you dog?
The matter wi' him is he's dead, stabbed. But there is something terrible in here: the thing you heard crowing.
SCREECH!
DOODLE-DOO!
'Sdeath and oddsfish, who is to bring me that doodle-doo?
I think I heard you volunteer, Starkey.
No, by thunder!
My hook thinks you did. I wonder if it would not be advisable, Starkey, to humour the hook?
I'll swing before I go in there.

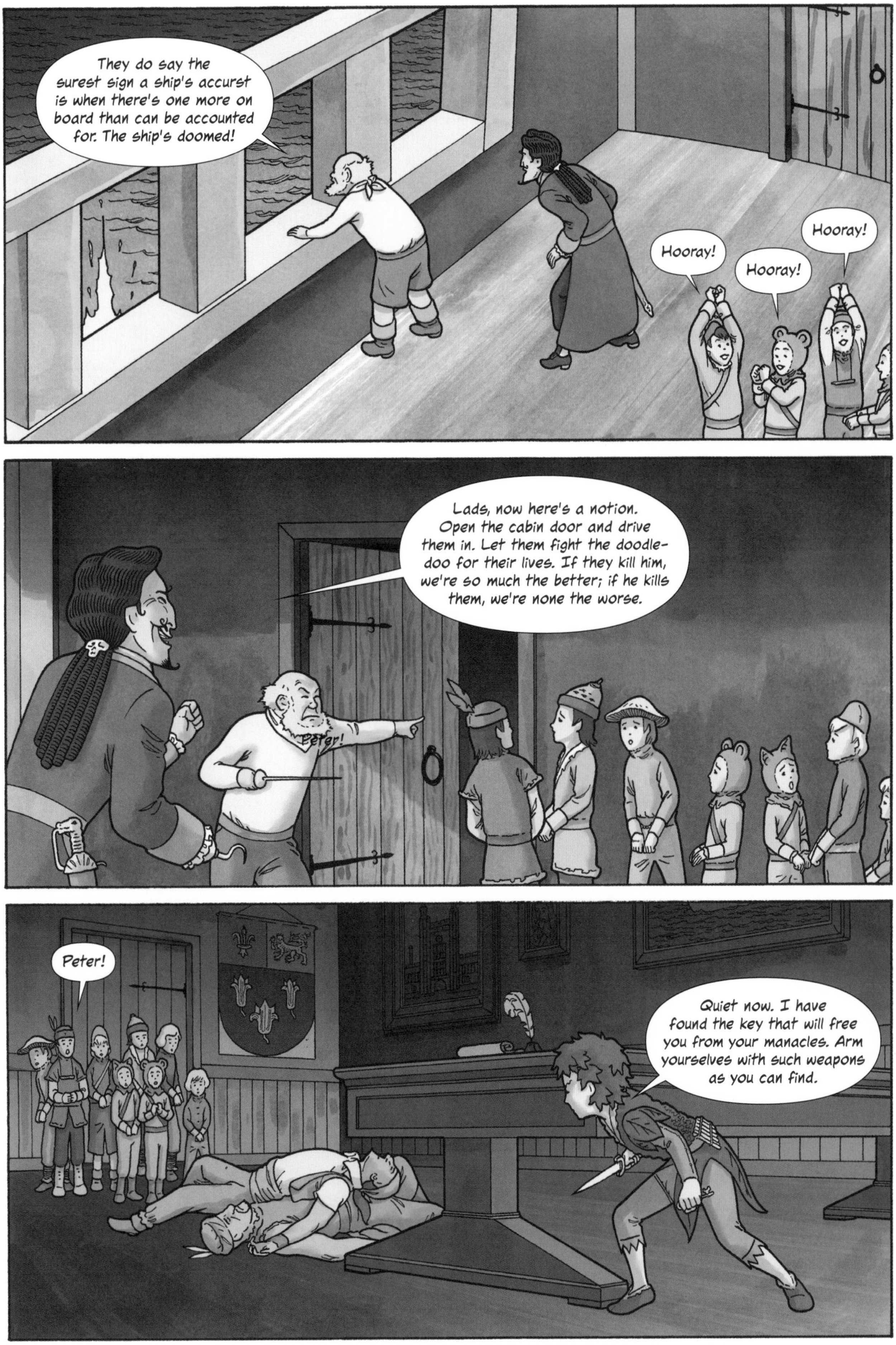

They do say the surest sign a ship's accurst is when there's one more on board than can be accounted for. The ship's doomed!
Hooray!
Hooray!
Hooray!
Lads, now here's a notion. Open the cabin door and drive them in. Let them fight the doodle-doo for their lives. If they kill him, we're so much the better; if he kills them, we're none the worse.
Peter!
Quiet now. I have found the key that will free you from your manacles. Arm yourselves with such weapons as you can find.

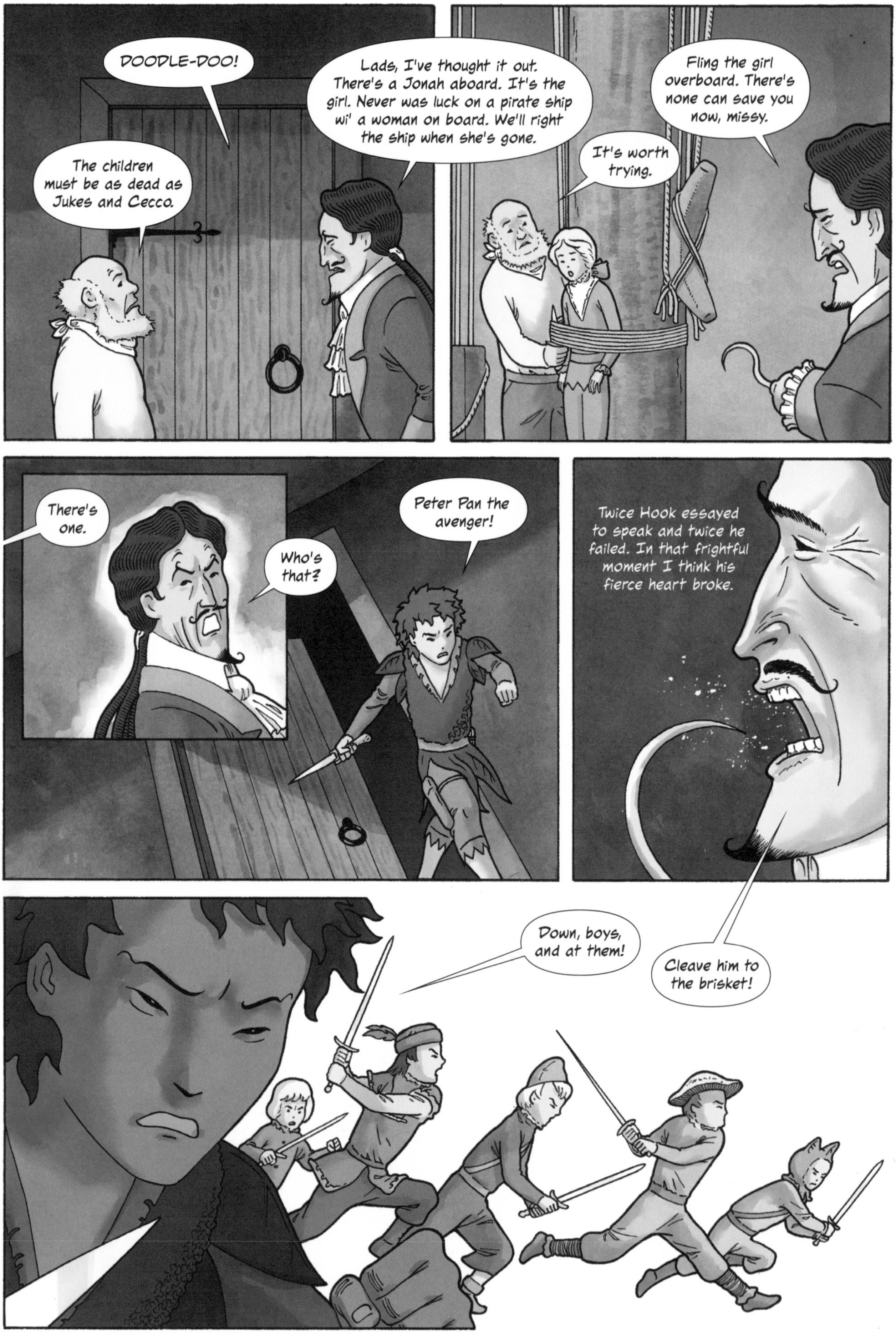
DOODLE-DOO!
The children must be as dead as Jukes and Cecco.
Lads, I've thought it out. There's a Jonah aboard. It's the girl. Never was luck on a pirate ship wi' a woman on board. We'll right the ship when she's gone.
It's worth trying.
Fling the girl overboard. There's none can save you now, missy.
There's one.
Who's that?
Peter Pan the avenger!
Twice Hook essayed to speak and twice he failed. In that frightful moment I think his fierce heart broke.
Down, boys, and at them!
Cleave him to the brisket!

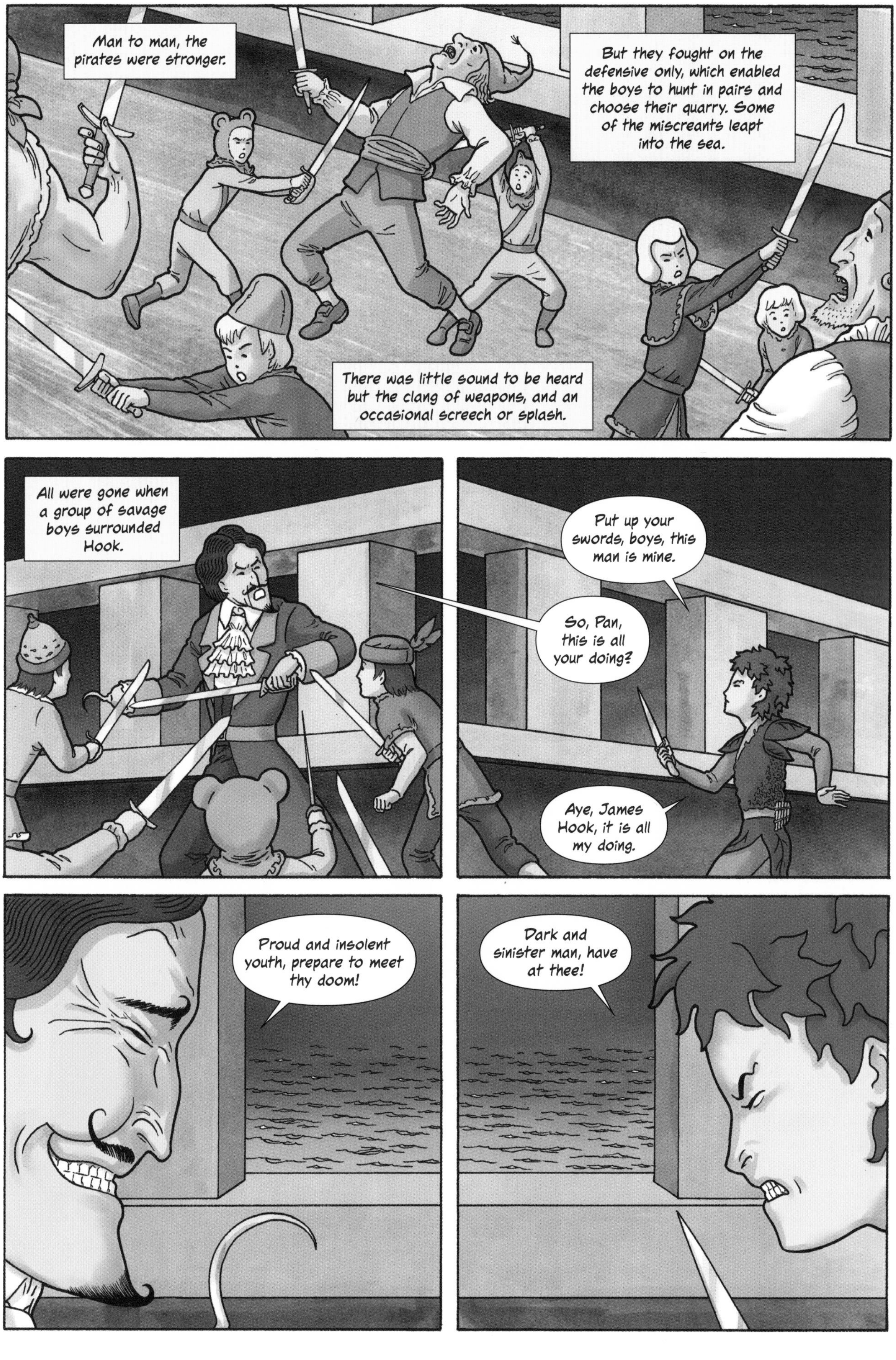
Man to man, the pirates were stronger.
But they fought on the defensive only, which enabled the boys to hunt in pairs and choose their quarry. Some of the miscreants leapt into the sea.
There was little sound to be heard but the clang of weapons, and an occasional screech or splash.
All were gone when a group of savage boys surrounded Hook.
So, Pan, this is all your doing?
Put up your swords, boys, this man is mine.
Aye, James Hook, it is all my doing.
Proud and insolent youth, prepare to meet thy doom!
Dark and sinister man, have at thee!

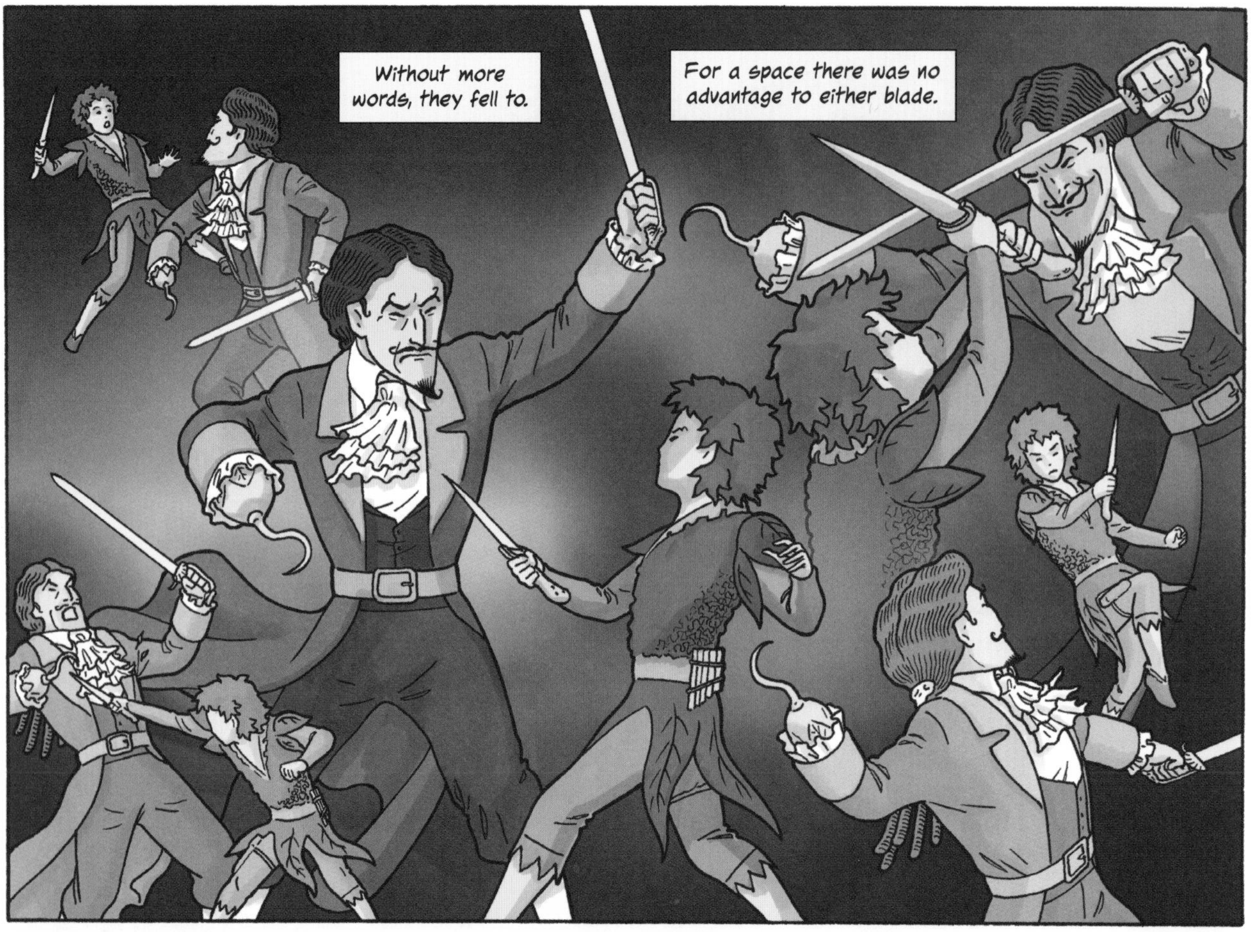
Without more words, they fell to.
For a space there was no advantage to either blade.

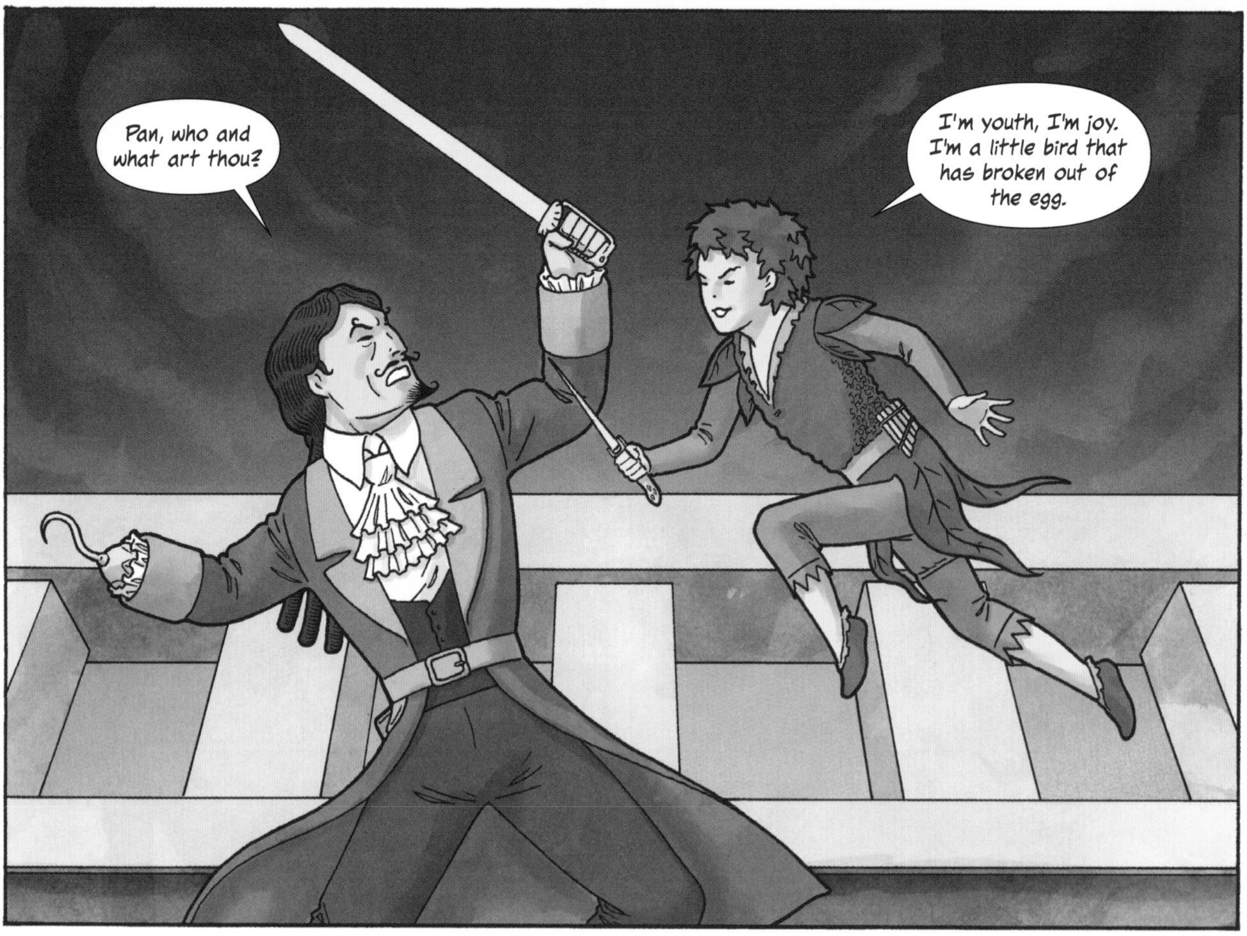
Pan, who and what art thou?
I'm youth, I'm joy. I'm a little bird that has broken out of the egg.

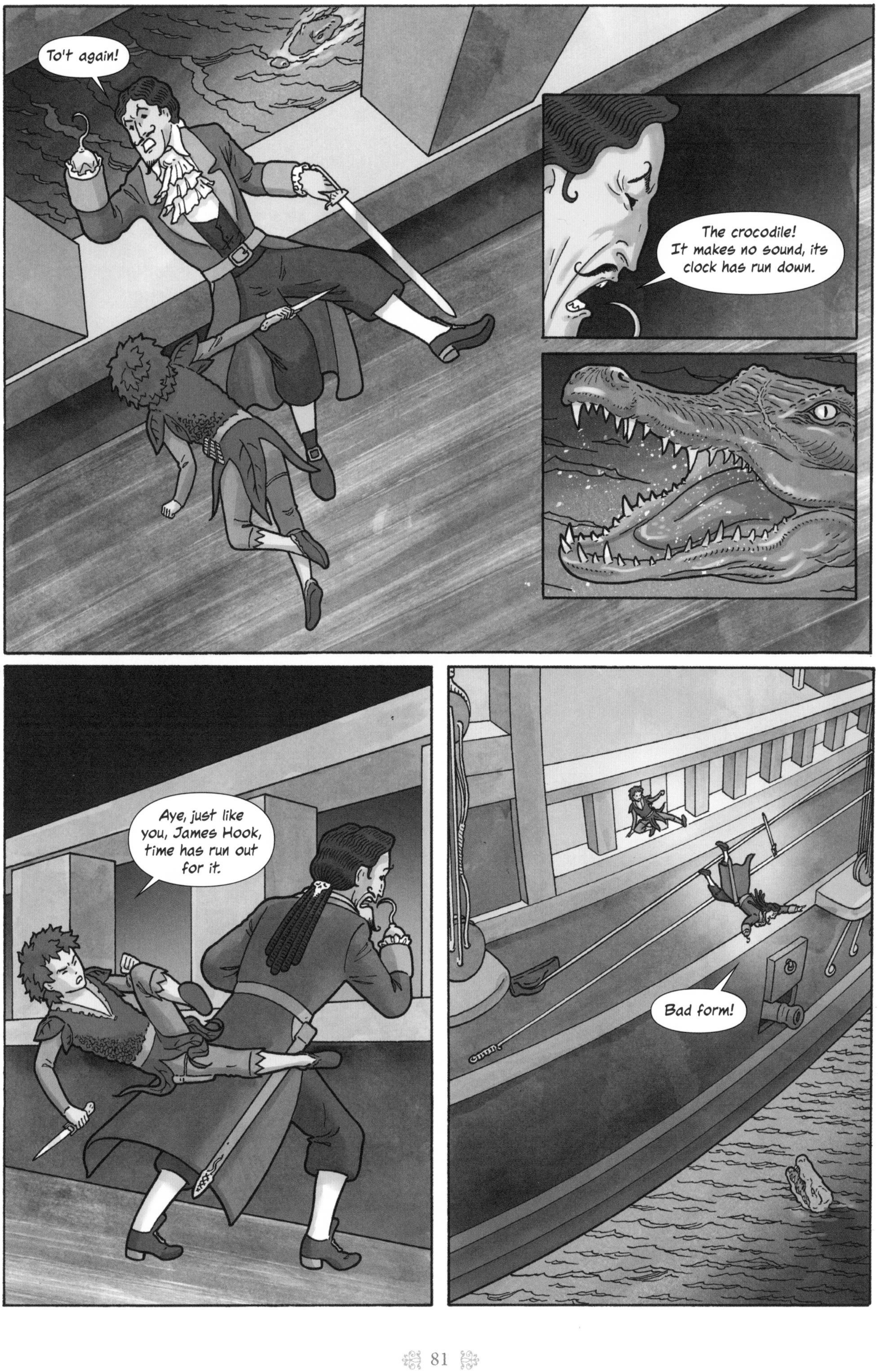
To't again!
The crocodile! It makes no sound, its clock has run down.
Aye, just like you, James Hook, time has run out for it.
Bad form!

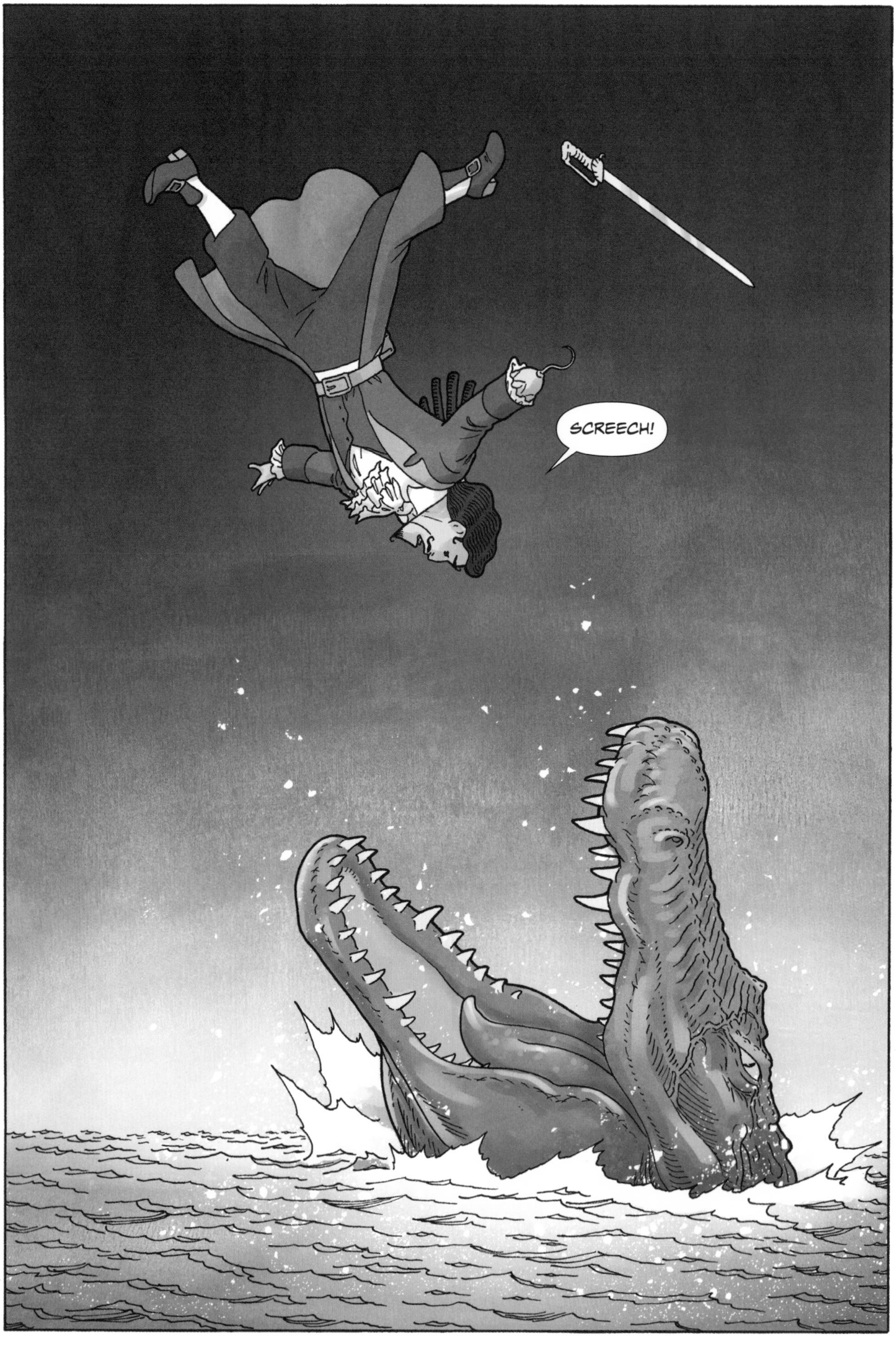
SCREECH!

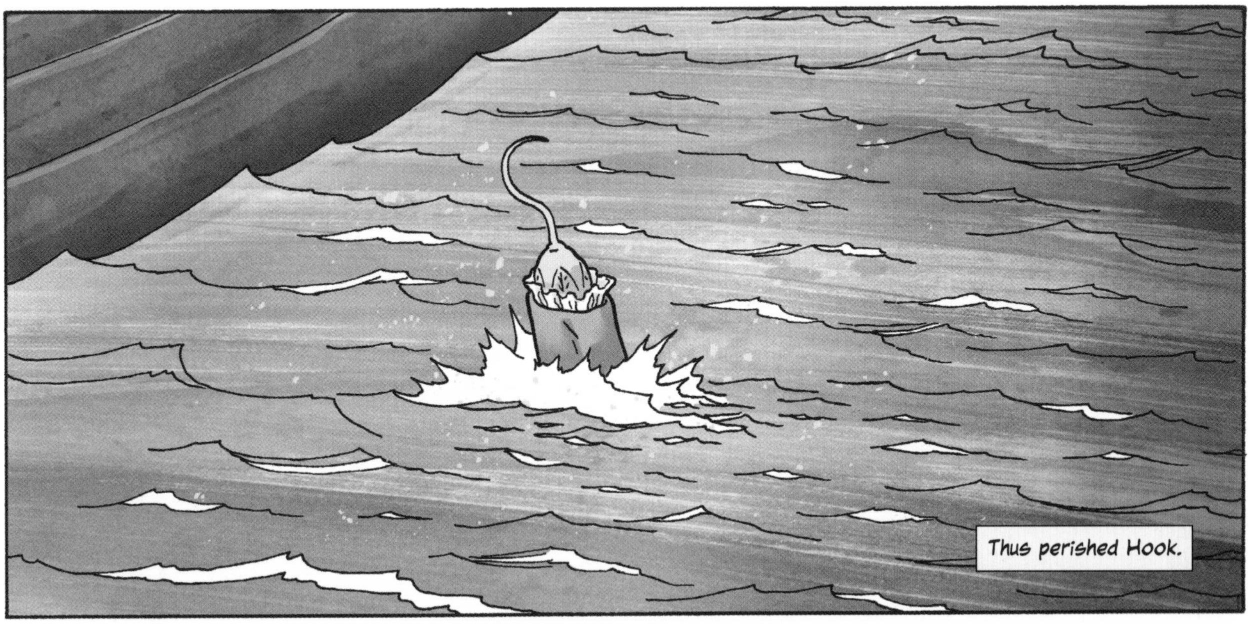
Thus perished Hook.

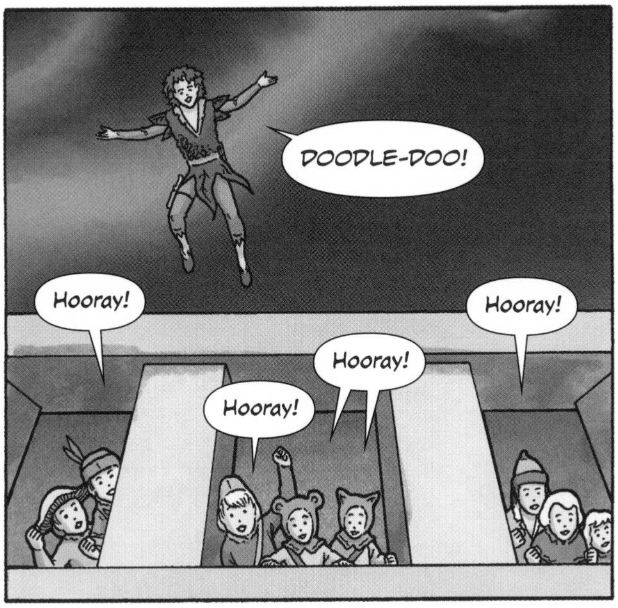
DOODLE-DOO!
Hooray!
Hooray!
Hooray!
Hooray!

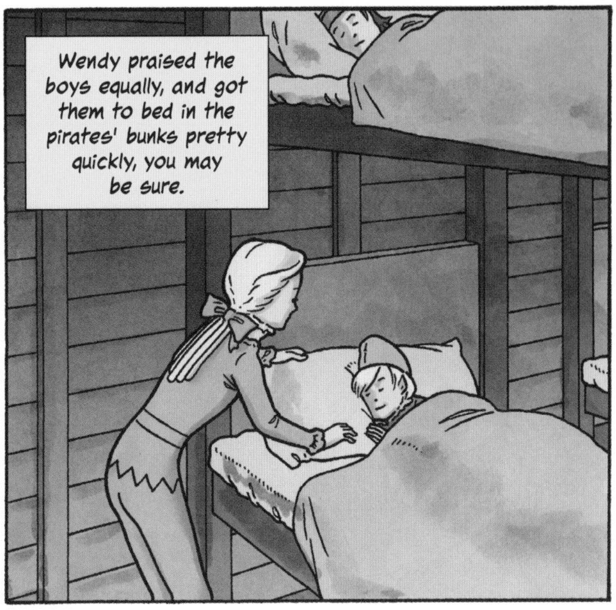
Wendy praised the boys equally, and got them to bed in the pirates' bunks pretty quickly, you may be sure.

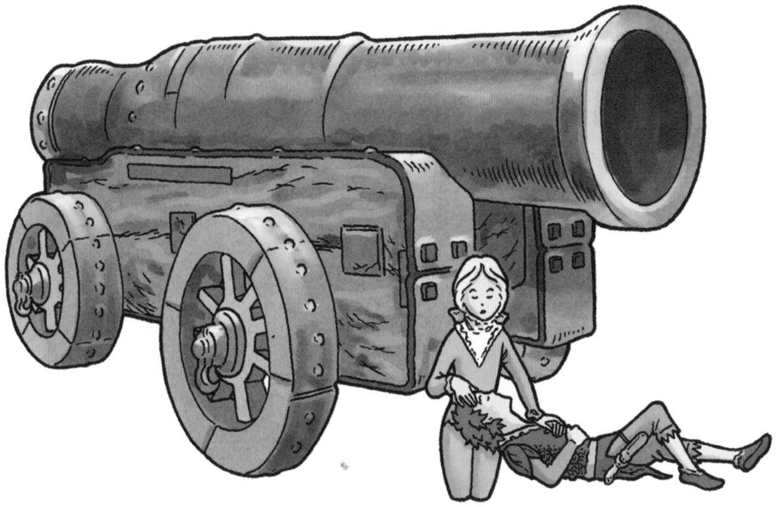

All but Peter, who strutted up and down on the deck, until at last he fell asleep by the side of Long Tom. He had one of his dreams that night, and cried in his sleep for a long time, and Wendy held him tightly.

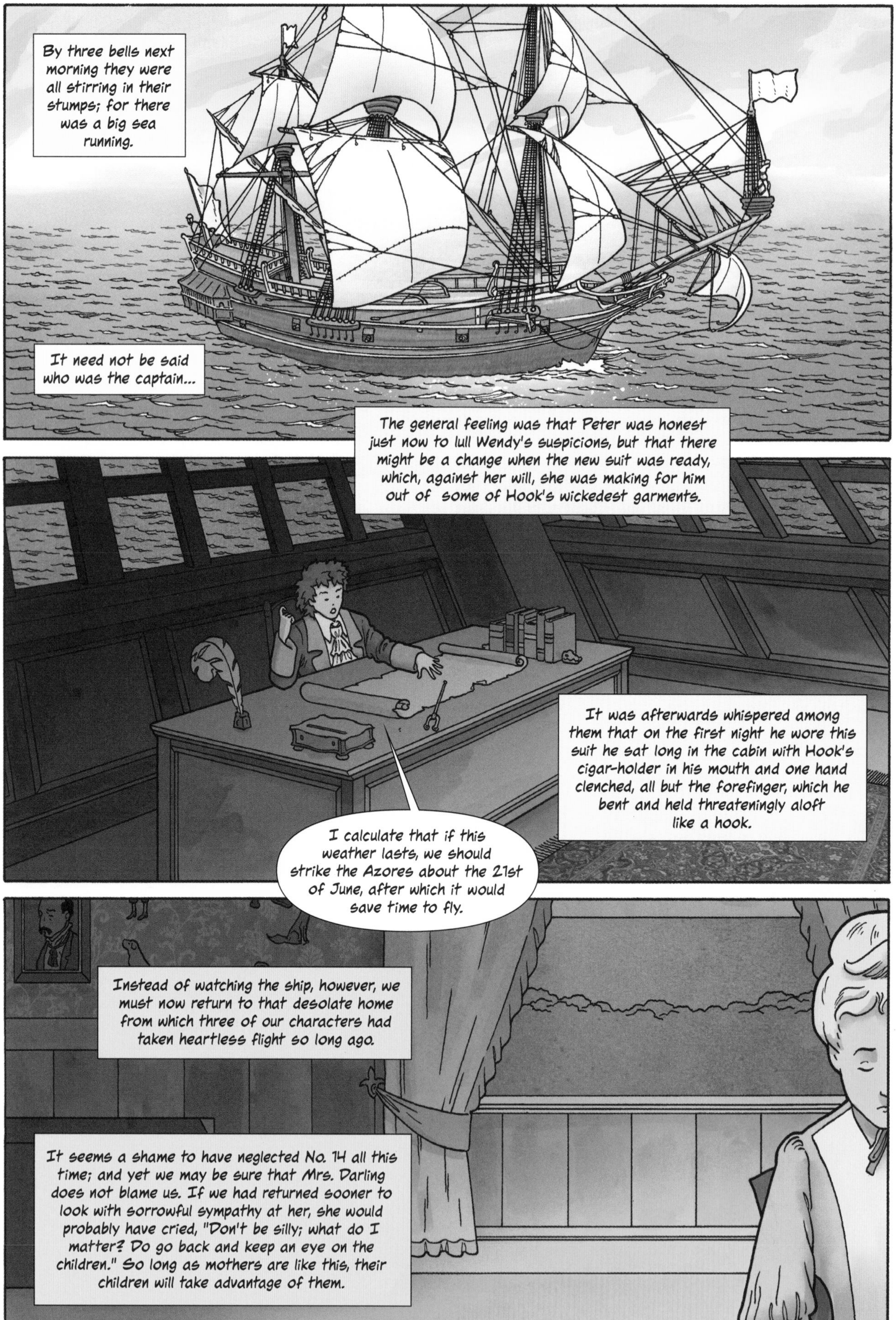
By three bells next morning they were all stirring in their stumps; for there was a big sea running.
It need not be said who was the captain...
The general feeling was that Peter was honest just now to lull Wendy's suspicions, but that there might be a change when the new suit was ready, which, against her will, she was making for him out of some of Hook's wickedest garments.
It was afterwards whispered among them that on the first night he wore this suit he sat long in the cabin with Hook's cigar-holder in his mouth and one hand clenched, all but the forefinger, which he bent and held threateningly aloft like a hook.
I calculate that if this weather lasts, we should strike the Azores about the 21st of June, after which it would save time to fly.
Instead of watching the ship, however, we must now return to that desolate home from which three of our characters had taken heartless flight so long ago.
It seems a shame to have neglected No. 14 all this time; and yet we may be sure that Mrs. Darling does not blame us. If we had returned sooner to look with sorrowful sympathy at her, she would probably have cried, "Don't be silly; what do I matter? Do go back and keep an eye on the children." So long as mothers are like this, their children will take advantage of them.

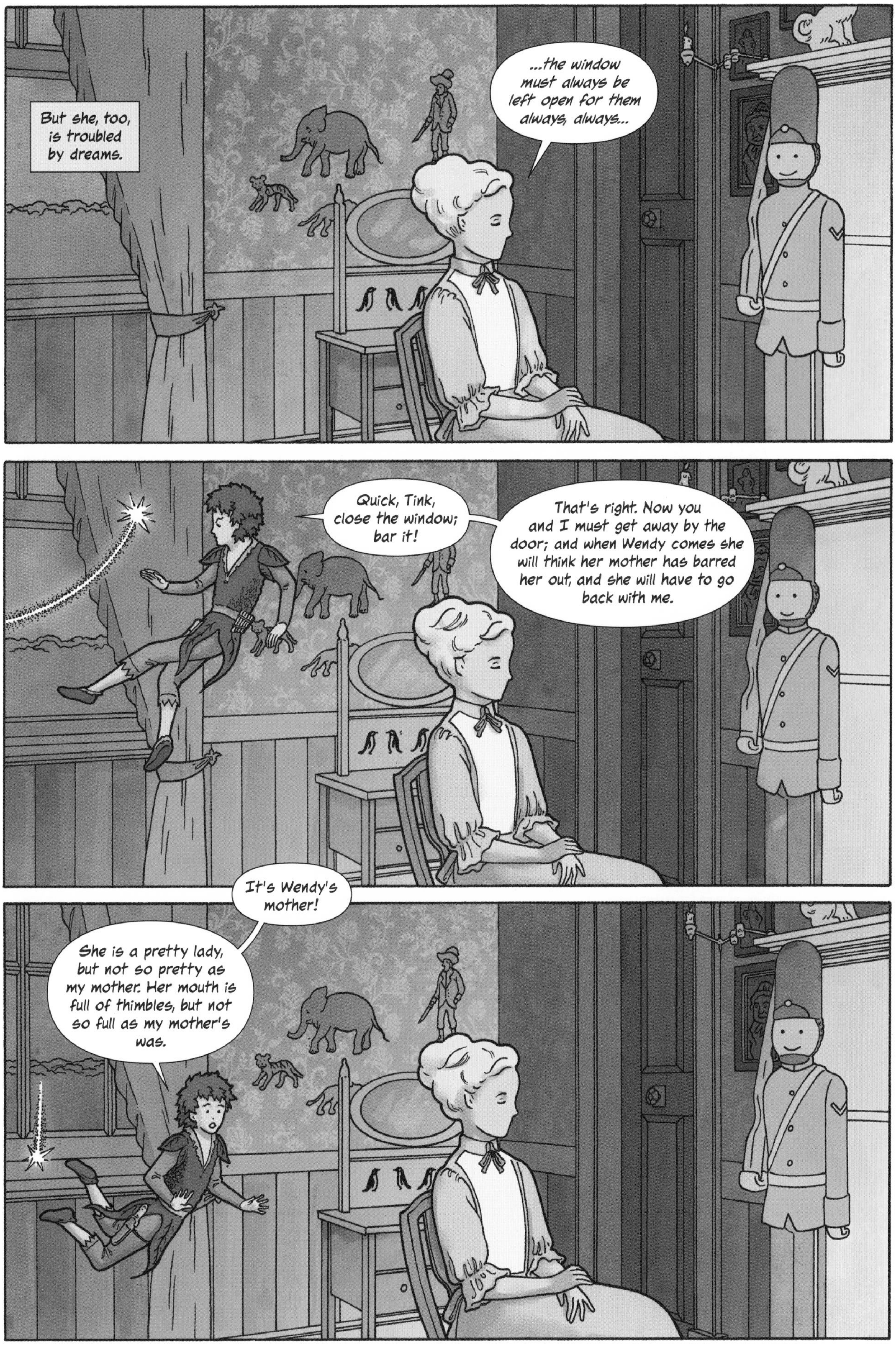
But she, too, is troubled by dreams.
...the window must always be left open for them always, always...
Quick, Tink, close the window; bar it!
That's right. Now you and I must get away by the door; and when Wendy comes she will think her mother has barred her out, and she will have to go back with me.
It's Wendy's mother!
She is a pretty lady, but not so pretty as my mother. Her mouth is full of thimbles, but not so full as my mother's was.

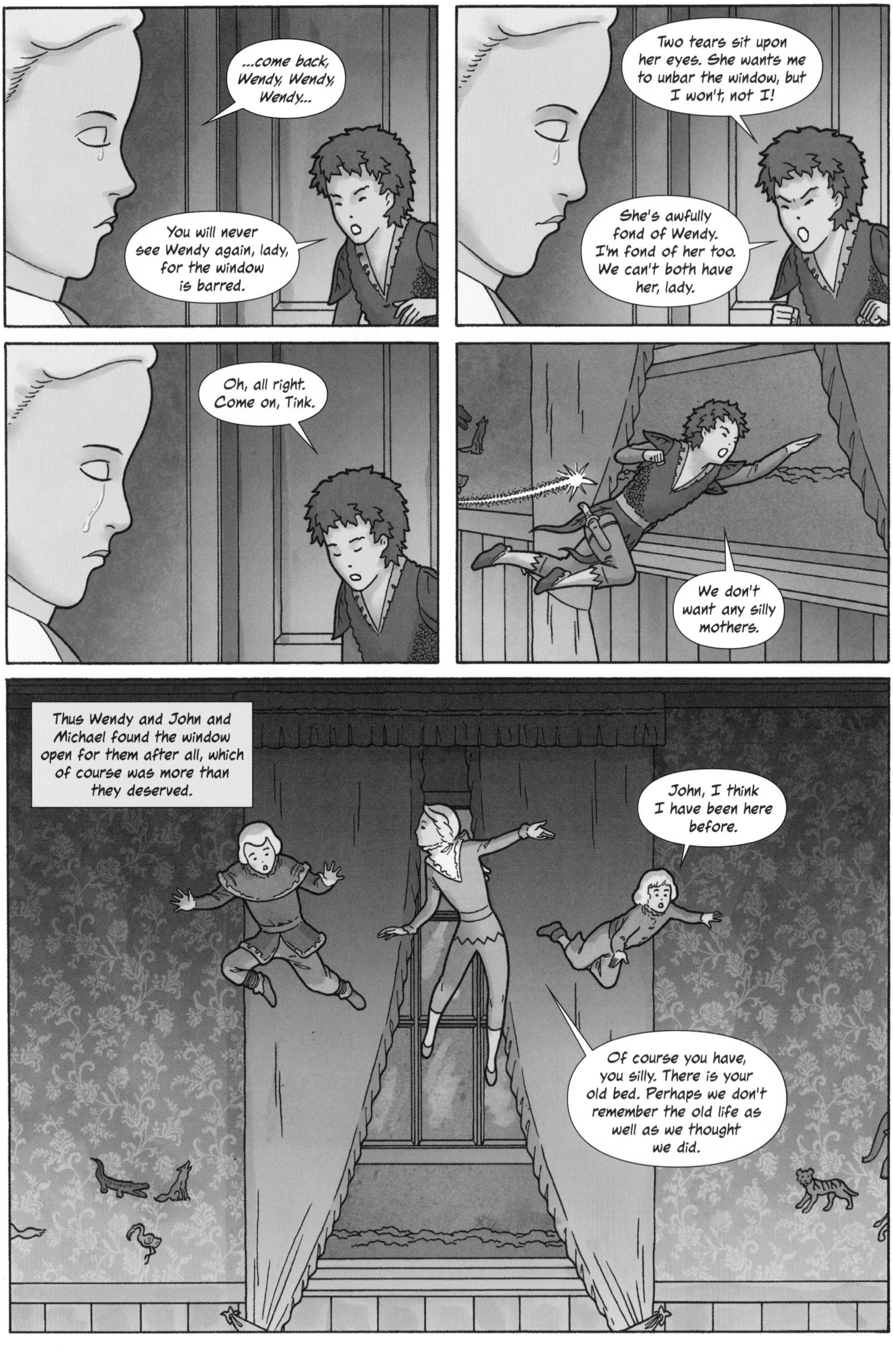
...come back, Wendy, Wendy, Wendy...
You will never see Wendy again, lady, for the window is barred.
Two tears sit upon her eyes. She wants me to unbar the window, but I won't, not I!
She's awfully fond of Wendy. I'm fond of her too. We can't both have her, lady.
Oh, all right. Come on, Tink.
We don't want any silly mothers.
Thus Wendy and John and Michael found the window open for them after all, which of course was more than they deserved.
John, I think I have been here before.
Of course you have, you silly. There is your old bed. Perhaps we don't remember the old life as well as we thought we did.

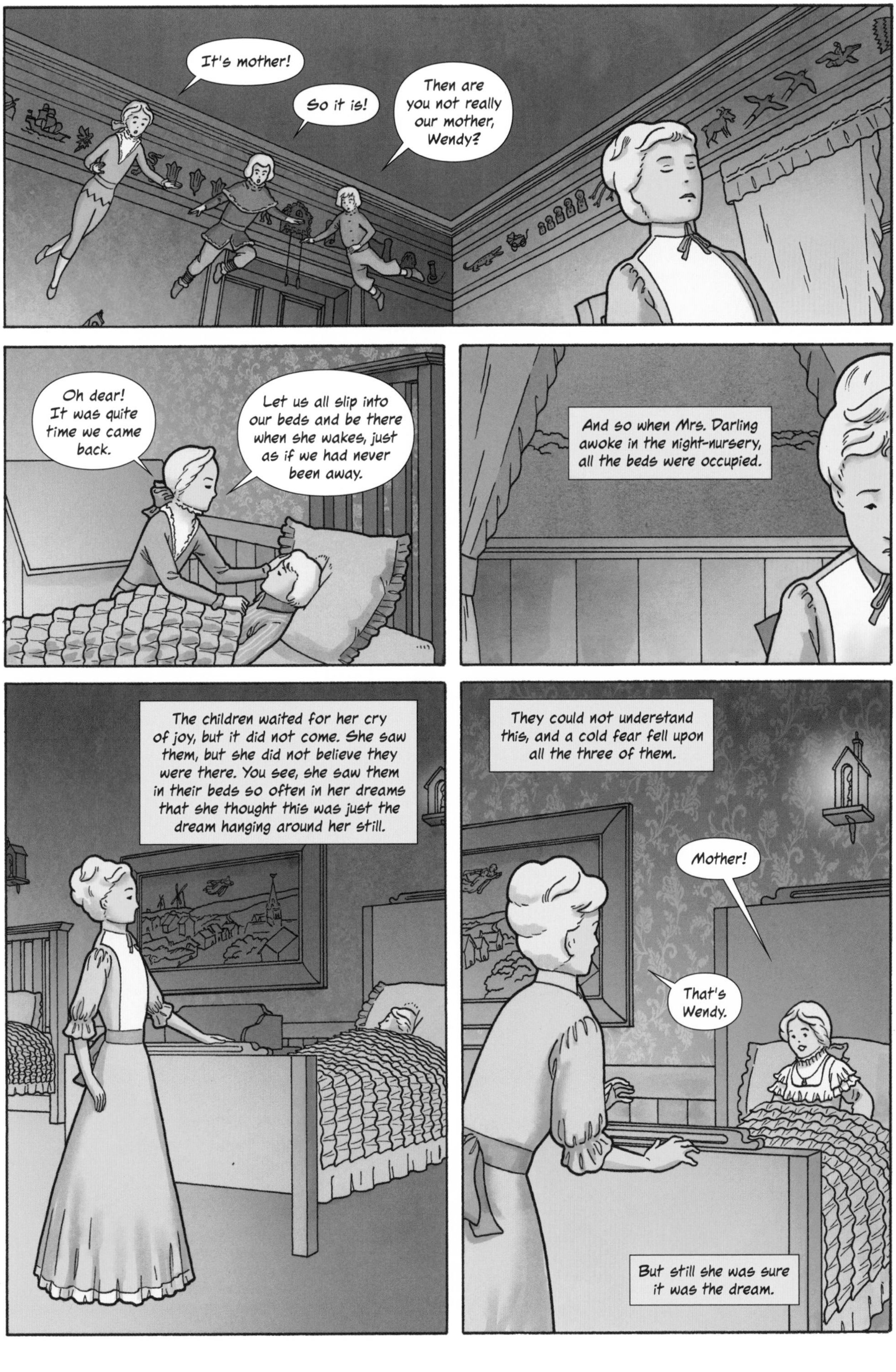
It's mother!
So it is!
Then are you not really our mother, Wendy?
Oh dear! It was quite time we came back.
Let us all slip into our beds and be there when she wakes, just as if we had never been away.
And so when Mrs. Darling awoke in the night-nursery, all the beds were occupied.
The children waited for her cry of joy, but it did not come. She saw them, but she did not believe they were there. You see, she saw them in their beds so often in her dreams that she thought this was just the dream hanging around her still.
They could not understand this, and a cold fear fell upon all the three of them.
Mother!
That's Wendy.
But still she was sure it was the dream.

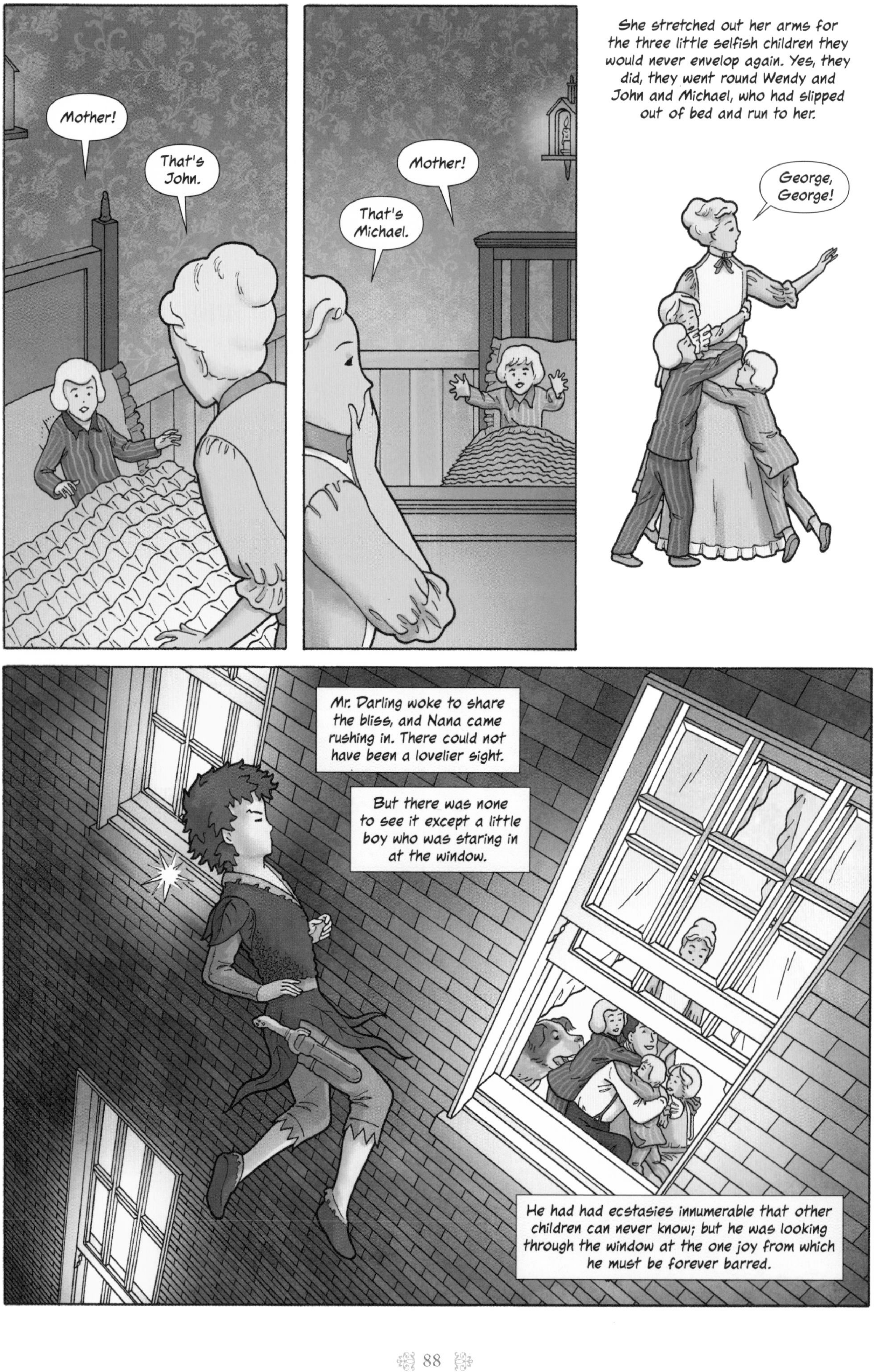
Mother!
That's John.
Mother!
That's Michael.
She stretched out her arms for the three little selfish children they would never envelop again. Yes, they did, they went round Wendy and John and Michael, who had slipped out of bed and run to her.
George, George!
Mr. Darling woke to share the bliss, and Nana came rushing in. There could not have been a lovelier sight.
But there was none to see it except a little boy who was staring in at the window.
He had had ecstasies innumerable that other children can never know; but he was looking through the window at the one joy from which he must be forever barred.

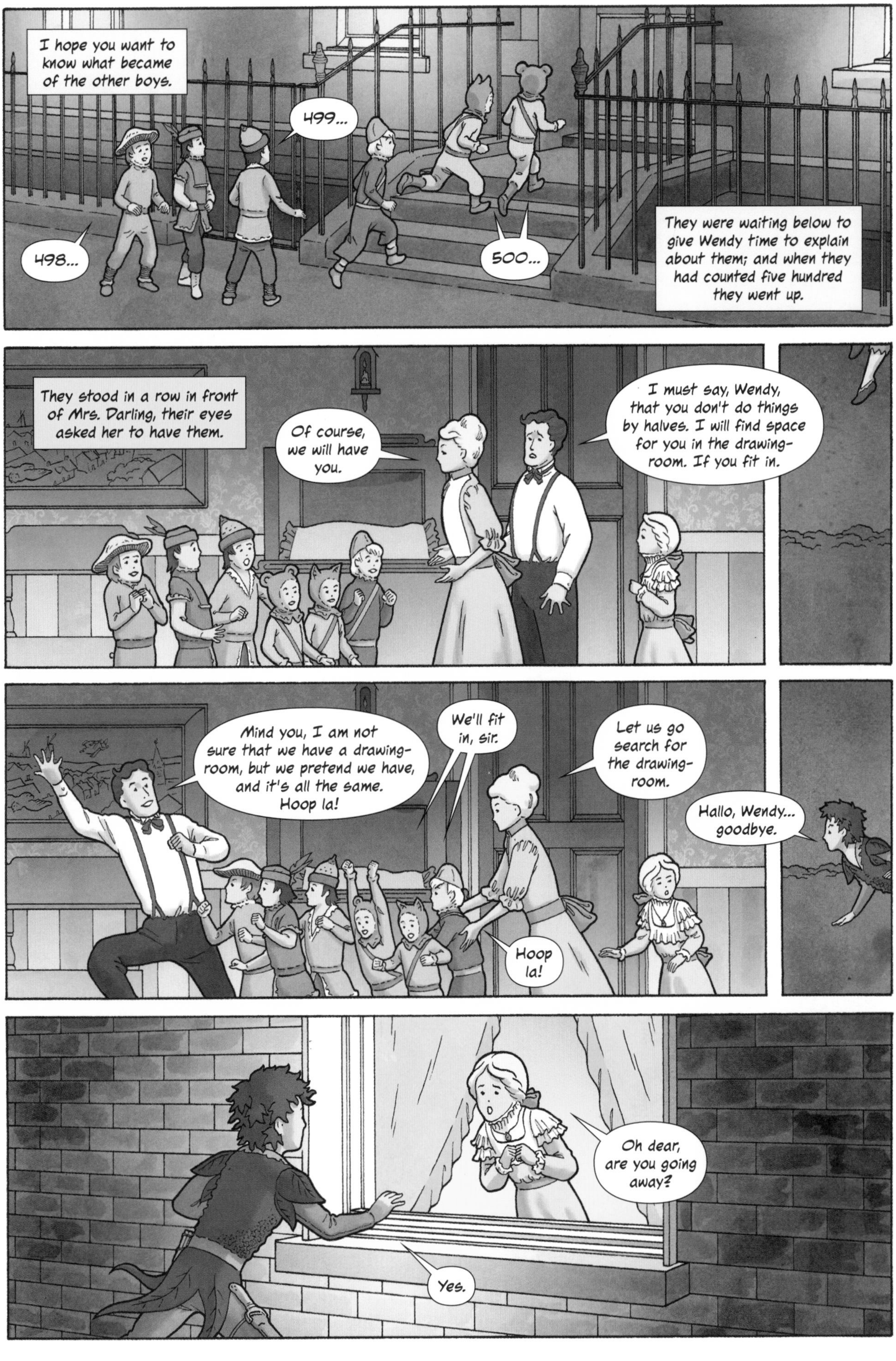
I hope you want to know what became of the other boys.
499...
498...
500...
They were waiting below to give Wendy time to explain about them; and when they had counted five hundred they went up.
They stood in a row in front of Mrs. Darling, their eyes asked her to have them.
Of course, we will have you.
I must say, Wendy, that you don't do things by halves. I will find space for you in the drawing-room. If you fit in.
Mind you, I am not sure that we have a drawing-room, but we pretend we have, and it's all the same. Hoop la!
We'll fit in, sir.
Let us go search for the drawing-room.
Hoop la!
Hallo, Wendy... goodbye.
Oh dear, are you going away?
Yes.

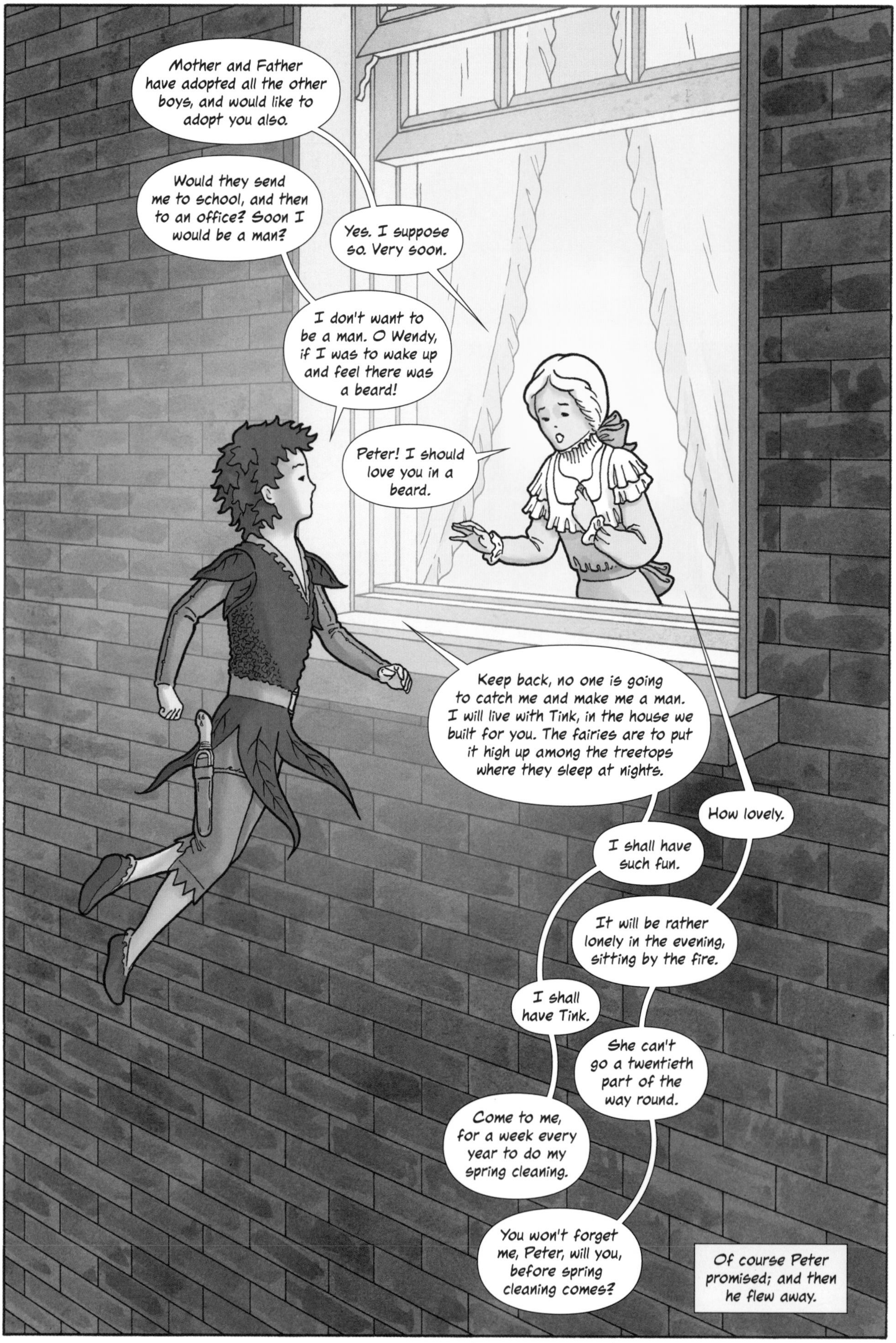
Mother and Father have adopted all the other boys, and would like to adopt you also.
Would they send me to school, and then to an office? Soon I would be a man?
Yes. I suppose so. Very soon.
I don't want to be a man. O Wendy, if I was to wake up and feel there was a beard!
Peter! I should love you in a beard.
Keep back, no one is going to catch me and make me a man. I will live with Tink, in the house we built for you. The fairies are to put it high up among the treetops where they sleep at nights.
How lovely.
I shall have such fun.
It will be rather lonely in the evening, sitting by the fire.
I shall have Tink.
She can't go a twentieth part of the way round.
Come to me, for a week every year to do my spring cleaning.
You won't forget me, Peter, will you, before spring cleaning comes?
Of course Peter promised; and then he flew away.

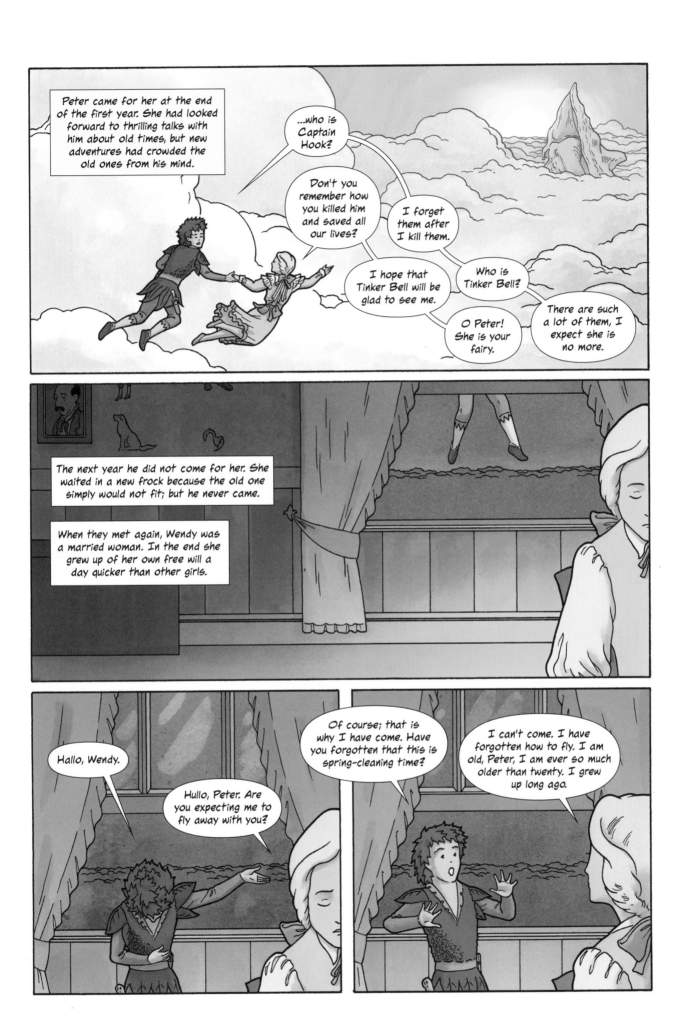

Peter came for her at the end of the first year. She had looked forward to thrilling talks with him about old times, but new adventures had crowded the old ones from his mind.

...who is Captain Hook?

Don't you remember how you killed him and saved all our lives?

I forget them after I kill them.

Who is Tinker Bell?

I hope that Tinker Bell will be glad to see me.

O Peter! She is your fairy.

There are such a lot of them, I expect she is no more.

The next year he did not come for her. She waited in a new frock because the old one simply would not fit; but he never came.

When they met again, Wendy was a married woman. In the end she grew up of her own free will a day quicker than other girls.

Hallo, Wendy.

Hullo, Peter. Are you expecting me to fly away with you?

Of course; that is why I have come. Have you forgotten that this is spring-cleaning time?

I can't come. I have forgotten how to fly. I am old, Peter, I am ever so much older than twenty. I grew up long ago.

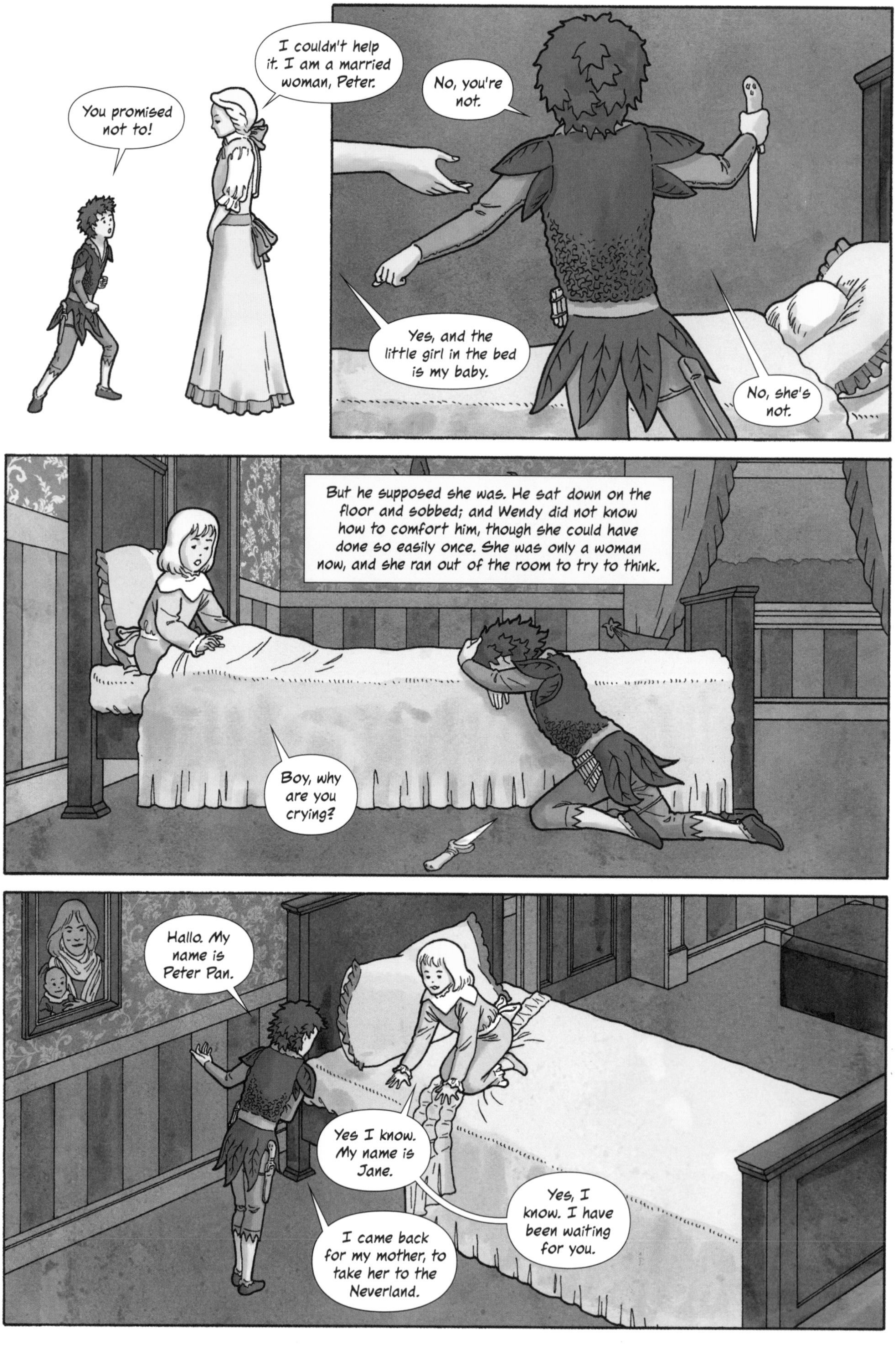
You promised not to!
I couldn't help it. I am a married woman, Peter.
No, you're not.
Yes, and the little girl in the bed is my baby.
No, she's not.
But he supposed she was. He sat down on the floor and sobbed; and Wendy did not know how to comfort him, though she could have done so easily once. She was only a woman now, and she ran out of the room to try to think.
Boy, why are you crying?
Hallo. My name is Peter Pan.
Yes I know. My name is Jane.
I came back for my mother, to take her to the Neverland.
Yes, I know. I have been waiting for you.

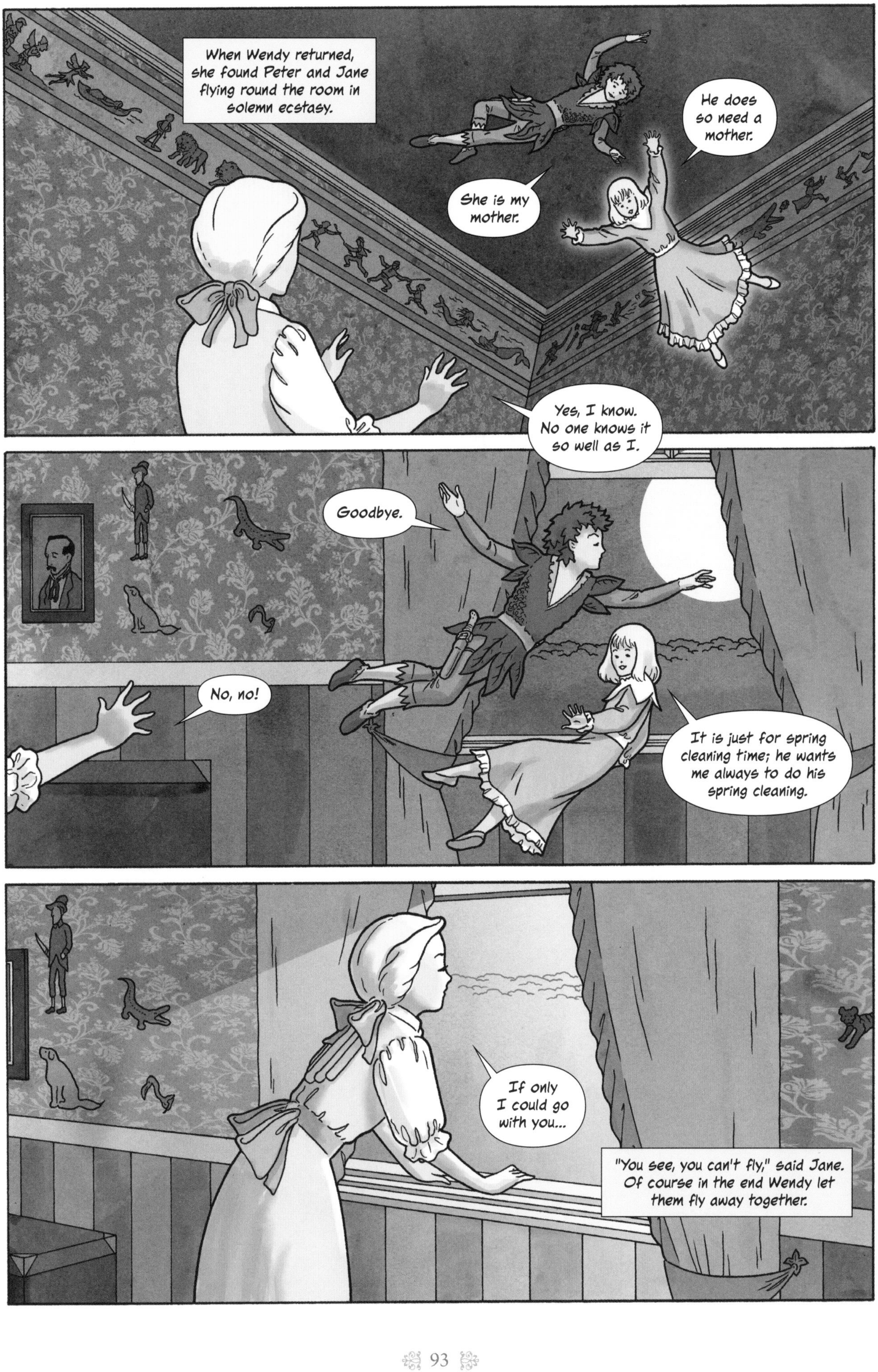
When Wendy returned, she found Peter and Jane flying round the room in solemn ecstasy.
He does so need a mother.
She is my mother.
Yes, I know. No one knows it so well as I.
Goodbye.
No, no!
It is just for spring cleaning time; he wants me always to do his spring cleaning.
If only I could go with you...
"You see, you can't fly," said Jane. Of course in the end Wendy let them fly away together.

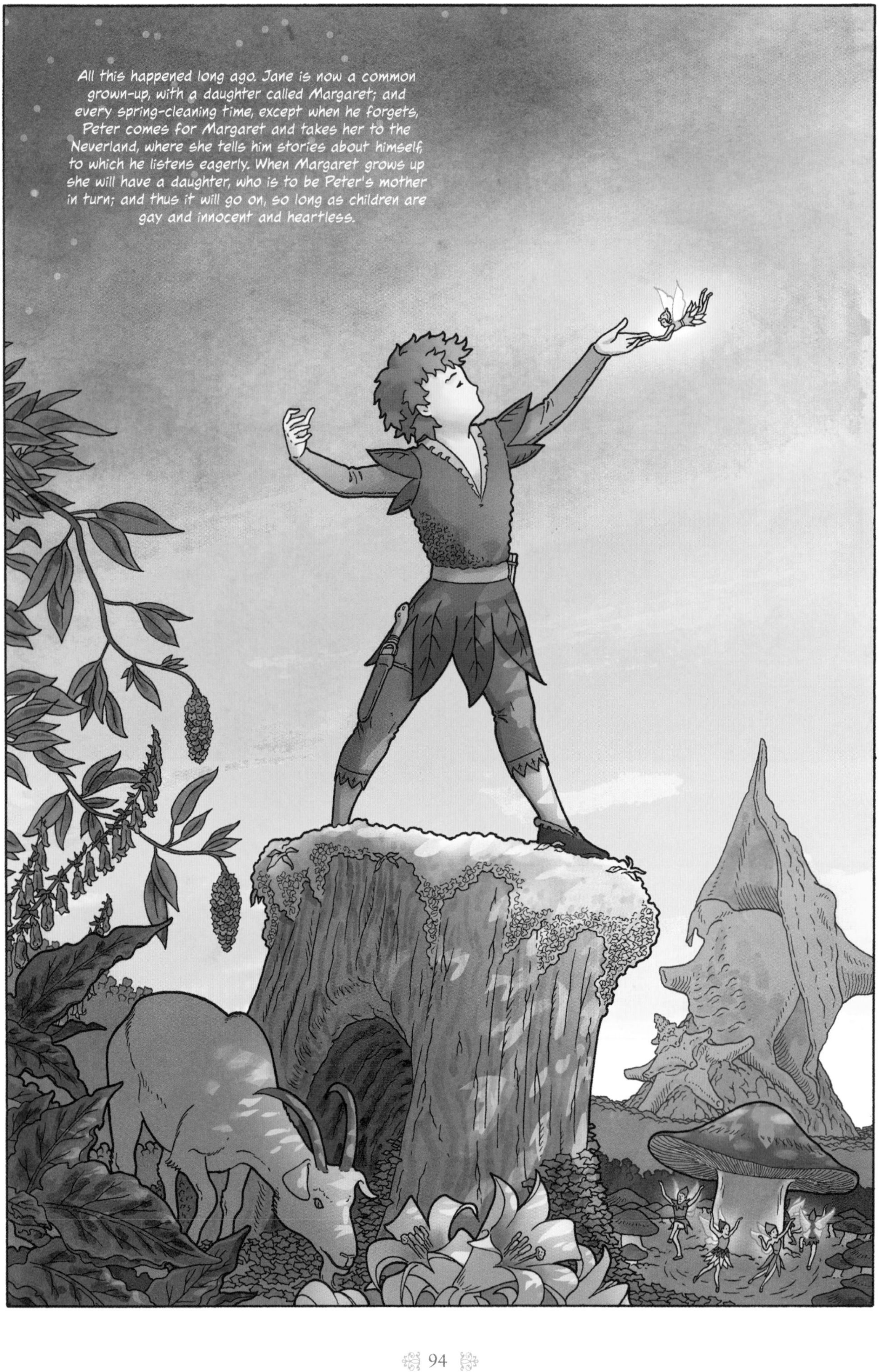
All this happened long ago. Jane is now a common grown-up, with a daughter called Margaret; and every spring-cleaning time, except when he forgets, Peter comes for Margaret and takes her to the Neverland, where she tells him stories about himself, to which he listens eagerly. When Margaret grows up she will have a daughter, who is to be Peter's mother in turn; and thus it will go on, so long as children are gay and innocent and heartless.

*This book is respectfully dedicated to
the memory of James Matthew Barrie,
and the Five*

J.M. Barrie, Peter Pan *and* Great Ormond Street Hospital
'All children, except one, grow up'

Since Sir James Matthew Barrie first staged *Peter Pan* at the Duke of York's Theatre in London on 27 December 1904 and later published his novel *Peter and Wendy* in 1911, his story has never been out of print and has been translated into more than sixty languages. It has been published in a multitude of shapes and formats, from novels and picture books to board books and pop-ups.

Stref's (Stephen White's) stunning graphic novel is the first ever published in the UK. His passion for the integrity of the original work and his attention to detail shine through. His graphic novel is also a celebration of Barrie's and Peter Pan's roots in Scotland – from the glens of Kirriemuir to the banks of the River Nith in Dumfries – which inspired much of the background and scenery in Stref's work.

The Hospital for Sick Children opened its doors on Great Ormond Street on 14 February 1852 with just ten beds, the first children's hospital in Britain. In 1929, twenty-five years after Peter Pan first made his appearance, Barrie stunned the world by making his gift of the copyright to the hospital. This meant that all proceeds from books, stage productions, films, etc. would now benefit directly the hospital's little patients.

Barrie was known to be a generous man and was familiar with the hospital, having lived around the corner in Bloomsbury during his first years in London – his lodgings in Grenville Street becoming the inspiration for the Darlings' house. He had long been a supporter of the hospital and indeed said in a speech in 1930: 'At one time Peter Pan was an invalid in the Hospital for Sick Children, and it was he who put me up to the little thing I did for the hospital.'

A memorial tablet to Barrie in the chapel records the hospital's gratitude to his wonderful gift. The Peter Pan Ward, the Tinker Bell play area and the Peter Pan statue at the entrance of the hospital are among the constant reminders to patients and visitors of this amazing legacy. Barrie's name – and Peter Pan's – will always hold a special place in the hearts of patients and their families, as well as everyone who works at the hospital.

More fairy dust was sprinkled over Great Ormond Street Hospital Children's Charity in 1988, when the House of Lords, prompted by Lord Callaghan, voted for a special clause in the Copyright, Designs & Patents Act that gave the charity a right to royalty from *Peter Pan* in perpetuity in the United Kingdom.

Eighty years on, the timeless adventures of *Peter Pan* are continuing to help towards making the hospital the incredible centre of hope it is today, and Stref's *Peter Pan* will be part of Barrie's legacy, following in the steps of so many illustrious artists.

CHRISTINE DE POORTERE
Peter Pan Director
Great Ormond Street Hospital Children's Charity
www.gosh.org